The Girls' Global Guide to Guys

"With *The Girls' Global Guide to Guys*, Theresa Alan delivers a brisk, funny, keenly observed portrait of a woman who wants more out of life than a soul-killing job and a tepid romance—and finds it on exotic shores." —Kim Green, author of *Paging Aphrodite* and *Is That A Moose In Your Pocket?*

"A wonderful and fun read not to be missed!" —*Chicklitbooks.com*

Spur of the Moment

"The players come across as real—kudos to Theresa Alan for accomplishing this feat. The sensitivities of Ana and the uniqueness of each member of the troupe as she perceives them make for a solid character study with overtones of a family drama and chicklit tale." —*The Midwest Book Review*

"Alan shows that she's capable of handling sensitive issues with an effectively gentle touch." —*Romantic Times*

Who You Know

"Alan does a masterful job . . . As the three women face the trials and triumphs of life, they assist each other in ways that only best friends can—through unconditional love, unrelenting humor and unwavering support. Reminiscent of *Bridget Jones's Diary* and *Divine Secrets of the Ya-Ya Sisterhood*, Alan's is a novel to be savored like a good box of chocolates." —*Booklist*

"A delightful chick-lit." —*The Midwest Book Review*

"A gorgeous book, superbly written with compassion and caring. *Who You Know* should absolutely be number one on everyone's list." —*Rendezvous*

Books by Theresa Alan

WHO YOU KNOW

SPUR OF THE MOMENT

THE GIRLS' GLOBAL GUIDE TO GUYS

GIRLS WHO GOSSIP

Published by Kensington Publishing Corporation

Girls * Who * Gossip

Theresa Alan

Strapless

KENSINGTON BOOKS
www.kensingtonbooks.com

KENSINGTON BOOKS are published by

Kensington Publishing Corp.
850 Third Avenue
New York, NY 10022

All Kensington titles, imprints, and distributed lines are available at special quantity discounts for bulk purchases for sales promotion, premiums, fund-raising, and educational or institutional use.

Special book excerpts or customized printings can also be created to fit specific needs. For details, write or phone the office of the Kensington Special Sales Manager: Special Sales Department, Kensington Publishing Corp., 850 Third Avenue, New York, NY, 10022. Phone: 1-800-221-2647.

Strapless and the Strapless logo are trademarks of Kensington Publishing Corp.
Kensington and the K logo Reg. U.S. Pat. & TM Off.

ISBN 0-7582-0760-3

First Kensington Trade Paperback Printing: April 2006
10   9   8   7   6   5   4   3   2   1

Printed in the United States of America

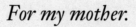

For my mother.

Acknowledgments

Thanks to Sara Jade Alan and Susan Arndt for their help editing this manuscript and to Burton McLucas for his love and support.

Chapter 1

What was I thinking?

When I see Aunt Claudia waving and smiling at me amid the tumult of shrieking children and businesspeople charging by, cell phones in one hand, luggage trailing behind them, I realize that I wasn't thinking. If I'd thought this through, I wouldn't be here right now, facing a summer with my aunt, my father, and my mother's ghost.

A man in his fifties bumps my left arm hard and mumbles something irritably, and I realize that I've stopped in the middle of the gate, blocking traffic. I adjust my backpack, pull my wheeled suitcase behind me, and approach Claudia. Despite the fact that airlines only allow carry-on bags that barely give you enough room to pack a tampon and a breath mint, I haven't checked any bags. My place in New York is small, so I left most of my wardrobe behind when I left for school; it's just been waiting here for me.

Claudia is wearing a top-of-the-line silk suit and has an expensive haircut with expert blond highlights. Her bejeweled hands, ears, and throat reflect and refract light into glittering beams. She has a perfect French manicure on pricey synthetic nails. How does a former actress who has been largely unemployed for the last thirteen years manage to look like Ivana Trump?

I haven't been back since the funeral. I don't really know why I'm coming back now. I've been going on automatic pilot for the last two months, and I guess when Dad's secretary sent me the plane tickets to Denver, I didn't stop to consider what I was doing. Now I wonder why I would volunteer to spend the summer with my father, a man who is essentially a stranger to me, the first man to break my heart. Maybe I came because I desperately needed something to do after the semester ended. Anything to keep myself distracted from the barrage of thoughts that are stuck in my mind like a never-ending CNN crawl.

"It's so good to see you!" Claudia says. "Are you happy to be home?"

I say nothing. I just can't find the words. She seems so happy and I simply don't understand. Her only sister just died two months ago. Shouldn't she appear at least a little shaken? I look at her, as if trying to figure out what she's saying, like I've forgotten how to speak English.

"I know Denver's not quite as exciting as New York, but your dad is sure excited to have you here!"

I try to smile, but I'm afraid I probably look like a drunken stroke victim. Aunt Claudia's heels clip sharply against the tile floor. How strange it is that Claudia is picking me up instead of sending our housekeeper, Maria. I've only seen Claudia a few times in my entire life, and yet here she is, driving me home from the airport just like Mom would have done.

"He's really sorry he wasn't able to make it to the airport. An important meeting came up, you know how it goes." Yes, I do. "You'll definitely get to see him tonight, though. We've been planning a wonderful dinner. I've been running around all week, planning the menu and buying the wine. My friend Polly is going to be there.

She works at an entertainment magazine here in Denver. She might be able to get you a job writing movie reviews or something. Would you like that?"

"That might be cool," I say, but I don't mean it. In my current mental state, I don't think I'd even accept a job with DreamWorks or Miramax.

"I mean you could work for your father this summer, or just hang out if you want, but I know you like to write."

I shrug. How does she know that? Oh. Mom. Mom must have told her I write movie reviews for the campus newspaper.

"And internships are the key to getting a good job after college," she continues.

Seeing as Claudia has lived off the charity of my mother and rich older men for most of her life, her advice is akin to a tobacco lobbyist lecturing on health and nutrition.

The automatic door whooshes open, and we walk outside. Claudia keeps talking, but I have a hard time focusing on what she's saying. Her voice melts into white noise along with the sound of my wheeled suitcase rumbling along the parking lot pavement. Claudia stops at a silver Lexus and says, "This is me." Unless she landed a movie deal I don't know about or won the lottery recently, she must be borrowing it from Dad.

She opens the trunk and I throw my backpack and suitcase inside.

I gaze out the window for the forty-minute drive home. Claudia talks and talks about nothing in particular. I stare at the rush of gray pavement in a kind of trance.

That's really the only state I know how to be in anymore, a perpetual blurred daze. I went back to school after the funeral to finish out the semester, mostly because I didn't know what else to do with myself, but the days passed in fog. I just went through the motions of living, going through the routine of life like an automaton. Strangely enough, I think I managed to do okay on my finals. It's amazing how life goes on, even if you're not really there, even if you're not paying any attention.

Like the way Claudia suddenly stitched herself into the fabric of my family's daily life. How did it happen? Why is she still living with my dad after my mother, her sister, has been dead for two months?

Until about a year ago, Claudia lived in California, but we never saw her. Claudia would call Mom from time to time and hit her up for money. I overheard Mom on the phone many times inviting Claudia to come to Denver for a visit or asking if there would be a convenient time for us to fly out to California to see her, but these visits never materialized. Then about a year ago, Claudia's boyfriend of three years went back to his wife and kicked Claudia out of the penthouse she'd been staying in rent-free. Homeless and penniless, Claudia decided a visit to Colorado wasn't such a bad idea after all. She's been here ever since.

I hadn't noticed the way Claudia had been seeping into every part of my family's life. It's not entirely my fault. I was in Europe last summer and away at school all year. The only time I came home was over Christmas break, and I spent most of the time with friends. I didn't pay much attention to Claudia. And of course I came home for the funeral, but I spent that time completely out of it. I drank a lot and cried a lot and have vague memories of well-dressed strangers telling me how much they'd miss my mother, how wonderful she was, what a shame it was that this terrible thing happened.

But now that I'm facing an entire summer with Claudia, now that it's her picking me up from the airport, it's finally hitting me that something about this situation is not right.

Many years ago, Claudia was a big deal movie actress. She'd had a couple of small parts in low-budget movies, and then when she was twenty-four, right about the time my mom was celebrating her first anniversary with Dad and giving birth to me, Claudia became a bit of a celebrity for her role in *Becoming*. The title had a double meaning, both that she was an attractive, "becoming" woman, and also that she had been a demure, sweet female, who during the course of life's twists and turns "became" a violent thief and killer. In the movie, Claudia played a woman who had been brutally attacked, and her attacker was let off because the police mishandled some of the evidence. After overcoming a series of small obstacles by being a bad ass—stabbing a fork into a groping man's hand, stealing from the register of a condescending male clerk, things like that—her character ultimately decided that she couldn't wait around for justice, and she murdered her assailant. At the time, it was a pretty big deal for a woman to go around killing people, even bad guys. Some people argued that she portrayed a strong woman who wouldn't sit back and passively be victimized, others said she was just embracing male violence and was certainly no role model. In any case, Claudia was often in the news back then, being interviewed on TV and getting her picture on the cover of magazines.

I used to watch Claudia's movies when I was a kid, and I would brag to my friends about how Claudia was my aunt, as if her fame, however small, made Claudia more important than the rest of us, and therefore me more important by extension.

Of course as a kid, I didn't know the difference between a movie star and a fading star. It wasn't until a couple years ago when I picked up a "Where Are They Now?" issue of *People* magazine that I learned Claudia's fame was short lived, that she couldn't keep the momentum going after *Becoming*. The next three movies she was in bombed.

While her career was sinking, Mom was quickly being launched into the highest stratosphere of the wealthy elite. Dad cofounded a company with his college roommate, Charles Sinha, an engineer, a few years after they'd graduated. Chuck designed the original products, and Dad raised the capital and developed the strategy and business model. Within three years the company was profitable, and it just kept growing. By the time I was nine, Able Technologies was a Fortune 100 company, with offices around the world. My father has graced the covers of *Fortune* and *BusinessWeek* and seen the insides of *Time*, *Newsweek*, and *People*. Dad isn't Bill Gates- or Angelina Jolie-famous, but anyone who knows anything about business and the stock market knows who he is.

When we get home, Claudia tells me I have an hour to get cleaned up for dinner.

"'Kay." I bring my bag up the long flight of winding stairs. Our home is the stuff upscale home decorating magazines are made of. The carpet downstairs and on the staircase is a rich, plush burgundy, and all the furniture is heavy mahogany. My bedroom has light wood floors, white walls, and pale green accents on the bedspread, sheets, shades, and drapes. The furniture is light maple, and all the lighting fixtures are made from brushed silver. My bathroom is cream, with cream granite tile floors, a cream-colored Jacuzzi bathtub, and an all-glass shower. It's very, very different than the cramped space I share with my roommates, Kendra and Lynne, in New York, but somehow I miss my New York apartment already. I shut my bedroom door behind me, dump my bags on the floor, and collapse on my bed next to my two remaining teddy bears. Before I left for college, I took all of my childhood stuffed animals to Goodwill. I used to have so many there was barely enough room left for me on the bed. I used to worry about whether I was loving each animal equally; I didn't want anybody to feel left out. Giving them away was a fit of insanity, I see now. I think maybe I'd been trying to make a statement about wanting to feel grown-up. Also, there was the practical issue of owning too much stuff and wanting to get rid of the clutter. But now, I sort of feel like I donated memories of my childhood, rather than just a zoo of stuffed animals smiling friendly smiles.

Of the two bears I have now, one is a cheap but cute all-black bear that I won last summer at a fair by tossing a Ping-Pong ball into a tiny fish bowl. It was triumphant proof that the hours I'd logged playing beer pong my freshman year of college had honed valuable skills in me.

The other bear is white and so soft you feel compelled to burrow your face in it. It was a gift from my high school boyfriend, Dan. I used to think I loved Dan, but now that I'm twenty and much more mature, I realize that really it was just infatuation and not true love at all. I like to think I'm much wiser about these sorts of things now.

I sprawl across the bed and dial Marni's number.

"Hey babe," I say.

"Helaina! Are you in town?"

"Yep. I have this family dinner deal tonight, but I thought maybe you me and Hannah could get together afterward. I'm pretty sure I'll want to get very, very drunk tonight."

"Are you—how are you doing?"

"I don't know. I really don't." I don't say anything for a moment. "Call Hannah to see if she can make it, would you? Where should we meet?"

"It doesn't matter. Where would you like to go?"

"You decide."

"Turnsol?"

"Fine, we'll catch up then."

"Cool. See you later."

I hang up the phone and lie on my back on my bed, staring at the stippled white paint on the ceiling for several minutes, wondering why I came back to Denver and how long I should stay before going back. When Claudia's knocking wakes me up, I'm completely disoriented. It takes me several seconds to remember where I am. I look at the clock. An hour has passed.

I open the door. "Yeah?"

"The guests are here."

"Guests?"

"Polly and her stepkids. The kids are about your age, maybe a little older."

I nod and dutifully start making my way down the hall.

"That's not what you're wearing, is it?" Claudia asks.

"What's wrong with what I'm wearing?" My outfit consists of black jeans, Doc Martens, and a black vest. I'm a film student, what can I say? Black makes up a healthy portion of my wardrobe. If you dressed me in pink, I'd probably go into shock and have myself a seizure or two."

"It's just that you look like a rock star."

"So?"

"I suppose you don't think your family is worth dressing up for? And God, your hair. When's the last time you had a trim? I can set you up with my hairdresser. He used to be your mom's—"

"Eric? Yeah, Eric used to do my hair too. I'll make an appointment with him soon."

"I can give you some money."

"Claudia, my father is one of the richest men in

America, money is not the issue. The issue is that my mother died two months ago. I've been a little distracted, and I haven't been able to practice my usual vigilance against split ends."

"Are you at least going to change? Polly may be able to give you a job."

"Claudia, lay off, okay?"

She rolls her eyes. She is wearing a sleek red dress with spaghetti straps that reveals her neck, shoulders, cleavage, and back. At forty-four, she's still an incredibly beautiful woman. She reminds me of my mother in that way. They both had such grace and elegance about them. I always wish I had more myself; maybe I'll grow into it.

"You'll like her kids too," Claudia adds. Then, in a whisper, "They lost their father two years ago."

I pause. I think she means that they can identify with my loss. I know that other people have been through this, but right now it feels unique to me alone.

As we come down the long, winding staircase, I see my father, who is still wearing a suit and tie from work. I feel a nervous jolt, as if I were about to go on a first date. There are other people next to him: a woman in her early fifties and a guy and a girl in their twenties. I can feel their eyes on me, but it's my father's gaze that seems to sear beneath my skin.

"Hello," he says, hugging me.

"Hey, Dad." I hug him back awkwardly, stiffly. His arms seem to be keeping me at a distance rather than bringing us closer.

I step back, and Claudia introduces me to Polly. Polly is so thin she looks brittle, as if she got one good hug she'd crumble. She's wearing old-lady perfume that makes me want to keep my distance.

"It's nice to meet you," I say and shake her hand.

"This is her stepdaughter, Laura, who just graduated from Wharton with her MBA," Claudia says.

I nod. Laura is extremely thin, all elbows and angles. She has a sharp chin and a tight smile.

"But instead of coming to work for me, she accepted another job," Dad says, shaking his head in mock disappointment.

"I didn't know you personally when I accepted the job with Erikson," Laura says. "I've already gotten my first international project. I'm very excited about it. I fly out to St. Petersburg tomorrow to help a company prepare for their IPO."

"She speaks German and Russian fluently," her stepmother adds.

"After a couple of years at Erikson, I'll be able to bring you more experience," Laura says to my father.

"And negotiate an even higher salary," Dad says.

"But of course." She smiles.

"Let's not start talking business right away. We haven't even gotten the introductions out of the way," Claudia says. "Helaina, this is Polly's stepson, Owen. He's getting his MFA in poetry at the University of Iowa. He's spending the summer writing for Polly's magazine. Owen, Helaina writes too. She's a film major at NYU."

"I just play around, nothing serious." I shake his hand.

"It's nice to meet you." He looks like the only member of the family who eats regularly. He's not a big guy, 5' 10" maybe, but broad shouldered, with thick, muscular arms and legs. He has curly, honey-colored hair and hazel eyes.

"Well, help yourself to the cheese and crackers." Claudia gestures to the credenza behind her. It's an elaborate spread of exotic cheeses and crackers, and there is way too much food for just the six of us. I wonder why she's going to all this trouble. She's standing in front of my father, and that's when I see it, the way Dad brushes his hand across her back. It lingers for too long a moment. It's too intimate for a man and a sister-in-law. It's the touch of one lover to another. How long have they been sleeping together? Did they start before Mom died or after? Which would be worse?

Did Mom know? My God, if so . . . the betrayal she must have felt. She must have been devastated.

Is it possible the accident wasn't an accident?

I can't see Mom committing suicide, though.

Is it possible her death was a murder?

No, no. Of course not. Grief is making me delusional. It's a ridiculous thought.

Except . . . it's awfully convenient for Claudia to have Mom out of the way. Mom's frequent financial handouts supplemented Claudia's career as a mistress and helped her through the difficult dry periods between men. But without Mom around, Claudia can cash in on all the financial benefits of being Dad's full-time girlfriend without anyone or anything to get in her way.

I don't know how long I'm gone for, falling into that fugue state that seems to creep up on me more and more, but the next thing I know, Claudia is standing in front of me with a bottle of wine in each hand.

"Helaina? Helaina?" she asks. I don't know how many times she has said my name before I hear her.

"What?"

"Red or white?"

"Red, please, thanks." Dad hands me a wine glass, and Claudia pours the Merlot. I take the glass and swallow half of it in a single gulp. Shouldn't I be feeling rage and anger right now? Instead I feel weighed down, sluggish, and tired, as though I'm wearing a lead vest like the kind the nurse puts on you when you're getting an X-ray, this heavy burden around my heart.

"Helaina?" Claudia interrupts my thoughts again. "Did I tell you that I met Polly at a meeting of the Denver Women Entrepreneurs?"

"No. What were you doing there?"

She laughs. "I'm an image consultant, didn't you know that? Anyway, we got to talking and she told me she runs a magazine. I asked her if there was a section on fashion, she said there wasn't, and I said, 'Let's change that,' and she said, 'You know, I think that's a good idea.' So now I write a column on fashion every month. Here's the most recent issue." She picks up a magazine from the coffee table.

"You write?" I ask.

"I'm a woman of many talents."

The magazine is called *Local Color*. I flip through the thick, glossy pages. There's an article comparing different local country clubs; a feature about a woman who'd built one of the most successful interior design firms in the area, complete with interior shots of some of the palatial homes she's decorated; and a profile of a chef at one of the elite restaurants in Aspen. Then I get to the page with Claudia's picture on it. There's a bio beneath the picture that reads, "Claudia Merrill starred in blockbuster hits such as *Becoming, Behind Closed Doors* and *Longing* before launching her consulting firm, Prima Facie, which is dedicated to helping people 'dress for success and always look their best!'"

I try to remember the definition of prima facie from when I memorized all those vocab words for the SAT—I think it means something like "on first view or appearance."

The headline reads, "Does this trend fit you?" There

is a picture of an unhappy-looking, overweight woman wearing a t-shirt that stops just below her bust, exposing the rind of flab curling over the waistline of her jeans. Beside her is a picture of Britney Spears, wearing a similar outfit. The caption reads, "Not all trends are right for everyone!" Ah yes, hard-hitting journalism at its finest.

"Did you come up with the name of the company yourself?" It's all I can think of to say.

"Your father did. And don't worry, if you go to work for Polly this summer, you won't have to be concerned about running into me at the office. I'm on the road a lot going to fashion shows, visiting department stores, or working from home, studying fashion magazines and industry news releases."

She works from home a lot—so that's why she's trying to get me a job this summer. She wants me out of her way.

"Would you be interested in working for us?" Polly asks. "We have film reviews in each issue. Normally our editor writes them, but I know she'd like the help. The pay is not that great, but you'll get some good experience and some nice clips for your portfolio."

If I wanted, Dad would just buy me my own magazine to run. But maybe it'd be good to have something to keep me busy, something to occupy my thoughts. "Yeah, sure. I guess I need something to do this summer." I wonder if I'm passing for normal. I'm trying really hard to be polite; I learned that from my mother. Even if she'd had a shitty day or was feeling sick or tired, she was always gracious and friendly, and she always had a smile to share.

"I've always loved movies myself. I remember how much I looked forward to going to the movies when I was a little girl. Every Saturday afternoon . . . " Polly begins telling me about every movie she's ever seen in her entire life—the plot, the actors, her personal opinion on the strengths and weaknesses of each film. I glance around hoping to alert some kind soul that I'm in need of rescue, but Dad and Claudia are glued together, smiling intimately, and Laura and Owen are deep in conversation, oblivious to my plight.

Polly continues telling me about her personal cinematic history *in real time.* I've studied some of the films she's talking about in my classes, and I open my mouth to add to the conversation but can't get any words out because she just keeps right on talking. I end up opening and closing my jaw futilely like a fish out of water.

After several decades have passed (we're up to when Polly was in college and saw the premiere of *Zorba the Greek* and how handsome she thought Anthony Quinn was in that film), and I can feel the crow's-feet forming around my eyes and the gray hairs growing on my head and my subscription to AARP's magazine about to arrive in the mail any day now, Maria peeks out from the kitchen door and announces that dinner is ready.

"Wonderful," Claudia says. She gives a little backward wave of her hand signifying we should follow her, which we do. As we walk, I realize, *we're following Claudia,* as if this were her home. In the hallway we pass one of my mother's paintings. The painting is a delicate still life of a vase of freesias. Mom painted this piece when I was just a baby. If you know where to look, you can see where my little baby sneeze made the colors run, just a bit. I love this painting. I love that I was so close to my mother when she was working on it that my sneeze made its mark as indelibly as the paint itself.

The table is immaculately set. I'm not sure the table ever looked this decked out for holidays or for parties with Dad's executive-type pals. The china is out, as are the crystal wine glasses. The burgundy cloth napkins have been starched and are folded in a complex style that reminds me of the swooping, sail-like shape of the Sydney Opera House. I watch Claudia take her napkin and unfold it precisely, laying a sharp triangle of it on her lap. Who is it that she is so eager to impress? Has she always been like this? Has she always needed everything to be just so? It feels like she is auditioning for a part, but I don't know what role she wants to play.

I pour myself another glass of wine. There are baskets of bread on the table and tomato and fresh buffalo mozzarella salads at each place waiting for us.

Claudia picks up the bread basket and hands it to Polly. "Care for some French bread? Our chef, Paul, makes the most divine bread."

"Oh no thank you, I never eat bread. The carbs!" says Polly.

"Laura?"

"I don't eat bread either."

Claudia takes a slice of bread herself, and then Owen takes some. I take two slices and spread them lavishly with butter. After a couple bites, my throat tightens and I can't eat anymore, even though the bread is unbelievably good and still warm. Normally, I would devour Paul's bread, but since Mom died, I haven't had much of an appetite.

"I've passed all my diet secrets on to Laura," Polly says. "I know that people say that you should just be yourself, but if you want to get a husband, the only way you can be yourself is if you're naturally skinny, naturally even-tempered, and always pleasant to be around." She offers a tittering laugh. "It helps to have long hair too and of course the right clothes and accessories are essential. Even if you are all those things, a little extra effort never hurts. Men are so lucky. Take Owen. He never works out and he's in great shape."

I look across the table at Owen. He's smiling sardonically. He has nice, full lips. "I walk a lot," he offers with a shrug.

I nod in what I hope is an attentive manner while wondering how his arms got so strong if not from lifting weights.

Polly dismisses the idea with a wave of her hand. "You simply have an ambulatory form of brooding, like someone who paces when they're upset. It's not like you're going out to get exercise."

He looks at me and says confidentially, "It's only exercise if you suffer."

I smile.

"This home is so beautiful. Ellen did a beautiful job," Polly says.

"She didn't have anything else to do with her time," Claudia says with a shrug.

I narrow my eyes at her, not quite able to believe what I just heard. Does this woman really have the audacity to knock her dead sister? "My mother was actually very busy," I say. "She volunteered a great deal of her time to various charitable organizations and she was a docent at the art museum."

"She was a wonderful woman," Polly agrees.

Maria, our housekeeper of eleven years, clears the salad plates and brings dinner. Everyone else is having some kind of game hen; Maria brings me a plate loaded with grilled vegetables instead of poultry.

"Thanks," I say to her.

Claudia looks at my plate, horrified. "Did you request a special dinner? Are you on a diet or something?"

"I'm a vegetarian. I've been a vegetarian for about

eight years. Maria and Paul know to make something without meat for me. They don't have to ask."

She gives me a puckered look, then quickly recovers with a forced smile. The smile comes so quickly I wonder if I really saw her make a face or if I imagined it.

"So what do you learn in film school?" Laura asks me.

A wave of relief washes over me. I can talk about movies all day. I'm on comfortable ground here. "We study films like an English major would study novels—the cultural implications, themes, meanings, that sort of thing. I also learn the technical stuff like lighting and shooting a camera. I've played around with writing screenplays. Originally I thought I wanted to be a writer, but now I've decided that I really like being part of every aspect of making movies. I recently completed a short film for a class, and my professor thinks it has a good shot of being accepted at some national and international film festivals."

"That's great," Owen says.

I shrug. "It's only seven minutes long, but it took hours and hours and weeks and weeks to complete. It was a lot of work, but also a lot of fun."

"I'd love to see it," Owen says.

"Me too," Dad chimes in.

The comment takes me aback. I hadn't even thought about showing it to Dad. My professors really liked it, but they were probably just comparing it to other students' work; Dad will have no other basis of comparison except big-budget movies. "Um," I say.

I'm grappling for a response when Claudia says, "I like to think I had a little something to do with getting you interested in film."

"Maybe," I say, though I don't mean it. If anything, Claudia is a cautionary tale against the erratic, unpredictable world of Hollywood.

"I find film to be such a plebian medium," Laura says.

I decide that I don't like Laura all that much.

"We'd love to see your film," Claudia says. "We don't get to see many movies. Usually we see live theater. We just saw *Glengarry Glen Ross*. It was very well acted. It made me miss working in live theater."

Laura asks about Claudia's career, and Claudia launches into a monologue in which she carefully drops many names of bigwigs she's hobnobbed with over the years.

As Dad, Laura, Claudia, and Polly talk, Owen asks me why I decided to go vegetarian.

"It's kind of a long story."

"I've got time."

"It's not profound or anything. I was twelve years old and watching this IMAX movie about the jungle and it was following the life of this endangered species, I can't even remember what it was anymore, from birth to nearly adulthood, and out of nowhere it gets eaten by a lion, and I just started crying my eyes out. I mean I know about survival of the fittest, but I just thought it would be so nice if the lion could eat one of the shrubs nearby, full of fiber and antioxidants or whatever. I understand that to keep a balance in the ecosystem there have to be predators and prey, but humans raise animals just to eat them; it's not about keeping a balance. I just decided I didn't want to be part of that."

"So beneath your cool exterior you're really just a softy."

"I can be tough when I need to be."

"I believe it."

His gaze is captivating. I think about how I should avert my eyes from his, but somehow I can't manage to.

After dinner, everyone settles down in the great room, cradling glasses of brandy. I observe rather than listen to the conversations going on around me, like I'm watching a muted television, until Owen says, "So, do we get to see your movie tonight?" He says it loudly enough so that all other conversations stop abruptly. Everyone looks at me.

I hesitate. Maybe I should say that I don't have a copy with me. In fact, I have several that I'm planning to submit to independent film festivals this summer. "Sure, I'll go get it." I run upstairs and grab a copy of the video from my suitcase.

When I return, everyone has moved from the great room to the family room where there is a television the size of a small movie screen. As they settle in, I pop the movie into the VCR. We have a DVD player, but we keep the old VCR for me. Dad has to help me figure out four different remotes before I can actually get the movie to play and sound to come out.

The movie is a comedy spoofing the women Mom considered her "friends," country-club types who were shallower than communion wafers and as trustworthy as a safety net with a giant hole in it.

On-screen, four middle-aged, well-dressed women are sitting at a patio table near a pool, saying horrible things about other women at the club.

"Did you hear about Donna Kennecott? I heard her husband is sleeping with his twenty-four-year-old marketing assistant. And frankly, I can't blame him. She's put on, what, twelve, thirteen pounds? I mean look at her, she's just popping out of her swimsuit. Has she ever heard of a little thing called self-control?"

The woman they've been talking about starts coming their way, so the four women quickly shut up and put smiles on their faces.

"Donna, hi! Good to see you! What's new? How are things?"

"Wonderful. I just had an oxidizing facial the other day and I have to tell you, run, don't walk, *run* to get one yourself. My skin feels so much more hydrated, and the whole experience was so relaxing. I really needed the break."

"It's so important to take care of yourself, to just take a little time out from the everyday grind," one of the four women at the table says. As she says this, she takes a sip of her mixed drink, pushing the paper umbrella aside. She swings her feet back and forth, and for a moment, the camera just focuses on how quiet the country club is. The crystal-blue pool sparkles serenely behind them.

The second Donna walks away, the four women's faces all flash these terrifying looks of horror-movie monsters. I am proud of the effect and how well the makeup turned out. After a flash where we get to see their true inner monsters, they look normal again and begin saying negative things about Donna as cattily as can be.

I look away from the movie for a moment to look at my audience. Dad and Claudia are facing each other on the couch, giggling quietly, totally ignoring my film. Polly looks confused. Only Owen looks engaged.

It stings like a slap that my father isn't watching this. He has no idea how much work this took.

On-screen, the women go on dissing people and then being sweet as aspartame when these same people happen by, and the monster-face flash thing happens a few more times. Owen laughs out loud several times at my jokes, but Dad is paying no attention whatsoever. The movie ends and Dad suddenly comes to when Owen starts clapping.

Shit, shit, shit. Why did I show this to my father? How many times do I have to let him do this to me before I figure it out already? What do I care if he doesn't like it?

What does he know about film or literature or poetry or anything except making money? Although maybe I did rely on stereotypes too much. Maybe it is really a stupid, unfunny piece of shit.

"That was *outstanding*," Dad says. He says it so convincingly that even though I know he didn't watch any of it, I actually want to believe him. Of course, it's his very ability to sell people on anything that has made him such a successful businessman, but you'd think that as his daughter I'd be immune to his charms. Maybe it's simply that I desperately want to believe he's impressed.

"Very . . . unusual," Claudia says.

"I don't get it," Laura says.

"That was awesome, totally cool," Owen says.

I give Owen a grateful smile. "Well everyone, thanks for dinner and thanks for watching my movie. I need to get going," I say. "I've got plans to meet up with some friends. Dad, is there a car I can borrow?"

"Well, we have six. I could probably spare one."

"I want whichever one you like least. I don't need anything fancy."

"Are you going to be drinking tonight?"

"Dad, I'm not 21. There are laws." The lie comes easily. I am Gary Denner's daughter, after all. In fact, I've had an awesome fake I.D. since I was seventeen.

"You can take the Jaguar or the BMW—"

"Which car does Maria use?"

"The Jeep."

"The Jeep? Isn't that like three years old?"

"Yes."

"Why do you still have a three-year-old car?"

"I keep it around for Maria, so she has something to go grocery shopping in."

"I'll take the Jeep. That'll be great, thanks."

"Why would you take the Jeep over the Jag or the Beamer?" Laura asks.

"I don't drive much in New York; I'm not a great driver. And in high school I got into a little fender bender—I mean a seriously tiny fender bender—some guy rear-ended me when I was driving Dad's Porsche and the Porsche got a scratch on the fender like yea long"—I indicate with my thumb and index finger a distance of about two inches—"and ah, well let's just say Dad's pretty serious about his automotives and I'd just prefer to take the Jeep."

"Helaina, you'll need a car to get around this summer," Dad says. "You'll need something to get to work in. I was thinking of trading in the Viper soon, why don't you drive it this summer and I'll trade it in after you go back to school in the fall? Maria will give you a set of keys."

"Okay, I'll take the Viper. Thanks. It was nice meeting all of you." I look at Owen. He gives me a slight nod and smile. I turn to Polly. "Polly, thanks for the job opportunity. I'll see you on Monday."

I go into the kitchen and give Maria a hug.

"How are you doing, kiddo?"

I shrug. "I don't know."

She nods with a sad smile. She's forty-something like Claudia, and she's another woman who has aged well. I hope I'm not the first woman to come out of this house to break this trend. She has clear skin and dark hair that she pulls back into a thick ponytail. She lives in a little cottage on the property with her husband, who takes care of our yard. She's always felt like a member of our family; she just wears jeans and t-shirts, no dorky, black-and-white maid's uniform or anything.

"How are *you*?"

"I miss your mom."

"Yeah. Hey, what's the deal with Claudia? Are you working for her now?"

"She seems to think so."

"What's that been like?"

"Let's just say I really, really miss your mom." Her tone is light. Her sad smile warms her face.

"I'm sorry."

"It's a job."

"I guess. I'm going to go meet some friends and get out of this nuthouse."

"Lucky you."

"Dad said I could use the Viper this summer."

"You can take the Jaguar or the BMW or the Lamborghini. The only car I'd advise you to stay away from is the Mercedes. That's his latest baby. But you can take something more exciting than the Viper."

"Being Gary Denner's daughter is all the excitement I need. Thanks, M."

As I drive down to the club, I simmer with anger at myself. Why did I set myself up like that with my movie—exposing myself, like a kid on a bicycle shouting down the street, "Look Dad, no hands!"—hoping to get a little attention, a little approval.

Is my movie any good? Why had I even made it? The process of making it taught me a lot. That's the important thing, not so much whether it's good, right? God, listen to me. Half an hour ago I was going to send it to film festivals and now I'm certain it's worthless. Why do I let Dad do this to me?

Marni and Hannah are already at the bar by the time I arrive. It's still early, only 10:30 or so, and they've managed to snag a booth. There are only a few people on the dance floor.

Marni and Hannah slip out of either side of the booth and hug me. They tell me something, but with the throbbing music, I can't hear what they're saying.

I slide in the booth next to Hannah. Now that we're facing each other, we can do a shout-and-read-the-lips thing that makes communication possible.

"Girlfriend, I know they say you can never be too rich or too thin, but I think you're taking this whole anorexic look a bit too far," Hannah says.

"I know, I haven't had much of an appetite lately, but I'll be back to my pizza-and-ice cream-swilling ways in no time, don't worry."

Hannah is home from Cornell for the summer. At 5' 8", she's tall for a Korean woman. Her long dark hair is as shiny and sleek as the black leather uniform of a dominatrix. Even though Hannah goes to school only five hours away from me, we never see each other during the school year. Instead, we content ourselves to stay in touch by phone and email.

Marni is home from Stanford. She's petite and curvy. Her dark shoulder-length curls are adorably untamable. I feel suddenly self-conscious about my own appearance. I have wavy hair that in New York I can scrunch into curls or blow-dry straight, but in the dry Denver air, it looks wilted and defeated, no matter what I do to it.

I look at these two women, my friends since junior high, and smile. When we were in high school, I did all right academically, but Marni and Hannah were straight-A wunderkinds. Marni has been working toward her goal of being a surgeon pretty much since she emerged from the womb. Hannah is so damn smart she just needs to show up for a test and she aces it. She can write an essay an hour before it's due and it comes out flawlessly the first time—no outlines, no rough drafts, no editing required. It's admirable and infuriating both. You'd think that hanging out with them so much, some of their smarts would have rubbed off on me, but I've managed to remain staunchly average despite their positive influence.

Hannah lights a cigarette and asks me how dinner with my family went.

"Remember Hiroshima? It was a little like that. Dad and Claudia are sleeping together."

Marni nearly chokes on the sip of martini she'd just taken. "You're joking."

"I wish I were."

"Oh my God, hon," Marni says, "that's so brutal."

"That bitch," Hannah says.

"Yeah, that pretty much sums it up. She's walking around like she owns the place. It's creepy."

"Your dad gets bored easily enough. She'll be out of there in no time," Hannah says.

"Yeah," I say with a bitter half laugh. I feel this sudden swell of anger about the way Dad and Claudia have been acting. Did their treatment of Mom before she died, regardless of whether they'd been sleeping together, have anything to do with Mom's death? Was her death an accident or was it Mom's way of escaping?

"You know, it's funny, the other night I saw a vision of your mother. Hannah saw her too."

"Marni, we were tripping on X at the time."

"Yeah, I know. Still, I think she wanted to tell us something. Don't you think it's strange that we both saw her?"

"No, we were thinking about Helaina coming home. We were worried about her. We love you, Helaina, you know that."

"Did this apparition of my mother say anything?"

Hannah shoots Marni a pointed look.

"Uh . . . " Marni stammers.

The waitress comes by just then and I order a Long Island Iced Tea. When the waitress leaves, Hannah changes the subject. There is obviously something they aren't telling me, but I decide not to press the issue right now. "This might make you feel better. My sister is flying in from New York this weekend to go to a party in Vail. Brad Pitt might be there. In any case, it should be a killer party. She'll let us crash if you come with us. She's been dying to interview your dad."

Hannah's sister, Gilda, is a gossip columnist for a New York tabloid. She writes about celebrities and rich people in general, and my dad sort of fits into both groups. He's always making *Fortune*'s most influential and wealthiest people in America lists, but unlike a lot of the people on those lists—lots of rich old men on there—my Dad looks like a model or a soap opera star. He's profiled in magazines all the time and his picture regularly shows up in *People* and *Us*. My mom's death made the newspapers and magazines too, but it wasn't her picture that was highlighted, it was Dad's. *Look at the poor widower.* Though no writer said it outright, the message was clear: my father could now be added to another list, that of the most eligible bachelors in the country.

"That sounds cool."

"I hoped you'd be up for it. I think a little road trip is exactly what we need. I have to meet some guy worth shagging," Hannah says. "The last guy I shagged lasted like thirty seconds and I was like, well you can try some other ways to get me off, and he was like, no I don't think so. I was raging mad," Hannah says with an indignant roll of the eyes. "It's like, why did I even bother taking off my clothes? It took me longer to unbutton my shirt than the entire coital process lasted."

I smile. It feels good to be with these guys again, pretending like life is normal.

Hannah lights another cigarette and looks at me with one eyebrow cocked. "Any interesting dreams lately?"

She loves reviewing dreams. She's read all the "what your dreams mean" kind of books and is the one person I know who doesn't roll her eyes when you start a sentence, "So I had this dream last night . . . "

I think about the dream I had where I was outside in a parking lot and it began raining basketballs. None of them hit me, but a corpse in a body bag came thumping down, landing on the hood of my car. (Even though I don't have my own car in real life, in the dream I understood that it was mine.) Somehow I knew the body in the bag was my mother's. I woke up from the dream trembling and sweating. I got the feeling that my mother was trying to get me to look at her dead body, that there was something I was supposed to find. In real life, Mom's body was so battered by the crash that there was no possibility of an open casket. Anyway, Mom always wanted to be cremated and have her ashes released into the mountains, which is what we did after her funeral, so there is no body. Just a handful of us went—Dad, Claudia, me, and a few of Mom and Dad's friends. I shook the ashes out, and we watched her remains swirl in the breeze.

I don't want to tell Hannah my dream, though. Maybe it meant something, maybe it didn't, but I don't want to talk about it. So I say instead, "I haven't been remembering my dreams lately."

Hannah nods understandingly.

"Marni, how's Jake doing?" I ask.

"He's good." She smiles. "He's in Europe for a month. I miss him." She has this dreamy smile on her face at the mere mention of him, like a woman who has just fallen in love, not like a woman who has dated the same guy for

27

four years. They go to college together at Stanford. I'm pretty sure that this month he's traveling through Europe is the longest they've ever been apart. They're planning to get married after graduation. She'll have four years of medical school and he'll work for two years and then go back for his MBA in finance—they have it all planned out. I wonder what that would be like, to have some idea of what the future holds. I can't even figure out what I'm going to do next week.

"Ooh, he's cute," Hannah says, eyeing a guy who passes our table. "I'd do him."

"He's okay. He's not Jake," Marni says.

"If you marry Jake, you'll only be able to sleep with one guy in your entire life. Don't you want to know what you're missing?" Hannah asks.

"It's love." Marni shrugs. "That's all that counts."

"See, that's where you and I are different." Hannah points her cigarette at Marni to emphasize her point. "You're a romantic idealist and I'm a horny realist."

Marni smiles. She knows it's true.

We have a couple more drinks and gossip about people we know from high school.

Marni says that Stephanie Woodland had a nervous breakdown and dropped out of school. Stephanie was one of the smartest people in our class, so this news bums me out. I'm about to say as much when Hannah chimes in with a dig on Stephanie's substantial girth. "Ah yes, Stephanie Woodland, the girl voted 'Most likely to fill out the yards of fabric of her graduation gown.'"

I don't mean to laugh but I do, and then I immediately feel guilty. I'm acting just like the women I made fun of in my movie. About forty times a week I vow to become a better person, yet somehow I always manage to stay my imperfect self.

Hannah is sharing the latest news on another girl we went to school with when three guys approach our table and ask if we want to dance. The guys are cute, so when Hannah and Marni look at me, the newly motherless orphan, to see if I'm up for it, I shrug and nod.

The six of us dance in a circle. Hannah, Marni, and I promptly start joking around, dancing with '80s-style moves like the Wave where you start rolling with the fingers of your right hand, then lift your right elbow, then shoulder, then move to the left shoulder, elbow, then hand. When Marni starts moonwalking, it's all I can do not to collapse with laughter.

"You are so beautiful," the guy dancing next to her says.

"I have a boyfriend," she says, but it's obvious his compliment makes her feel good. Marni often gets ignored by guys when she's with me and Hannah, not because she's not cute, she is, but because she has such a good-girl, I'm-in-a-monogamous-relationship-so-don't-even-think-about-it attitude about her. The alcohol is making her flirty.

I know it's this confidence and excited energy that leads to what happens next.

"You guys, watch this!" Marni yells. "I'm going to do the Snake."

I'm about to suggest this is maybe not the best idea when Marni goes diving down. She was supposed to go down on her hands, then do a roll with her chest and then hips rolling across the ground. Instead, in her inebriated state, she crashes against the floor chin first.

"Are you okay?" I run up to her. I hear Hannah laughing behind me.

Thankfully, Marni is drunk enough not to feel any pain, and she cracks up too. She's got a bloody nose, but otherwise seems fine, so after I grab a few cocktail napkins to staunch the flow of blood, I laugh too. All six of us lose it, like it's the most hilarious thing we've ever seen. "Hey you guys, watch this! I'm going to do the snake!" We tease her relentlessly and can't stop laughing. I don't care if my laughter is aided by alcohol. It's been a while since I've laughed like this, and it feels good.

I don't drink anything but water for the last two hours until I'm sober enough to drive home. When I get there, Claudia is passed out on the couch, an empty bottle of wine on the table in front of her. How vulnerable she is right now.

I try to think of what I could do to get back at her for hurting Mom. Sleeping with her husband whether before or after her death is such an unimaginably shitty thing to do. Right now is the perfect opportunity. But all I can think of are juvenile antics like putting her hand in warm water. Oh how I would love for Dad to wake up and find Claudia slumbering in a puddle of her own urine. He would be irate if Claudia ruined his imported, custom-made couch. I could get rid of Claudia just like that, with an eighth-grade sleepover stunt.

Instead, I get a blanket from the closet and cover her.

Chapter 2

The next morning I wake up late, my body demanding an urgent injection of caffeine. I go downstairs and pull out the coffee beans and skim milk from the well-stocked fridge, pausing a moment to marvel at the brushed stainless steel refrigerator's gleaming interior stuffed full of fresh food. I suspect my refrigerator in New York would go into shock if we tried to fill it with colorful produce rather than the murky take-out it has grown used to. I grind up the beans, and then use the high-end espresso maker to whip my milk into a gentle froth. Sipping my latte, I return to my room and get the shower started.

Even after the caffeine and the shower I still don't feel even close to human. I blow-dry my hair and spend half an hour trying to curl it, gel it, and get it under control with hairspray, but no matter what I do, I look like an electrocuted Farrah Fawcett. With each minute that passes, I get more and more frustrated until my frustration swells like a roiling boil, and I collapse on the closed toilet seat and burst into tears. I feel like shit, but do I have to look like shit too? Why does everything have to be such a huge ordeal? Why does everything have to be so hard?

I look at myself in the mirror and am greeted by an image of an ugly girl with ratty hair and bloated, red eyes.

You can see glimpses of both my mother and Claudia in my features. Just little hints in my smile and my eyes. We all have the same light brown hair, though both Claudia and Mom have lightened theirs since they were teenagers.

Maybe if I start looking better I'll start feeling better. It's worth a shot, so I call Eric for an appointment. Usually I have to schedule an appointment weeks in advance, but he must feel sorry for me because he says he can squeeze me in this afternoon. I get dressed, put a little makeup on, and wait until it's time to go.

Eric's salon is downtown. As I drive around looking for a parking spot, I can't get over how much open space there is here in Denver compared to New York. I don't mean bigger because obviously it's rinky-dink in comparison. I mean it's airier here and there are so comparatively few people. It's a beautiful summer day, just a few gauzy clouds dappling the sky. It's not too hot, and the gentle warmth of the sun feels good on my skin. Somehow, though, all this emptiness has the effect of making me feel vulnerable and exposed. I miss the asphalt and the anonymity and the endless pulse of New York.

Eric hugs me when he sees me. "I'm so sorry, darling," he says. He's still as skinny as ever and is still wearing his dark hair short and gelled with as many hair products as his follicles can handle. He wears tight clothes to reveal every last one of his ropey muscles.

"I know. Me too."

He sits me down in the chair and runs his fingers through my hair.

"How are you doing?"

"I'm surviving."

Eric just stands there for a minute, looking stricken. "I keep thinking about one of the last times I saw her. I can't help but feel guilty."

"Why?"

"I think . . . I think I may have told her something that really hurt her. I just worry that maybe she was upset and distracted, and maybe that's why she didn't make the turn." He's talking in a whisper.

"About Dad and Claudia?"

"You know?"

"I suspected."

"Well, you know I've been doing Claudia's hair since she came to Colorado."

"Yeah?"

"Well, Claudia told me, told everyone here, really, that she was having an affair with your . . . with Gary. I thought your mother should know."

"I knew they were sleeping together. I wasn't sure if it started before or after Mom's accident," I say, more to myself than to Eric. To Eric I say, "You can't blame yourself."

"I just wonder if she was preoccupied, I don't know, thinking about it and maybe that's why . . . "

"It was an icy mountain road, it should have had a rail," I say, not convinced. Mom had been driving to Grand Junction when it happened. She'd gone to visit a friend who owned a winery there. Now I know why she went by herself. She needed to get away from Dad and Claudia.

"Hey, you know, can we not talk about this? I'm dealing with too many tragedies these days. Like my hair," I say, trying to lighten the mood.

"Yeah, I noticed. What's going on here?"

"I've just been a little preoccupied lately."

"Well, we'll get you all fixed up. Come on." I follow him back to the sink where he washes my hair, spending extra time massaging my scalp. We return to his station and as he trims my hair he tells me about his date with a good-looking but stupid guy. He's trying to cheer me up, distract me. He tells me about how they dated for a few weeks and the sex was great but it was so painful trying to hold a conversation with this guy that he eventually broke it off. I try to laugh in the right places but I'm having trouble concentrating. I wonder what it must have been like for Mom to have her hairdresser report that her husband was sleeping with her sister. Claudia must have known that telling Eric would have been the same thing as buying an ad in the *New York Times* declaring Dad's infidelity.

Mom knew. Mom knew. Why didn't she kick Claudia out? How could she live with that betrayal right under her roof?

Driving off the road into a dramatic death—at least it was a fitting end for my mother. She wouldn't like to have died quietly in the night. She'd been too quiet in life for too long.

Anger toward Dad and Claudia simmers within me, and I wonder what I can do to make things right.

When I get home from the salon, I stop in the bathroom to study my new haircut. I have to say I look much better. I'm quite certain I won't be able to style it myself with all these flips and waves and wisps and body, though. Tomorrow I suspect my head will look like a cat that got caught in the rain, but for today at least, I look pretty good.

I find Maria in the kitchen and ask her to tell Dad and Claudia that I'm not feeling well and I won't be joining

them for dinner. She gives me a look that I can't qu[ite]
read—pity, maybe? Had Dad and Claudia not planned
having dinner with me anyway?

It's going to be a very long summer.

Fortunately, Hannah chooses that moment to call me.
"What are you doing?" she asks.

"Nothing."

"Good. I'm going to come pick you up and take you to
the salon. We need to get you all fixed up for the party
Saturday."

"You'll be happy to know I just got back from the
salon. My hair is in a considerably better state of affairs."

"Thank God. But what about a bikini wax? Manicure?
Pedicure? Tan?"

"Um, no."

"All right then. There is still work to be done. I'm
picking you up in twenty minutes. We are going to be
partying with celebrities this weekend. We have to look
like starlets. This is a beauty emergency."

I laugh. "Okay, I'm yours. Mold me into the starlet
you believe I can be."

When Hannah picks me up in her sporty little Lotus
Elise, she tells me how she was able to finagle last-minute
appointments for a bikini wax for each of us.

"I don't know, Hannah, I've never had a bikini wax before. You know I'm not a fan of pain."

"I'm sorry, but who knows how many pool parties
we'll be invited to this summer? We simply must attend
to proper bikini-area maintenance."

I don't really have the energy to fight, so I just nod.

Hannah takes me right back to the salon I just came
from. I put a smile on my face because I don't want Eric
to know just how rattled I feel, but it turns out to be un-
necessary because Eric has already left for the day.

The bikini waxes, to my regret, are first. Hannah ds off with Gretchen. My appointment is with Zelda, ick, thirty-something Russian with heavy-lidded eyes a commanding presence. She looks like she could stle a bear and come out the winner, which doesn't help my nervousness one bit.

I follow Zelda into a room with violet walls and soft gold candelabra-looking lights, feeling nervous. I've usually relied on Nair for this sort of thing, and while I know Hannah and Marni are devotees of this, it's all scary and new for me.

Zelda hands me little white tissue-paper panties with pink rims and gives me a moment of privacy so I can change into them. They are so large they just float around the area in question, basically just posing as a sheath to maintain my decency, though in fact they aren't remotely concealing.

"Vat is dis?" she exclaims, when she returns to see the mess she has to work with. "You use razor."

"Um, sometimes."

She shakes her head, very unhappy with me. "Vat you want, you want Brazilian?"

"No, no. Just a simple bikini-line job so I can look tidy and neat in my bathing suit," I say.

"But everyone iz getting Brazilian."

"Yeah, I'm sure they are, but I'm really just kind of a nature girl at heart. You know, but a tidy nature girl."

"Everyone has Brazilian. You want a Brazilian. Very freeing. Very sexy."

"You know, that's fine, but I'm not so much into looking like a 12-year-old."

Zelda sighs. "Okay, ve do it your way."

I spend the next twenty minutes with legs splayed, feeling like an idiot. When Zelda rips the wax off, it's every bit as agonizing as I was expecting. And then I look down.

Zelda has gone far over the neat triangular look I was hoping for, and in fact, I have something resembling a landing pad down there.

Zelda leaves so I can get dressed, and I go to the mirror to inspect the situation more closely. This is when I discover that not only do I have rectangular-patterned pubes, Zelda applied the wax slightly askew, so I have a dyslexic lightning-bolt sort of a look going on.

It is, I'm afraid, nothing like sexy.

"What's wrong?" Hannah asks I emerge into the waiting area where she is sitting with a copy of *Vogue*.

I tell her of how my beauty plans went hideously awry and she snorts with laughter.

"Thank you. That's just the sort of support I need. I really appreciate that."

"Come on, we'll get our nails done really bright red. It will distract men from your creative pube arrangement."

"I don't expect any men to be able to inspect my 'pube arrangement' anyway."

"You can't lose heart, Helaina."

We get our toes painted first. We sit side by side in large black-leather chairs and put our feet in our own personal little Jacuzzi tubs for feet. We each have an Eastern European woman working on us. Mine is a stout woman who has a distractingly large mole on her nose that I can't stop staring at.

This isn't the first time I've gotten my nails done, but I always feel a little guilty about it. I stink at doing my own nails, but it seems like something that should be within my realm of talents, so I feel weird paying someone to do it for me. It does feel nice to be pampered a little, though. My nails are in terrible shape. I can see why Hannah felt compelled to march me to a salon. In our world, it's all right to *feel* like you're dying inside, but it's not okay to look like you're falling apart.

When we're done, Hannah says, "Let's go to my place. My parents are in Paris for the summer."

"Vacationing?"

"Are you kidding me? My parents don't vacation. No, they're doing a consulting project to help this French guy open up a series of Chinese restaurants."

"But you're Korean."

"True, but the French guy doesn't know that. Anyway, a restaurant is a restaurant and my parents know how to launch one."

Hannah's parents' place is beautiful. They're gone so much for work, Hannah basically lives here alone when she's home from school. It's large and has a gorgeous view of the mountains from the balcony on one side. Her living room has vaulted ceilings. It's done all in creams with splashes of red and black throw pillows and black vases with exotic red flowers.

"Do you want a drink?" she asks when we get inside.

"Sure."

She makes a pitcher of vodka and Crystal Light lemonade and takes the pitcher along with two glasses upstairs to her room, which is bright and funky. She has three white walls and one bright pink wall. There is a bright-orange chair, a lemon yellow bedspread, and a royal purple beanbag that I sprawl across, my limbs splayed. She slips an Incubus CD into her CD player.

"Helaina? Helaina?"

"Hmmm? What?"

"Earth to Helaina. Where are you?"

"Sorry, I was just thinking that it's so weird that my father seems fine with the death of his wife of twenty-one years. He didn't cry at the funeral. He didn't really seem upset at all, for that matter."

"Come on, Helaina. I know you're upset, but let's try to think of cheery things."

"Sorry, Hannah, but I don't want to be cheered up right now. I just want to be sad."

"What should we talk about then?"

"We can only talk about depressing things. Like the downfall of Edgar Allen Poe."

"What was the downfall of Edgar Allen Poe?"

"Well, some say alcoholism."

"That fits. Speaking of which, you need another drink. Gimme." She extends her hand for my glass and I give it to her. She makes another round of drinks. "How are things at school?" she asks.

I smile. Hannah prefers to just ignore unpleasant things. Personally, I think that sometimes a good cry is highly underrated. I think too many people think emotions should be like air-conditioned offices where the temperature never changes no matter what's going on outside.

I tell her about my film.

"That's so exciting! International film festivals. You're going to be famous."

"Very few directors are famous-famous, and that's fine with me."

We're on our fourth round of drinks when Hannah's eyes grow big. "Oh! I forgot. We're not quite through with our beauty makeover extravaganza." She jumps off her bed and runs into her bathroom.

"What's left?" I call after her.

When she emerges, she shows me a tube of Lancôme self-tanning cream, running her hand beneath it like a model on *The Price is Right*. "We must be tan!"

"You already have lovely caramel skin," I say.

"But I want chocolate, not caramel. Chocolate trumps caramel every time."

I nod blurrily. She seems like a wise and thoughtful leader at this moment.

We slather on the self-tanner. As I spread it across my skin, I realize just how tired I am. As soon as I'm sufficiently covered in tanning cream, I stumble over to Hannah's bed. "Tired," I mumble as I hurl my body across the mattress. She nods and lies beside me.

I wake up at some point, desperate for a pee. I stumble to Hannah's bathroom, use her toilet, and when I'm washing my hands, I see what I've done and let out a scream that jolts Hannah from her slumber.

"Wha? Huh?"

I rush out and see that Hannah also looks like an idiot.

Here's a tip for you: Don't self-tan while you've been drinking. You are supposed to wait ten minutes before sitting or putting clothes on after rubbing the stuff into your skin. You are patently *not* supposed to immediately sprawl across a bed and toss to and fro, because if you do, you'll smear the stuff in such a way that you'll look like you have Maori tattoos.

"What the hell are we supposed to do? We look like total dorks," I say.

"Maybe we can apply more."

"Won't that just make the places we're already dark even darker?"

"Maybe."

"Shit!"

"It'll come off in a few days. Just loofah like crazy. Shit. I hope Brad Pitt isn't at the party this weekend. I can't meet him looking like this."

"Ooooh," I moan. My plan to start feeling better by improving my appearance has thus far proven to be a spectacular failure. "What time is it?" I look at my watch. It's only a little after eleven at night, but it feels like four in the morning. I must still be jet-lagged. Also, I'm guessing it didn't help that we drank so much without eating. I feel completely sober after my nap, though. "I should go home."

"Are you sure? You can stay if you want."

"Thanks, but I think I want my own bed. You did cheer me up though. Except for the retarded tan and unfortunate pube situation, of course."

"I love you."

"I love you too."

When I get home, I go to the kitchen looking for something to eat, but then I realize I can't really imagine eating solid food.

I hear a noise in the living room and go to check it out. It's Claudia. She's sitting on the couch humming to herself. An almost empty bottle of red wine sits on the table in front of her and she has a full glass in her hand. She's wearing a glazed expression.

"Hello!" she trills.

"Hi. Where's Dad?"

"Oh!" She gives a dismissive wave of her hand. "He flew to Chicago for the night. Business. You know."

I'm curious to know more about this woman who is essentially a stranger to me. Plus, she knew my mother twenty-six years longer than I got to know her, and I covet her memories. I want Claudia to tell me everything she remembers about my mother's childhood, adolescence, and life before me.

"What's the matter?" Claudia asks. First I think she's asking me why I look like an orange-striped zebra, then she says, "You look blue."

"I am blue. My mother just died. Aren't you blue?"

"Oh, it's sad, sure," she says, not sounding sad at all. "Helaina, sit down."

I pause a moment, then sit on the ottoman in front of the couch so I'm facing her.

"Have you been avoiding me?" she asks.

I shrug.

"I'm not that scary I promise. You just need to get to know me."

"How could I get to know you? You've never been around. My mother invited you to every Thanksgiving and Christmas we had for years and you never came."

"Yeah, well . . . you know, your mom and I were never that close."

"Why not?"

She pauses a moment. "We just didn't share the same interests." She inspects her glass of wine. "In school, your mother just quietly got good grades and stayed out of trouble. It was like she never wanted anyone to pay attention to her at all. Me? I didn't want to just be in all the plays, I wanted to be the *star*. I didn't understand why your mother wasn't . . . *hungrier*."

"Didn't you have anything in common?"

"Not much. Although . . . I remember when I went to your mother's wedding. It was so beautiful. I remember thinking that I wouldn't have done anything differently. And that was weird because we did everything differently. We wore different clothes and different shoes. We had different friends and different goals. We had different taste in food and men."

Not all men, apparently. "You both dyed your hair."

Claudia laughs and rakes her fingers through her hair. The gesture leaves a tuft of a curl sticking out comically askew. The Claudia in front of me now who is drunk and wobbly and slurring her words is such a contrast from the image-perfect Claudia I saw at the dinner party the other night. It's all very Jekyll and Hyde if the part of Dr. Jekyll were played by an über-fashionable version of Martha Stewart. Maybe playing the part of a perfect beauty and perfect hostess gets too tiring and she needs to be a drunk slob for a while to let go. Seeing Claudia drunk reminds me of the articles I read about how her drinking caused bloat and weight gain that contributed to her acting career falling apart.

"Her wedding was perfect," she continues. "I remember thinking she was one lucky lady. But this"—Claudia takes her free hand and gestures to the large room—"I never could have imagined this. I knew your father was a bright, ambitious man, but I couldn't have imagined just how successful he would become."

She's not giving me the information I crave. I want to know what funny things my mom did when she was young. What games did she play? Did she dream of having a pony? I want to know everything, but I start with this question, "Did you and Mom *ever* have fun together?"

"Sure, I suppose we did." She drains her glass of wine and studies the bruise-colored drops clinging to the otherwise empty glass. "Oh, I know. I remember one time, your mother and I were in the backseat of the car on a road trip to visit our grandparents, your great-grandparents. Our father had already died by then . . . let's see, I guess your mom would have been about eight and I would have been six. Anyway, it was Christmastime and there was several inches of snow on the ground. Your mother and I were getting stir-crazy as kids will get on a long drive. We were arguing with each other, driving Mom crazy. She kept telling us to knock it off, but we didn't. Finally she pulled over to a rest stop and forced us to get out of the car. We weren't wearing shoes or jackets, but she made us get out wearing just our socks. Then she got back in the car and drove off. She came back for us after just a few minutes, of course, but by then we were chilled to the bone and knew that she meant business."

"That's your happiest memory of Mom? Arguing with her and getting stranded in the cold?"

"We were in it together, don't you see? We were in it together." For the first time tonight, Claudia focuses her unfocused eyes on me. "You know, you could be such a pretty girl if you spent a little more time on how you looked. Where do you buy your clothes—Anarchists Are Us? How are you ever going to find a husband looking like that?"

"Claudia, I'm twenty years old. I'm not worried about finding a husband. I'm not even thinking about it. Anyway, it's not like you or Mom had much luck with your husbands. What makes you think being married is the answer?"

"You need a man."

"Why?"

"Security. Sad but true."

"Security? Haven't you ever heard of dead bolts?"

"Economic security," she says impatiently, as if she's explaining a very simple concept and I'm just too thick to comprehend.

"You need a man for his money? Are you serious? Claudia, I don't know if you know this, but women are allowed to have jobs these days. We can own property. We can even vote if we want." My sarcasm is probably lost on her, but I can't stop myself.

"I'm not saying it's fair, but it's the way the world works, sorry to say." Although the way she slurs it, it comes out more like "shorrrytosay." "Sure, sometimes you find a woman who heads a company and makes a lot of money, but most of the time, a woman just can't make enough money on her own."

"Claudia, are you really suggesting that you should marry a man for his money? What about love?"

"Love," she rolls her eyes and gives a dismissive wave of her hand. It's the nonverbal equivalent of "ba hum bug." "He'll cheat on you, you'll cheat on him, it's best if you've got some cash." She studies me again. Her gaze is so intense it makes me uncomfortable. "You're too skinny. Have you thought about implants?"

"*Breast* implants?"

"Of course."

"No. God, no."

"You really should think about it. They'd look good on you. Men like curves."

"Claudia, I have to go to bed. You should have a glass of water. You'll feel better in the morning."

"Pfff," she scoffs.

"Good night, Claudia."

I stomp into the kitchen trying to process the conversation I just had. Claudia was from the generation of women where women weren't necessarily expected to have careers of their own. That's the only thing I can think of to explain her horribly unromantic view of romance and marriage.

Or am I just being naive?

No, no, she just made her living with her looks and has always been dependent on men. I'm smart. I have talent. I refuse to buy into Claudia's ugly view of male–female relationships.

I grab a wine glass and a corkscrew, and then I go downstairs to our cellar to pick out a bottle of wine. Mom and Dad have taught me some things about wine, but I don't know enough to know which is the most expensive. I'm guessing an '89 Chateau Le Pin red Bordeaux is going to be pretty pricey, though, so that's what I choose.

I sneak up to my room, hoping not to be noticed. I hate that I am sneaking around my own house, like a criminal, an intruder.

I close and lock the door to my room, open the bottle of wine, and pour myself a generous glass and swallow it down in a couple gulps.

I pour another glass and set it down next to my bed. I turn my CD player on and hit the Mixed Play button. I look around for something to do. I've got an entire wall of shelves filled with books. Richard Wright, Margaret Atwood, John Steinbeck, Sylvia Plath. I've got lots of anthologies on film, and collections of poetry and short stories. I want something light, something that won't make me think at all. A comic book, a magazine. I've got a library-sized book collection and nothing light enough for my mood. I probably couldn't concentrate anyway.

I could watch TV or a DVD. I could listen to Brian Regan or Margaret Cho or another comedian's routine on CD. Laughing, that would be good right now. But I don't feel like listening to comedy. I don't feel like doing anything but not feeling. I should be feeling rage at Claudia and Dad. How could Claudia do this to Mom? Humiliate her like this after all Mom's done for her? All of Mom's friends go to that salon, they all must have known. But somehow I don't feel anger. Instead what I feel is the combination of anxiety, restlessness, depression, and confusion that has settled in my chest as a more or less permanent ache since Mom died.

So I take the obvious next step on the path to numb oblivion, I drink more wine. I should have asked Claudia about Mom in the last days of her life, but right now the pain is still too new, too raw. I don't yet have the courage. Would Claudia tell me the truth anyway? She's an actress. She could tell me anything and it would be convincing.

And if my mother's death wasn't an accident, what would I do then?

It seems to take forever for the wine to kick in. I've gotten to know the decorations on the wall intimately by the time my poster of Janeane Garofalo's Denver performance last winter starts to blur.

I'd seen Janeane over Christmas break, the last time I'd seen my mom alive. I was home for three weeks, and it seemed like Mom and I were fighting all the time. Why were we fighting? What were we even fighting about? Mom and I used to have a good relationship. Did she change or did I? I don't know, maybe both. Things began to change not long after we moved here from Boston when Dad moved Able Technologies' corporate headquarters to reduce operation costs. That's when Mom quit her job, but it was also just about the time I was hitting puberty, so maybe ornery hormones were to blame for the tension between us.

I was always harder on Mom than I was on Dad. Ever since I was little, it was practically like Mom was a single parent. Dad traveled so much for work and worked such long hours when he was in town that he seemed more like a myth, some guy Mom told me stories about, than my father.

I was nine years old when we moved to Denver. Until the move, Mom had worked as a creative director with an advertising-and-marketing agency, but the truth was that Mom's salary wasn't needed, and Dad needed her around more and more to plan dinner parties and attend events. Being a CEO's wife had become a full-time job.

It was toward the end of the fall semester when we moved, an awkward time for me to be switching schools.

I remember what a dork I felt like on that first day of school, all skinny and knobby-kneed. I had always been a pretty confident-and-outgoing kid, but on that day, the world seemed a frightening place. Suddenly other nine-year-olds were bloodthirsty pack lions in Nike gym shoes. No one talked to me. I silently observed my classmates all day, trying to work up the confidence to go talk to somebody. At my other school, I'd always just *had* friends, I had no idea how go about *making* them.

I knew right away that I wanted to be friends with Tammy Harris. She was pretty, brazen, and the other kids seemed to gravitate to her. At lunch, I tried to smile at her, but she either didn't see me or ignored me. All day I felt ignored or, worse, like the other kids were glaring at me. I couldn't figure out what I had done wrong.

I woke up the next morning with a stomachache, my insides knotted with anxiety. Those fifteen minutes at recess and fifty minutes of lunch loomed ahead of me like a dark hallway in a nightmare where no matter how fast or how far you run, it just keeps going on and on, never ending.

When Mom came to get me out of bed, I was already awake. I hadn't been able to sleep much that night.

Mom started singing her "Rise and shine and make that morning f-i-i-i-ne" song. She always deliberately hammed it up, dancing around and acting silly, and no matter how cranky I was to be woken up, it usually made me crack a smile. Not this morning.

"I don't feel good," I said.

"You don't look sick."

"Well I am. I have a stomachache."

"Is anything bothering you?"

I shrugged.

"I know things were lonely yesterday, but you're going to make friends soon, I promise. The only way you're going to make friends is if you're there to meet them."

"Everybody looked at me like I'm a great big friendless geek. Which I am. Why did we have to move now? Why couldn't we have moved at the beginning of the semester? Then there'd be other new kids. I *hate* Dad."

"If you're friendly and smile a lot, people will warm up to you."

I rolled my eyes. "Yeah, right."

"Just ask the kids about themselves. People love to talk about themselves. Just give it a few more days before you throw in the towel. Okay? For me?"

Grudgingly, I went to school. I remembered my mom's advice to smile and be friendly.

At recess, I watched Tammy jump rope with two other girls for about five minutes before I finally forced myself to approach her, looking as friendly as I could, and ask her if I could join them. She looked at me as if I'd suggested we bomb the school.

"We have all the people we need."

I nodded. Stood there. It was Tammy's turn to jump rope, but the three girls just stood staring right back at me.

"What are you looking at?" she demanded.

"Can I watch?"

"No. Don't you have any friends you can play with?"

I could feel my cheeks burn with embarrassment. In one simple statement, she'd done away with social niceties and revealed me for what I was: a friendless loser. Having it said out loud made it real. My loser status wasn't just a product of my imagination; it was a truth that others knew.

I backed up, then walked quickly to the side of the

school. I hid for the remainder of recess, wishing desperately that I could disappear.

That afternoon I came home crying to Mom that nobody liked me, that I had no one to play with. Mom consoled me with the promise that for my birthday in mid-December, we'd have a huge party. We'd invite my entire class, and everyone would have a great time and realize what a fun person I was.

Now that Mom wasn't working and we had a maid and a cook, Mom had little else to occupy her day, so she threw herself into planning this party as if it were her full-time job.

Every afternoon I would come home from school and Mom would share her new ideas with me. She would show me possible cake designs and flavors and party-favor options and we'd review different menu possibilities.

At our new house we had an indoor/outdoor pool covered by a glass atrium that we could open in the summer. Even though my birthday was so close to Christmas, we decided to have a luau—a Luau-in-December party. The invitations, which Mom designed, had a Christmas tree decorated in flower leis and sunglasses. The tree was topped with a sun wearing sunglasses and a smile. Inside the invitation, along with the when and where, kids were instructed to wear their swimming suits.

Dad agreed to play Santa Claus. I was giddy with excitement over the thought of Dad wearing Bermuda shorts and a Hawaiian shirt padded to give him a belly. He was going to wear a white beard and wig, sunglasses, and a baseball cap. He would bring a bagful of gifts that he'd give out as party favors.

We sent the invitations out on a Saturday. On Wednesday I waited for my classmates to rally around me, to beg me to sit with them at lunch and play with them at recess.

Wednesday came and went, and no one said a thing to me, no one even mentioned they got an invitation. On Thursday, when we were in art class, the last class of the day, I approached Tammy's worktable. She and Rose Pozen were working side by side talking. Their conversation stopped abruptly when I walked up to them.

"Hi, did you guys get the invitation to my party?"

Tammy glared at me, and then looked down at the painting of a flower that she was working on. "Yes."

"Are you going to be able to come?"

"I guess I have to," she snapped, still not looking at me.

"What do you mean?"

"I mean if I don't go your dad will probably fire my dad, that's what my mom said."

"What are you talking about?"

She rolled her eyes. "Whatever. Like you don't know."

But I didn't know. All I knew was that no one liked me and I was destined to be a social pariah. It was all I could do to make it through the rest of the class without crying.

Mom picked me up after school and immediately asked me what was wrong.

As soon as she pulled off school property, I burst into tears. Through jagged sobs I said, "Tammy says that Dad will fire her dad if she doesn't come to my party. What is she talking about?"

Mom sighed and explained that Dad's company was in the process of acquiring another company and that a lot of people might lose their jobs. Mom told me that maybe that was why the kids weren't warming up to me, but we'd throw such a great party that they'd forget all about who my dad was and they'd just be lining up to be my best friends.

On the day of the party, the girls showed up wearing

sundresses beneath their winter coats and boots, and the boys wore shorts and flowered shirts. They all wore the expressions of kids who were about to get punished for something they didn't do.

When Mom went into the kitchen to fill up a bowl of chips, I felt like I was facing a firing line. Dad was supposed to come in any minute now as Santa Claus bearing gifts. He had to work that morning, but he promised he'd be home by two o'clock for the party. I prayed he'd come soon to break up the horrible silence.

"You guys can help yourselves to something to eat or you can go swimming if you want," I offered hopefully. The table was filled up with lemonade and punch and barbequed hot dogs and hamburgers. There was corn on the cob and potato salad and brownies.

"You think you're so special just because you have a swimming pool?" Hamilton Farnsworth asked.

"Show off," Tammy said.

"No, I . . . " I stammered.

I could feel my throat get tight, tears threatening, when the atrium doors began opening and a rush of cold air filled the room. At first I thought one of the kids had flipped the switch accidentally, then I heard my Mom say, "If you kids want to fight, that's fine, but you should do it the old-fashioned way." She walked out into the snow wearing nothing besides her sandals and a sundress over her swimsuit. She grabbed a handful of snow and packed it into a snowball and hit Hamilton in the chest.

No one moved for a few seconds. We were too busy gaping, eyes wide, at my apparently insane mother.

"You think you can catch me?" Mom asked. Then she threw another snowball and this one hit me in the arm.

I shrieked and ran outside to get a snowball of my own. Hamilton and a few others followed, and in less than a minute, the scene was total pandemonium, a cacophony of shrieks and laughter.

We'd run outside, grab a snowball, pelt somebody, and then dash inside and run around the pool or hide behind a lounge chair just long enough to warm up. Gelsey was the first person to tear off her sundress, revealing the bathing suit she'd been wearing beneath it, and jump into the heated pool to warm up. The rest of us followed her example. Then a few brave souls jumped out of the pool, ran outside to pack fresh snowballs, and would throw a few snowballs before jumping back into the pool again.

Impromptu teams and strategies formed. Tammy told me and Allison Walden to sneak up on Jami Winters and get her with a full-frontal surprise attack. After we threw our snowballs at her, we ran laughing wildly into the swimming pool.

When we finally got tired out, our throats sore from so much yelling, Mom closed the atrium and handed out towels and hot cocoa. We ate lunch and cake and while everyone digested their food, Mom donned the Santa Claus cap and passed out the party favors. (Dad never showed.)

In retrospect, it's amazing that nobody got pneumonia. If anybody did get sick, I never knew about it. To this day, it was one of the best parties I've ever been to.

Mom had been right; the party broke down whatever barriers had been keeping the other kids at a distance. Afterward, I got invited to come over to other kids' houses after school or to go to the roller rink on Saturdays, which was *the* thing to do when we were nine. I even got invited to one of Tammy's slumber parties. Tammy and I hung out a few times after that, but it was Gelsey who became my best friend until she moved away.

Dad did end up buying the company and laying off

about 15 percent of the workforce, but most of the people who got the ax were receptionists or customer-support specialists or technicians who couldn't afford to live in our neighborhood and send their kids to my school.

I didn't think much about the layoffs until years later when I bumped into a drunk Rick Harwell at a party in high school. I didn't know Rick, but when I introduced myself to him, he said, "You're not related to Gary Denner, are you?" And he told me about how his dad had gotten laid off. He was out of work for ten months. Then he killed himself. It made me realize just how much power my father wielded: the ability to give jobs or take them away, to enable financial security or to rip it out from under families. My father could destroy lives as quickly and easily as he could sign his own name.

On the first day of junior high, where the kids from three grade schools were brought together, I sat next to Hannah during the school assembly. I loved her take-no-bullshit attitude and her dry sense of humor. It was obvious from the expensive clothes she was wearing that she, too, came from a wealthy family, and it would soon become apparent that our backgrounds were similar in other ways as well. Her parents and my dad were the kind of adults who found it hard to drag themselves away from making money to attend our plays and recitals, which explains a lot about how Hannah and I turned out.

We met Marni three months later when I saw her sitting by herself in the cafeteria at lunch. I didn't recognize her, but I recognized that desperate look in her eyes. "Hey, are you new?" I asked her.

She nodded. "My parents just got transferred to Denver General Hospital."

"Are they like doctors or something?"

"Surgeons."

"My name is Helaina. You want to sit with Hannah and me? We're over there."

"Oh yes, thank you." We took our trays over to where Hannah was sitting.

"Hey Hannah, this is . . . "

"Marni."

"Marni. She's new. Her parents just got transferred to Denver General. They're surgeons."

"Cool," Hannah said.

"It's nice to meet you," Marni said.

Hannah and I filled Marni in on the cool teachers, the crap teachers, the kids to hang out with, and the ones to avoid. Marni clearly admired Hannah's audaciousness and seemed to think I was hilarious. Marni had a gentleness and optimism that Hannah and I needed more of in our lives.

The three of us have been best friends ever since.

I think it would be safe to say that the wine has officially kicked in. I look at the framed photograph of Mom and me from my graduation that rests on my bedside table and blink away the tears that pool in my eyes.

Mom. Mom. God, I miss her. The ache is too ferocious, too much.

I consider, for a moment, slitting my wrists, making all this pain, all these thoughts go away. But I can't take the chicken's way out of this pain just yet. I need to figure out how to get back at Claudia and Dad for the way they treated her.

I look at the few drops of wine clinging to the bottom of my glass like tea leaves that can divine the future. If only they could distill the past and tell me whether my mother killed herself, or if her death was an accident. Did

Claudia shredding Mom's reputation make Mom want to die? Was Mom distracted, deep in thought, and that's why she didn't make the turn?

Mom didn't look great when I last saw her, but she didn't look bad either. She seemed happy enough. Of course, I know better than anyone about Mom's ability to smile and pretend everything was just fine. How many times had I heard her crying, then heard her pick up the phone with a cheery "Hello! It's so good to hear from you!" How many times had I caught her crying in the pantry during a dinner party, then seen her wipe her tears away and paste a smile on her face, acting like hostess extraordinaire, like nothing was wrong?

The wine finally makes me black out and I sleep in jagged, unrestful spurts.

I dream I see my mother. She's in my room, wearing her white silk pajamas and her white silk robe, untied. She's just watching me, like she'd just woken up in the middle of the night and wanted to check on me.

"Mom? Mom?"

Mom turns and walks out of my bedroom. I throw off my covers and run out into the hallway. She's walking toward her and Dad's bedroom, her open robe billowing behind her.

I follow her into the room. Mom looks at me, then glances around. What is she looking for? She looks at me again. She turns and walks to the adjoining room, her study.

I run in there after her but don't see her. I look around the room but she's gone. "Mom? Mom?"

I wake up with a start. I sit up and look around. It takes me a minute to catch my breath. I feel as scared as when that creepy guy was trying to break into my apartment in New York. When I'd woken up that night and seen his shadow in the window outside on the fire escape, the crowbar in his hand, I was terrified, my heart pounding, every part of me violently alert. I feel that way now, but that's ridiculous. Why would a dream about my mother scare me?

Maybe because it wasn't a friendly visit; she wanted something. Did she want me to follow her? She wanted me to see something in the bedroom, or her study, or maybe both.

But what? Maybe she wants me to look around the house and see if I can find anything about her or Claudia. Maybe I can find out what was going on before the accident. I'll just wait until Dad and Claudia are out of the house, and then I can look around.

I feel better now that I've finally decided to do something. Granted, my plans are vague, but I have a next step. I'm able to get back to sleep, and eventually manage to make it through the long hours of the night.

Chapter 3

At Hannah's request, I've packed an overnight bag for our little trip to Vail. Fortunately, my tragic attempt at self-tanning has lightened some, and with makeup I almost look presentable.

Hannah picks me up in her ruby-red Lotus Elise, a two-seater sports car that is packed with so many suitcases we could open our own mall. Marni is in the passenger seat with suitcases wedged in all around her.

"Where am I supposed to sit?" I ask. "Why do you have all this luggage? We're only going for one night."

"I want to be prepared," Hannah says. "What if there is swimming or some kind of formal event?"

"First of all, people rarely throw balls and banquets at the last minute, and even so, a ball gown and bikini don't require forty-six suitcases. And you still haven't addressed the issue of where I'm going to sit. Why don't we take Marni's Escalade? Or my Viper? There would be plenty of room for all of us."

"No! I have this great car and I want to show it off. There is plenty of room. Get in."

Rolling my eyes, I do. Hannah actually packs *around* my body, putting my bag and a suitcase in my lap. It's such a tight fit I can't move my limbs, tap a toe, or sneeze.

"Why am I friends with you?" I ask.

"Because you love me."

"But why?"

"We'll be there soon."

We've just pulled out of my driveway, but to bug her I say, "Are we there yet?"

"I'm going to turn on hip-hop if you make one more peep."

"No! Not hip-hop. I'll be good."

It's a two-hour drive to Vail and except for the extreme discomfort I'm in, it's actually a pretty fun drive. Teasing Marni and Hannah and getting teased right back is a surprisingly entertaining way to kill time.

When we get to the party, we see Gilda right away. Gilda is as skinny as her sister, with a blunt haircut that looks sharp enough to slice through skin. Her hair is shiny and black just like her outfit and her perilously high-heeled shoes.

"Sucks about your mom," she says.

"Yes, it most certainly does." I love her for not asking how I'm doing.

"No sign of Brad yet, but I hear that girl over there slept with Christian Slater."

"Huh," I say, looking at the girl and trying to sound impressed with this bit of information.

"So when are you going to get me that interview with your dad?"

"I don't know. How long will you be in town?"

"Till Sunday night."

"I might be able to swing a lunch date with him on Sunday, but I can't guarantee it. He doesn't have much time." I don't know if my Dad will agree to the interview. Gilda is known for her scalpel-sharp writing that skewers nearly everyone. Known, that is, among people who read

People and *Us* and watch *Entertainment Tonight.* My father is not one of these people.

Gilda gives me her card and tells me she has to go mingle but to give her a call. I look around. I don't see Hannah or Marni. I'm surrounded by people but suddenly feel out of place and very alone. If I wanted to express the feeling on film, I'd have my character in the middle of the room looking preoccupied about something. I'd pan the room and get snippets of the dozen conversations going on around the character, getting louder and louder until it sounded like the scream of a dozen teakettles going off at the same time, all competing for attention, then I'd zoom in with a close-up of the character, then look out from the character's perspective into the crowd like she was being encircled by a pack of sharks.

I go to the bar to pour myself another drink and decide to take the whole bottle with me. I look around, observing my surroundings like an anthropologist. *To indicate that she's in heat, the human female will open her eyes wide, toss her hair, touch her desired mate's forearm gently, and laugh extravagantly at unfunny jokes,* my notes would read.

The party is packed with people. Even though the house is enormous, everyone is so crowded around the bar that we're about one-tenth of a micron apart. I push my way out of the crowd and look around. There's a contingent of dreadlocked guys and girls swaying to reggae music around a portable CD player. What is it about people who like reggae music that they feel compelled to wear clothes that look like they were salvaged from the bottom of somebody's garbage can twenty years ago, that's what I want to know.

I spot Marni and Hannah, who are off on the side of what has been made into a makeshift dance area around the entertainment center. The music being blared over the area is techno.

"Hey, girls," I say.

"Hey," Hannah says. "What's going on with you in school? Any guys we should know about?"

"Nope. Nothing."

"Aren't there something like two million single men in New York? You'd think at least some of them would be straight and worth kissing."

"I'm sure there are. That's the problem. There are too many choices. I got asked out by two different Scotts on the same day at the same party. They were both cute and they both seemed nice and I just couldn't decide who I liked better so I didn't go out with either of them. Anyway, I think it's easier to just be friends with guys."

"So have you had an orgasm yet?"

I love Hannah's honesty . . . most of the time, but when Hannah's bluntness is turned on me, it's not always quite as much fun.

"No," I admit, "I haven't had anyone to practice with."

"You don't need a man in your life. Come on, Helaina, we're in a new millennium. Why haven't you been practicing the shower-nozzle masturbation techniques we discussed at Christmas break?"

Ugh. Shower-nozzle masturbation. What a hassle. "I've been busy. I'll get around to it."

"Hmmm," she clucks disapprovingly. "Speaking of orgasms, I need to find myself a guy. Don't be shy, girls!"

Hannah leaves us. She checks out the host's music collection and removes the techno music, replacing it with West Coast swing. Being her usual take-charge self, she miraculously convinces a respectable segment of the party to dance with her.

A drunk but cute black man asks me to dance. I nod

and follow him out to the makeshift dance floor. "What's your name?" he asks.

"Helaina. What's yours?"

"Xavier." Yeah, right. It's probably Bob. "Where are you from?"

"Denver."

He nods and we dance for a minute or two. I don't know how to swing dance, so we just make up our own moves. "What's your name?"

"It's still Helaina."

"I'm Xavier."

"We've covered this."

"What?"

"Nothing."

"What did you say your name was?"

I gesture that I'm done dancing since, clearly, meaningful dialogue is not to be had between the thundering music and Xavier/Bob's blood-alcohol content.

I stand around sipping my drink for a few minutes. I spot a good-looking guy with dark curly hair and make eye contact with him. He seems to smile at me, but maybe I'm imagining it. No, I didn't imagine it—he's coming this way!

"Not a bad party," he says, smiling. "Where are you from?"

"I grew up in Denver but I go to school in New York. That's where I plan to stay after graduation. You?"

"I work in Boulder. I'm Jeremy."

"Helaina."

"Would you like to dance?"

Before I can answer, Hannah comes over and says, "Get on the dance floor, you two!" She grabs Jeremy's hand and pulls him over to the crowd of dancers and they start dancing together.

Before I can even be disappointed, a man with white-blond hair worn in icy spikes grabs my hand and asks me to dance. "I don't know how," I say.

"I'll show you how."

"It's not th—"

He pulls me onto the dance floor so fast my drink splashes everywhere as I set it down on a glass end table. He starts whipping me around like a rag doll, and every time he spins me, I shriek and stumble over my feet.

"I Bruno," he shouts over the din of the music in a heavy German accent. I can't even tell him my name because I'm too busy concentrating on staying alive as he throws me around. Out of the corner of my eye I watch Jeremy and Hannah. They look like professional dancers, so young and cute and hip they could be in a Gap commercial. Jeremy does this move where he grabs Hannah's side and tosses her behind his back so her legs come swinging up on his other side. Bruno decides to copy this move, and it doesn't bother him in the least that I have thus far showed no dancing ability whatsoever. I'm shocked to find myself being hurled over someone's back, and I'm not sure how it happens, but Bruno loses his grasp on me and I go flying, skidding into several people before finally stopping when I crash into a wall. Fortunately, my hand hit the wall first, and I didn't ram my nose into the paint job, but still, there is simply no graceful way to recover from something like this.

"Ugh," I moan.

"Oh my goodness, are you okay?" some girl asks. I pause a moment to assess the situation and find to my surprise that, miraculously, I'm okay. I start laughing as much out of embarrassment as anything else.

I decide that in an effort to avoid mortal injury, it

would be safest for me to stay off the dance floor and focus on drinking myself into a coma.

When I wake up in the morning, the room looks like a World War II hospital, with bodies strewn everywhere. I get up, stagger around, and find Hannah and Marni in the poolroom. They are using sweatshirts as pillows (no doubt from the department-store's worth of clothes Hannah brought with her) and are curled up in tight little balls to keep warm.

We drive home, our mouths feeling mossy, our heads aching. Hannah tells me that I sat in a corner all night mumbling about how I couldn't get Mom out of my mind, that her ghost was following me around, and I wasn't going to let Claudia get away with it.

"It was pretty trippy," she says.

I don't have the energy to say anything. I do remember the corner but I don't remember saying anything. But then, I was pretty wasted.

When I get home I call my dad on his cell phone. He's at the golf course.

"Hey Dad, I wondered if you and I could do lunch tomorrow."

"I'd love to, hon, but I've got plans."

"Oh," I say. "It's just . . . I haven't had a chance to spend any time with you yet. I just feel like it's really important to be around family at a time like this. The thing is, I have this friend from New York who is trying to break into freelance writing, and she's in town only for this weekend, and an interview with you would mean so much to her career, and it would mean so much to me to be able to spend some time with you." I make up the bit about Gilda just launching her career because he'd never agree to the interview if he knew she was a tabloid gossip columnist.

"You know what, you're right," he says. "I'll have my secretary make reservations for us for one PM."

"Really? Thank you so much. It really means a lot to me."

I call Gilda and tell her the good news. I also warn her that Dad thinks she's a fledgling wannabe. She just laughs. "Whatever, as long as I get the story."

Chapter 4

Gilda and I are on our second round of Bloody Marys by the time Dad shows up at the restaurant half an hour late.

"Sorry I'm late," he says, wearing a politician's smile.

"Dad, this is Gilda Lee. Gilda, this is my father, Gary Denner."

"Very nice to meet you," Gilda says.

"Nice to meet you. How long have you lived in New York?" Dad asks.

"About six years now."

"Do you like it?"

"I love it."

"New York is a great town. There's so much to do there. I go there several times a year on business. I always try to catch a show or a Knicks game. Well, should we get started? I'm ready, fire away."

"There's no rush. We can wait until we've eaten," she says. What she means is, we can wait until you've had a drink or two.

When the waitress sees that Dad has joined us she stops by to get his drink order. Like all the waiters here, ours is young and eager looking, but Dad barely gives her a glance because she is plump in a chunky, uncomfortable way, not a cute way. She's wearing a button-up white shirt and black pants. White has always seemed to me like a ridiculous color for people who work at a restaurant to wear, but this is one of those upscale places where everything is so crisp and clean it's hard to imagine anyone ever dropping or spilling anything. This is not a restaurant where they serve orange juice and coffee but mimosas and espressos.

Dad orders a Bloody Mary after noticing that that's what we're drinking. "Are you ready to order?" he asks us.

We say that we are. I get an asparagus omelet, Dad orders steak and eggs, Gilda gets the Eggs Sardou.

My father hands the waitress the menu and his eyes follow a good-looking blond woman walking by. He doesn't even pretend to be subtle about it. Men are so weak. They feign an armor of money and power and stern gazes, but they waver like a leaf in the breeze, changing their affections every time they see another pretty girl.

He returns his attention to us. "Yeah," my father continues, "I love New York. There's always so much to see."

"I love that you don't need a car to get around," I say.

"Me too," Gilda says. "Cabs can be kind of gross, but it saves a lot of hassle. No oil changes or tune-ups, no forgetting you need to fill up on gas until you're dressed in a gown and heels and running on fumes."

The waiter brings Dad a Bloody Mary. Dad takes the celery stick and swirls it around in his glass.

"I have to respectfully disagree with you two. I love cars."

Yeah, but you also have a whole staff of people who take care of them for you. All you ever have to do is drive.

He goes into detail about his new Mercedes he bought—the million jillion horsepower, the whatever whatever, the this the that.

As Dad continues to recount his new car's many features, I try to take a bite out of my omelet, but it makes me gag. I can't swallow. I pretend to cough into my napkin and I spit the egg out. I watch Dad eat his steak. He likes it rare. He likes the blood. He likes to soak it up with his bread so he doesn't miss a single drop.

Dad sees me watching him eat his steak and offers me a bite.

"I'm a vegetarian."

He pauses, digesting this information. It finally dawns on him that this is not the first time I've told him this. "That's right, that's right, of course."

I wonder if there will ever come a day when it won't hurt to have a father who can't remember anything about me or my life. I feel unable to speak, but fortunately Gilda and Dad do all the talking.

I have to admire the subtle way Gilda works. Though she told Dad she wasn't going to start the interview until after brunch, it's clear she's noting every word he says.

"I have to say I did my best to prepare for our meeting today," she says. "I read everything I could find on you, but business is not really my area. I was a flaky journalism major, you know."

"I'll talk slow," Dad jokes.

"I've been thinking I should get into the stock market, but I'm worried it can't hold out like this forever. You obviously have confidence, or you wouldn't have purchased Avec Communications a year ago."

"There's no doubt we're going to see some slowing in the market. The last couple years have seen a proliferation of Internet and telecommunications companies, and not all of them will succeed. The strong will, though, and that's why we bought Avec. It's a good, strong company that complements our core competencies."

It goes on like this for about a hundred years until finally my father says he has another engagement and he has to get going. We say our good-byes and Dad goes to his Mercedes. Gilda follows me to the Viper. "I owe you one," she whispers.

"Yes, you do."

I watch Gilda drive off and turn my gaze to my father, who is in his car talking on his cell phone. I don't know what compels me to do it, but I run over to him and tap on his window. He raises his index finger, giving me the hang-on-a-minute gesture. I stand there stupidly for several minutes until finally Dad clicks his phone off and opens his window.

"What is it?" he asks.

What indeed? What the hell am I doing? "Dad, I just . . . I wondered if maybe you and I could talk, just the two of us, just for a few minutes."

"Helaina, I'm very busy. I have things to do."

"Dad, please?"

He sighs. "What do you want to talk about?"

"Could we just go and get some ice cream or something? It's kind of weird talking to you here in the parking lot with you in your car and me standing here."

He closes the window, gets out of the car, and presses the remote lock, which makes a high-pitched noise to indicate he's locked the car successfully. "Make it quick," he says.

He follows me as I walk down the street to an ice cream shop. Now that I have his attention I feel nervous. I want to ask him about Mom, whether he misses her and thinks about her, what the last days of her life were like when I was away at school, but somehow I feel too embarrassed to say the words.

The ice cream store is packed with people—and why

wouldn't it be? It's two thirty on a sunny, warm summer afternoon. Little kids stand in line frantic with excitement over the prospect of getting ice cream. They hop up and down, needing to physically express their thrill over the treat they will soon get.

It's noisy in the store with all the little kids squealing and chattering and laughing. One little kid wants a chocolate-dipped waffle cone and his mother says no, it's too big and it's too close to dinner—he can have a small cup or a sugar cone. He is done in by this disappointment and he begins to cry as if he'd been told he would never get a Christmas present ever again. It's an admirable performance. His lungs are impressively hearty.

"Can't these people control their children?" my dad says irritably and not quietly. "Parents shouldn't take children out of the house until they're ten."

I wait for him to smile to show that he's kidding or being ironic, but his expression is gravestone serious.

"You're joking, right?"

"I'm just saying parents need to be able to control their brood or they shouldn't have children. Look, I have things to do. My head is going to explode if I stick around this zoo any longer. It was good talking to you."

But we didn't talk! I never asked you what I wanted to ask!

I watch my father go. When he's out of sight, I get out of line. I don't really feel like ice cream. What's the point of eating ice cream anyway? It only takes a few minutes to eat and when you're done it's just a memory. Why not just recall what it's like to eat ice cream and save yourself the calories?

Maybe someday I'll be able to enjoy food again, but right now it's impossible to taste anything. Right now all the flavor is gone from my life.

Chapter 5

I start work the next morning. The office is much more dreary than I was expecting. It's small and looks more like an underfunded elementary school—concrete floors, chipped paint, and no attempt at decoration—than a hip magazine.

It's nine AM, the time Polly told me to show up, and the place seems mostly empty. I find a flustered-looking young woman wearing jeans, a pilly sweater, and decidedly untrendy glasses.

"Hi, my name is Helaina, I'm supposed to start working here today. Do you know where Polly is?"

"Polly doesn't usually get in till ten. I'm Amanda, I'm the assistant editor. You're going to write film reviews, right?"

I nod.

"Follow me."

I follow her through the maze of desks until she says, "This will be your home for the summer."

"Thanks." I sit down. The desk is buttressed against another desk, I guess so two people can share a window instead of only one getting the view. I hope I like whoever will be sitting across from me, because I'll be staring at him or her day in and day out.

Both desks have computers on them. My desk has some pens and pencils, a stapler, and a pad of sticky notes but is otherwise bare. The other desk is covered with cut-outs of *Tom Tomorrow* and *Dilbert* cartoons, a Ken doll wearing a suit and carrying a briefcase in one hand and a small picket sign taped in his other that says, "Thank God for corporate welfare." There's a dictionary, a thesaurus, two style guides, several notebooks, and dozens of sticky notes with various messages scrawled across them.

"Do you know if there are certain movies Polly wants me to review?" I ask.

"Polly didn't tell you what she wanted you to write about?"

"No."

"She'll be in at ten, you can ask her then."

"I just saw the movie *The Baskets*. I could write a review on that."

"I'd probably just wait to talk to Polly if I were you. I've got a deadline to meet and writers to deal with, so I need to get going. I'll talk to you later, okay?"

"Yeah sure, see ya."

I sit at my desk, turn on my computer, and look around for something to do. I look through my desk drawers, arrange paperclips and boxes of staples, then shut the drawer and look around again. Flies are buzzing around at the window. Gross.

Since I have nothing else to do, I decide I'll write about the movie I saw last week. I'll clear it with Polly as soon as she gets in.

I've got about two hundred words written when someone sits at the desk across from me. I look up. It's Owen.

"Howdy, stranger," he says.

"Hey."

"How's your first day on the job?"

"A little weird actually. I'm not quite sure who my boss is or what I'm supposed to do exactly."

He laughs. "You've got a pretty good grasp of things already. The trick here is to look busy when there is nothing to do, which is most of the time. I think technically your boss is my stepmother. She controls content from a distance, but the real editors are Amanda and Jill."

He points first to the woman in the glasses who showed me to my desk this morning, and then to another woman who is pretty in a sweet, stay-at-home-mom-who-knits-and-goes-to-bed-by-ten-every-night sort of way.

"So help me out. I want to look busy until Polly gets here, but I don't have anything to do. Any thoughts?" I say.

"Do you have email?"

"I have a Yahoo account."

"I'll write you. I've personally found that emailing is one of the all-time great ways of wasting time because you can make it look like you're working when you're not. What's your address?"

"Thalieia30@yahoo.com."

He types it right in. "Thalieia, the muse of comedy."

"Wow, I'm impressed."

"Do you consider yourself something of a comedian?"

"Unfortunately, no. But I like to laugh. Does that count?"

"Absolutely. Now hush. I'm going to write you."

To: Thalieia30@yahoo.com
From: owenkirkland@localcolor.com

So, what should we talk about?

To: owenkirkland@localcolor.com
From: Thalieia30@yahoo.com

Perhaps we should talk about why you, a grown man, uses words like "hush." No, seriously, tell me something about you that I don't know.

To: Thalieia30@yahoo.com
From: owenkirkland@localcolor.com

Well, since you hardly know me, it shouldn't be hard to find something you don't know about me. Let's see . . . I have two cats, Calliope and Salinger. Salinger is definitely a daddy's boy, and follows me constantly. Calliope is sort of a feline throw pillow who purrs at the slightest provocation. She loves attention, and lots of it. Salinger's claim to fame is a strange obsession with being held and petted immediately following my taking a shower. He will sit at the edge of the tub and yip at me (he has never really meowed much . . . he just sort of does this little "meep" thing) until I give him the go-ahead, and then he jumps up into my arms, where he proceeds to crawl around and purr like I am a human tower of catnip. I have no idea why, but he is pretty much guaranteed to be looking for attention 10 seconds after I shut the water off. Most of the rest of the time, he isn't at all interested in being held, but the shower is a whole other story. Calliope, on the other hand, is all about attention . . . her big event is bedtime, where she is guaranteed to demand some petting before I drift off. She typically sleeps right against my side—I have been largely immobilized in bed for the past several years. They were not at all pleased about having to make the drive from Iowa City back to

Denver. They love to play outside so you'd think they'd be big travelers, but no. They just like to sniff the leaves in their own backyard and paw menacingly but ineffectually at various bugs. They just don't care much for trips that involve cars. Go figure.

I smile. He had me at "meep." And imagining him just getting out of the shower . . . Mmmm.

To: owenkirkland@localcolor.com
From: Thaleia30@yahoo.com

I don't have any pets myself. My apartment in New York is too small for animal companions, unfortunately. Plus, I find that many landlords would prefer that you ran a meth lab out of your apartment than let you share your space with a cat or dog. As it is, trying to find a place to live in New York is like losing weight on an 8,000-calorie-a-day donut-only diet—it's impossible. Trying to find a place to live that allows pets is even harder.

All day Owen and I write emails back and forth. In between amusing ourselves in this way, I continue working on my review.

I don't see Polly until the afternoon, when she walks by my desk and then abruptly turns to look at me as if surprised to see me.

"Oh, hello there. So, how are you enjoying your first day?"

"It's going okay. I'm a little confused about what I should be doing. Is there like a training or an introduction I'm supposed to go through?"

"Oh no, there's no time for that here. The world of

publishing is a world of insane deadlines and constant action. It's baptism by fire here, sink or swim, sink or swim as they say."

"Okay, well, are there specific films you want me to cover?"

"Use your creativity. Usually our editor, Jill, writes the film reviews. She'll be so happy to have the help. She usually comes up with some ideas and runs them by me."

"Well, I wasn't sure what else to do today, so I just wrote up this review of a movie I saw last weekend."

I hand her the printout. She starts reading it, and then promptly starts shaking her head. "Oh no, no, this is much too dark for our audience, much too controversial. I've got an idea, why don't you write up a preview of the Telluride Film Festival that's coming up in August."

"Do you think I'll be able to see any of the films in time to review them for the August issue?" I wonder if I'll get the budget to fly to film festivals. I doubt I'll be able to get distributors to send me copies of films beforehand since I'm a no-name, writing for a small magazine.

"Probably not," she agrees.

"So where do you want me to get the information for the story—the press release?" I say it with a smile, knowing it's a ridiculous idea.

She nods.

"Oh."

"If you have any other questions, just ask Owen, he knows the ropes." Polly walks away and Owen and I look at each other.

"She gives me books to review like *The Best Places in Colorado to Hike With Your Dog*," he says. "I'm not even allowed to point out a book's flaws."

"You're kidding."

"We're nothing more than a four-color PR outlet. At

least it only takes me about two days to get a month's worth of work done."

"So how do you fill the rest of the time?"

"If I keep working here, I should have a novel finished in no time."

"I thought you were a poet."

"Actually, after graduation, I thought I'd get a job writing copy for book jackets. You know, stuff that promises a thrill-a-minute hilarious action-packed adventure fraught with romance. Lies, basically. God knows I've gotten enough experience doing that here. So what is *The Baskets* about?"

"It's about two German teenage war orphans from an internment camp who escape but are persecuted by the . . . "

He laughs.

"Yeah, yeah, I get it." I take the review I printed out, crumple it up, and toss it into the wastebasket. I look at Owen again. "So what made you decide to go to grad school when you have a nice cushy job right here?"

"I'd like a job that's a little more mentally challenging. Plus, right now I'm living with Polly. She's all right and everything, but . . . I don't know, to tell you the truth, I'm actually surprised I came back. After I graduated from Berkeley I moved to Portland. I lived there for a year, bartending at night and writing during the day. Then I somehow miraculously got accepted to the writers' workshop at Iowa. I came back here this summer because I need some publishing experience on my resume so that after graduation I can get a job in New York working for a publishing house."

"I know a few editors in New York. I can introduce you if you ever come out."

"Cool."

Owen smiles at me. His hazel eyes are glittered with flecks of gold.

"What made you decide to work for pitiful wages as an intern here when you could become the next CEO of Able Technologies?" he asks.

I pretend to gag. "No way. I don't want to have anything to do with corporate America."

"Sort of a rebellion thing?"

"It's not intentional. I just never envied the way my parents spent their days, all that backstabbing and artificiality. I remember going to company picnics when I was a kid and watching people slap my dad on the back and tell him how great he was looking and how good it was to see him, and then as soon as he was out of earshot they'd be bitching about what a penny-pinching jackass he was. Artists may be a little insane, but you usually know where you stand with them. I'd rather someone tell me flat out that they hated me than for them to say one thing to me and do another. What about you? Why would anyone willingly go to Iowa?"

He laughs. "Well, it's got the most prestigious writers' workshop in the country, for one thing. I actually really love Iowa City. The other towns in Iowa don't do much for me, but since Iowa City has the college, it gets film festivals and dance performances and national theater reviews. Famous writers and poets are always dropping in to do readings. And of course wherever you have writers you have a lot of bars."

"Of course."

"The people are nice. Really down to earth. They're predominantly white, but if you can get over the lack of diversity, it's a nice town."

"So why are you moving to New York after you graduate?"

"There aren't a lot of jobs for writers and editors there. The city is too small. Plus, it's not *that* great."

I smile. A summer of staring at him all day might make the time I'm here in Denver not so bad after all.

I go home after my first day on the job, run up to my room, lock the door, and look around and realize I have absolutely nothing to do. If I were in New York, I'd go out with some group of friends, go see a movie or a play or some stand-up comedy, or we'd just go to a bar and talk and drink and listen to a band, but here I'm at a loss.

I take off my shoes, lie down on my bed, and look up at the ceiling. I've become intimately acquainted with each bump and groove over these last few days.

I wonder what Owen is doing tonight. He's probably huddled over a notebook, crossing out words and rewriting lines of poetry. I can picture his soft, full lips as he chews on a pencil, deep in thought. I wonder what it would be like to kiss those lips.

I sit up abruptly. What the hell is wrong with me? My mother just died two months ago, and I'm acting like a schoolgirl with a crush, mooning over some guy I barely know.

I pick up the phone and call Hannah. "What are you doing tonight?" I ask when she picks up.

"Going stir-crazy. I'm so bored I think I may even get a job."

"Drastic. What would you do?"

"Bartend at one of my parents' bars maybe. I don't know."

"Want to get some practice on the other side of the bar tonight?"

"Absofuckinglutely."

"What's Marni up to?"

"Saving the universe no doubt. She's doing some crazy volunteer shit."

"What's up with that?"

"Apparently she's got too much time on her hands or something with Jake in Europe. She'll get over it when he gets back."

"I'll call her on her cell and see if we can drag her away from her Mother Teresa shtick so she can have a few cocktails. Where should we meet?"

"I don't care. What do you think?"

"I have no idea."

"How about the Purple Martini? I'll meet you there in an hour."

"Great. See you then."

Denver is dead at seven o'clock on a Monday night; Hannah, Marni, and I practically have the place to ourselves.

Hannah lights up a cigarette.

"Where did you get that nasty habit?" I ask her. "All of your friends hate smoke."

"I'm a true rebel. Instead of peer pressure to smoke, there's pressure not to smoke, thus I smoke."

"Can't argue with that," I say.

"Hon," Hannah says to me, "you know we love you, but that Fendi bag of yours is like what, a year old? And your shoes, I mean pretty soon you're going to have to wrap them with electrical tape."

I smile. "I'm going for an urban-grunge look."

"You live in New York, the epicenter of the fashion industry in America. There is just no excuse for you looking like this; we're going shopping tomorrow."

"I can't, I have a job."

"You have to go like every day?"

"Five days a week. Don't give me that look, Marni's working too. And just today you said you were thinking about getting a job."

"I'm not exactly working. I mean I'm not getting paid," Marni says. "I'm volunteering at the hospital so I can get in good with the doctors. I want to do my residency here."

"Both of your parents are surgeons there. Do you really think you're going to have a hard time getting placed there?" I ask.

She shrugs. I look down at my bag and think about my artist/actor friends in New York, who wouldn't know a Fendi from a brown paper bag. They buy whatever they can find that's on sale at a secondhand store. I feel guilty when I'm around them for noticing what designers people are wearing, like I can see through people's clothes to their labels and my New York friends can't. After being around them so long, my "skill" has faded. It's not as important. Not like in junior high or high school when you had to wear Esprit or Tommy Hilfiger or risk social suicide, like other brands were toxic. And to our social life, it probably was.

"Then we'll go shopping tomorrow night. Or this weekend maybe," Hannah says.

"I don't know. I don't really feel like it."

"What? This is heresy. You used to be able to shop with the best of us."

It's true. When we were in high school, the three of us could drop an impressive amount of money at the mall in a single afternoon, and I never thought twice about how much we spent. It wasn't until I moved to New York and started hanging out with struggling artists that I got some perspective on the whole thing. Like one time I went out with my roommate Lynne and I wanted to stop and get a cup of coffee. She said it wasn't in her budget and she really shouldn't. I told her I'd be happy to buy her a cappuccino. She told me she couldn't let me do that. "A cup of coffee is like three or four bucks," I stammered, utterly amazed to realize that some people budgeted cups of coffee. Cars and houses I could see. Needing to budget your wardrobe I understood. But somehow it never entered my mind that not everyone (barring the homeless or old folks living off Social Security) needed to concern themselves with every single dollar. Living with Lynne and Kendra has made me much more aware of how little of the stuff we buy we actually need. Which doesn't mean I don't like shoes and clothes and manicures, because I do. Right now, though, the idea of spending a bunch of money on cute outfits holds no allure for me.

Fortunately the conversation is dropped when a man in an expensive suit approaches our table. He's about thirty and good looking if you like that wholesome, Midwestern, toothpaste-commercial-smile kind of look.

"Can I buy you ladies a round of drinks?" he asks, looking at Hannah.

"That depends. Would we have to talk to you?" Hannah asks.

"Just for as long as it takes you to finish the round."

"We can drink pretty fast," I say.

"Fair enough." He orders us another round and slides in next to me, across from Hannah.

"I'm Todd Cook," he says.

"We're charmed I'm sure," I say.

"So Todd, what do you do for a living?" Marni asks.

"I'm a consultant. I live in Chicago, but for the next three months or so I'll be in Denver, at least during the weekdays. I'm living here at the hotel for the summer. Drinks are on the company. What do you all do?"

"We're college students, home for the summer," Marni says.

"What are you studying?"

"I'm premed, studying biology and English, Hannah is prelaw, she's double-majoring in history and political science, and Helaina is a film student at NYU."

"Prelaw, huh?" he asks, looking at Hannah.

"She remembers everything she reads, everything she hears, it's kind of creepy," Marni says. "I mean, in a good way."

"You have a boyfriend at college, Hannah?"

"Lots."

He laughs. "I bet." Nobody says anything for a minute. "Yeah, expense accounts are good. They helped me buy my new toy."

Nobody bites, but he tells about his new toy, an Audi, anyway, as I knew he would.

He goes on in this vein for about a million years, buying us drinks and bragging about the car he drives and the house he owns and the scuba diving trips he's taken. It's obvious that Todd isn't used to having money. I look at my watch. He's been sitting here for more than an hour. The free drinks aren't worth this. I need to be distracted, not bored.

I consider telling Todd that my father is Gary Denner. That would shut him up. No matter how rich you think you are, there's always someone richer. Unless, of course, you're Bill Gates. Otherwise, shut up already.

I can see that Hannah is warming up to him, though. Or maybe it's just the free alcohol making her horny.

"I'm hungry," Marni says. "Do you guys want to share some appetizers with me?"

"Sure," Todd says.

When the waitress stops by again, Marni orders a basket of onion rings and some jalapeño poppers.

"So who are you doing the consulting work for?" Hannah asks.

"Able Technologies."

"Small world," Marni says. I elbow her, but she keeps going. "Helaina is Mr. Gary Denner's daughter."

"Really?" Todd is suddenly interested in me for the first time all night.

"Yep." I meet people who work for Able all the time—it's the largest employer in the state.

"What kind of consulting do you do?" Hannah continues.

"Accounting. We're doing the company's due diligence."

"You actually went to college thinking, when I grow up, I want to be an accountant?" I say in a teasing voice. "That's inexplicable. I just don't get that."

"What's wrong with accounting?" Todd says.

"Nothing. It's just not creative enough for me."

"Oh, you'd be surprised. It can be plenty creative." He smiles sardonically.

The waitress returns with our appetizers and I take a bite from a popper, biting it in two. Half the cheese oozes down my chin. I rescue the cheese from my chin with one hand and Todd comes to my aid by handing me a napkin.

"Thanks."

"This is really a healthy food product," Marni says. "You have your fried outer layer, your dairy cheese insides, and all the vegetable you could ever need with the thin jalapeño skin."

"What could be better than fried cheese? Fried cheese in any form, that's what I say," Hannah says.

"Really the only way they could improve on this would be if they could somehow find a way to frost it," Todd says, and we all snigger. This is the kind of conversation that passes as witty after a few drinks.

When Marni gets up to go to the bathroom, Todd gets up to order us more drinks, and when he comes back, he slides in next to Hannah.

"You're a beautiful woman," he says.

"I know," she says.

"You're very smart, very funny."

She ignores what he's saying, and leans closer to him, sniffing his chest. "I like your cologne."

"I have the bottle up in my room if you want to see it."

"That's the lamest come-on line I've ever heard, and believe me, I've heard lots. You should tell me you have a bottle of Dom Perignon, and then you might get me up to your room."

"I'll go order some; it'll be waiting for us by the time we get there."

She shrugs indifferently. He leaves to order.

"He's pretty cute," I offer.

"He's okay. We'll see how he is in bed. I need something to occupy myself this summer before I go completely insane."

She leaves with him, and when Marni gets back, she says we should probably be going home ourselves, even though it's not even midnight.

When I get home, I do three shots of bourbon, but it still takes me forever to fall asleep. I can't stop thinking about seeing Owen in the morning. I never thought I'd be looking forward to going to a job, but I can't wait. Yet my fluttery feelings of excitement are punctuated by feelings of guilt. These days my emotions are a turbulent stew of ingredients, always threatening to boil over.

Chapter 6

At work the next morning, I try to start writing an article about the Telluride Film Festival, but flies buzz around me, hit against the window and ceiling, and flit between the window and shades. They are making me crazy. I can't concentrate.

When Owen strolls in at 10:30, I say, "Would it be hypocritical for a vegetarian to slaughter flies?"

"Depends. Aren't you a vegetarian for moral reasons?"

"Yeah, but mostly it's just that meat grosses me out. The idea of eating dead animals just depresses me."

"So it's more about the consumption of dead things, not the killing of them."

"Yeah, but I wouldn't wear a fur coat or go around hunting deer or killing small animals for fun or anything. I guess I'm a specieist. I think it's sad when people kill rabbits or pigs or whatever, but I really wouldn't mind at all if someone just took these flies out, just killed them dead. Actually, I'm a situational specieist. I wouldn't kill a fly outside, but when it's flying around inside it's really like breaking and entering, don't you think? How about this, how about you kill these flies that are driving me crazy, then I can keep my conscience clear?"

"So you have no problem sending in a hit man to do your dirty work for you."

"None at all."

"What about the sexist implications of asking a man to do a job that could just as easily be done by a woman?"

"Oh for Christ's sake, I'll do it myself." I pull the shades up to expose the window the flies are inexplicably drawn to. I take a notebook and use it as a fly swatter. In two minutes I've killed at least ten flies.

I sit down and face Owen. "My karma is so screwed."

The window looks like a morbid version of a Pollack painting, with smears and dollops of fly innards splashed across the screen. There is a fly wing on my keyboard.

"Gross. There's fly shrapnel everywhere." I blow on the wing and it floats to Owen's desk. "Oops, sorry about that."

He blows it back my way.

"Hey, I didn't do it on purpose." This time I blow on it from the side, and it wafts to the ground.

"I'll call maintenance and see if they can do something," Owen says. "So what did you do last night?"

"I nearly died of boredom."

"Maybe we can catch a movie sometime."

Is he asking me on a date? "If it's a movie I'm going to review, it better be a Disney movie."

"Let's make it a movie you won't review."

"Yeah, okay, sounds good." I turn to my computer screen and pretend like I'm concentrating on my work.

There are still a few flies flitting up against the window and ceiling light like they're all having epileptic fits at the same time. I try to tune them out and focus on the article I'm writing, but all I can think about is whether I just agreed to a date or if he was asking me out just to be friendly. I don't know which I want it to be. Owen's cute and he seems cool, but I'm not sure I can handle the drama of dating right now. This is what I'm thinking when the maintenance guy stops by.

"What?" I say, startled.

"Having some trouble with flies?" he asks again.

"Yeah, they're driving me nuts."

"I brought some fly paper. That's really all we can do."

"Where are they coming from?"

"From outside."

Duh. "Right, what I meant is, where are they getting in? Is there someplace we can patch up so they can't get in?"

"Flies are really common in the summer. Lots of buildings are having problems," he says, ignoring my question. He puts a couple strips of fly paper out, one on the floor and one on the windowsill. The guy looks like he's only in his thirties or so, but a haggard, run-down thirties. He has a big brown mustache and his jeans, t-shirt, and work boots are covered in dust, like he's been rolling around in dirt.

"They're attracted to the glue. It'll kill 'em," he tells me.

"Okay, thanks, I guess."

"No problem. You have a good day now."

I look at Owen again.

"Charming work environment we have here," I say.

"Only the best for our employees."

I've finished my article by early afternoon. I check my e-mail account, read the online *New York Times*, and look at a couple of movie Web sites. Even though this is a stupid job, curiously, I'm finding it kind of fun.

I look at the strips of fly paper. There are already at least half a dozen flies on them, but they're not dead, just stuck. They are trying to get their feet, or whatever you call them, off the paper, but they can't. They are just a swaying mass of dying bodies.

"Gross!" I shout.

"What?" Owen asks.

"These poor flies. They're just stuck here, dying a slow death from starvation. I can't believe I'm witnessing fly torture."

"How'd you think the fly paper got rid of them?"

"I don't know, I wasn't really thinking. Maybe I thought they died a nice, painless little death just a little sooner than they would have died naturally. What's he doing? Can't he see that all his little friends are dying? Why is he crawling on there? Stop, little fly, don't do it. Why don't his little friends warn him?"

We watch a fly crawl onto the fly paper and get stuck himself.

"I don't think they're really all that bright."

"Apparently not." I look away. "I can't watch this. This is so depressing."

"What are you doing tonight?"

"Avoiding Dad and Claudia."

"How about we catch that movie tonight?"

"I'm supposed to meet my friends Marni and Hannah at Hannah's place. She's having a little soiree. Her parents are in France for the summer. Why don't you come with me?"

"Cool. What time?"

"Nineish?"

"Sounds like a plan. I'll pick you up then."

Getting ready that night is a nightmare. On the one hand, I don't need any more flak from Hannah about my suddenly absent fashion taste, but on the other hand, I don't want Owen to think I'm some pretentious label hound. I try on about forty outfits. I don't want to look underdressed or overdressed or too fashionable or not fashionable enough. Shit.

Of course, if I wear my black Carmen Marc Valvo pants and blouse, would Owen have any idea how much it cost? Doubtful. It's decided, then. Excellent.

I sit at my mirror and straighten my wavy hair with a straightening iron. I put the iron down and look at my reflection in the mirror. It's not a pretty sight. I looked tired and malnourished, skinny and weak.

I hear the bell to the gate at the end of the driveway. I buzz Owen in the gate and run downstairs to meet him. He's driving a very old Subaru.

"Hey," I say.

"Hey." He opens the passenger door, closes it after me, and walks around to the driver's side. "Where to?" he asks.

I give him the directions.

"You look gorgeous tonight," he says.

"Thanks."

I feel a shiver of excitement followed by a tremor of guilt. I know Mom would want me to be happy and get on with my life, but it's too early for me to date. I feel like I'm doing what Dad's done, forgetting Mom like a movie ticket stub left in a jacket pocket, casually put away and forgotten.

"Make the next left. Go two lights up and turn right."

When we get to Hannah's, Hannah and Marni give me these casual, raised-eyebrow looks when I introduce Owen, like, "*hey, not bad.*"

"He's my boss's son," I say in a tone that means, *don't get your hopes up.* I don't even know if this is a date or if I should be dating right now. I don't want my friends to get too excited about this.

Hannah's parents' rec room looks like a modern design catalog. In part of the room there is a brushed-steel bar, a pool table, a foosball table, and a pinball machine. In the other half of the room there are several different brightly colored U-shaped chairs in a half circle around the wide-screen TV. I tell Owen to grab one. I choose the apple green, he chooses the violet. We drag them into the corner so we have a little privacy to talk.

"Ready for another?" I ask.

"I don't think so."

"Lightweight."

"Designated driver," he protests with a smile.

"So what's the story with Polly? How long has she been your stepmom?"

"My mom died when Laura and I were pretty little. Polly was an entertainment writer for the magazine at the time. Dad married her maybe a year after my Mom died; I guess I was about ten or so. When my Dad died a few years ago, Polly took over as publisher and editor-in-chief."

Owen is just wearing blue jeans and a green t-shirt, but he fills the jeans out divinely and the t-shirt looks great with his coloring. There is something about the cross between his Russell Crowe build and the idea that he's some tortured poetic soul that I find very sexy. He looks like he could easily pass as some frat boy asshole, but there is something about his easy smile, something about his eyes that makes me feel I can trust him absolutely.

"Do you get along with her?" I ask.

"I don't know, I don't take her very seriously. She doesn't do a very good job running the magazine. I mean, you and I never have anything to do, and poor Amanda and Jill work obscene hours. We all get paid crap wages, but still, it's not like the magazine is making a killing or anything."

I feel a presence hovering over me and look up to see Dillon Fraiser. "Hey, Helaina."

"Hey."

Dillon looks at Owen. "Dillon," I say, "this is Owen. Owen, this is Dillon Frasier. He was a couple of years ahead of me in high school."

"Nice to meet you," Owen says.

Dillon nods. "Right on." Dillon looks at me again. "How's school?"

"Great."

"You're in New York."

"Yeah."

"I'm going to Boulder. I'm majoring in computer science."

"Great."

"I graduate in December."

Aha. "Cool."

"You think Able will be hiring programmers?"

"Probably."

"Maybe you can put in a good word about me to your dad."

"No problem."

"Well, it was good seeing you again."

"Sure. See you around."

We watch Dillon walk away. "Is that your ex?" Owen asks.

"Good God, no."

"Any boyfriends back in New York I should know about?"

"No. It's pathetic when you think about it. I'm surrounded by thousands of unmarried men my age and, well, I mean it's not that I never get asked out on dates, it's just that I get asked out by these ugly, boring, dweeby guys."

"Am I an ugly, boring, dweeby guy?"

"Definitely not."

"I asked you out."

"Yeah? So this is an official date?"

"That depends. Do you want it to be?"

I have no idea. "Sure."

"Well, a date it is then."

"That means you have to kiss me, you know."

"I didn't know that."

"Oh yeah. If I go on a date with a cute guy, I fully expect a smooch."

"Good to know the rules. Any others I should be aware of?"

"I make them up as I go along. I'll let you know."

He laughs. "Sounds fair. When do you want that smooch?"

"Now's good for me."

We lean across the curved arms of our chairs. He kisses me lightly at first, then harder. I feel like I'm watching myself from a distance, outside myself, filming the documentary of my life. The kiss is nice, but if I thought it would be like the kiss that woke Sleeping Beauty, jarring me from my slumber and helping me feel emotions again, it didn't work. Then he slips his tongue into my mouth and that's when I feel faint stirrings. Unfortunately, he doesn't have time to melt me completely because we're interrupted by Hannah clearing her throat.

We pull away from each other and smile.

"I see you two are getting along well," Hannah says. She sits on the arm of my chair. "So Owen, the boss's son, tell me all about yourself."

"Let's see, I was born in Denver, Colorado . . . "

"No, no, start with the good stuff. How much money do you make, are you a good kisser, are you going to treat my good friend Helaina like she deserves to be treated?"

"I can answer the first two," I say. "Absolutely none because he's getting his master's degree in poetry, and excellent."

"Well, Helaina has enough money for the both of you. The kissing is the important thing. How does Helaina's kissing stand up?" she asks him.

"Outstanding."

"Ugh, don't say that word," I say.

"What's wrong with 'outstanding'?" Owen asks.

"My dad says it, but he says it in this artificial way . . . you know how if you drink too much tequila and puke your guts out for like twenty-four hours straight, then anytime you ever see or smell tequila again or even if someone mentions the word, it just kind of makes you nauseated? That's how I feel with that particular 'O' word. My dad just has this way of saying one thing but doing another and when I hear that 'O' word, I just brace myself for a knife in my back. Like in ten seconds you'll be telling everyone I know that I slobber when I kiss and have all the passion of a rutabaga."

"I can see I'm really going to have to watch what I say around you. Okay, let me put it this way, Helaina's kiss has the perfect blend of tenderness and passion that takes your breath away. Like a strawberry whose sweetness takes you by surprise or that moment when you pour oil into a hot pan and it sizzles with that pleasantly startling spark."

"Hmm, food analogies, is somebody hungry?" Hannah asks.

Owen laughs. "Not me. Really."

I try not to smile. *A strawberry whose sweetness takes you by surprise*. Excellent answer.

"Owen," Hannah says, "I didn't realize they let muscular guys into poetry workshops. How much do you lift?"

"I don't lift."

"She's right. You've got perfectly sculpted arms," I say. Oh God. Tell me those words didn't really come out of my mouth. Why don't I just flutter my eyes and call him Big Boy as I stroke his brawny biceps coquettishly? I obviously have an unfortunate case of Dating Tourette's.

"So how's Todd, is he here?" I ask, in a futile bid to distract everyone from my geekiness.

"He's here." She points to him. He was obviously watching her because he sees her pointing at him and he waves. "He's good in bed, has good taste in wine, and he doesn't completely bore me to tears. That's about as good as I'm going to get this summer. I like him, actually. Until he starts talking about work. Bo*ring*."

"He's an accountant, what did you expect?"

"I don't care if he works with numbers all day. I just don't want to hear about it."

"Is there a bathroom around here?" Owen asks.

Hannah points to it just as Marni comes up to Hannah and me.

"I'll be right back," he says.

"He's cute," Marni says.

"He's a poet," I say.

"A poet, wow. He looks more like a firefighter. I always think of men who write poetry as being skinny and gay."

I shrug.

"You like him?"

"I don't know him well, but yeah, I like him. He seems like the opposite of my father. Hence the attraction."

"It makes sense that you would meet him now," Marni says.

"What do you mean?"

"People come into our lives when they do for a reason.

You're going through a tough time emotionally, so you meet a guy who obviously knows about emotions. You can't be a poet if you don't."

"Maybe. I like him, but it's not like this can go anywhere. I'm going back to New York at the end of the summer, and he's going back to Iowa. We're just having fun."

Owen returns. As he reclaims his seat he says, "I can honestly say that I've never seen a bathroom that has a wall-size aquarium filled with exotic fish. I'm fairly certain that is the coolest bathroom I've ever seen in my life."

"It is pretty cool, isn't it?" Hannah asks. "My parents love fish. It's too bad nobody's ever here to see them except the housekeeper who feeds them." Hannah turns, her gaze extending across the room. "What is *he* doing here?"

I follow her gaze and shift uncomfortably. "Yeah, doesn't he know about the caste system?" I try to joke.

"Helaina, what's wrong?" Owen says, but I don't have time to answer.

"Rick, hi. This is my friend, Owen. Owen, this is Rick Harwell," I say.

They shake and exchange nice-to-meet-yous.

"How are things going?" I ask, straining to breathe. Can your lungs suddenly deflate like a popped balloon—a sort of spontaneous combustion of your respiratory system?

"Things are very ironic. I'm dating a woman who works at Able."

"Really?"

"Can't seem to get away from it in Denver."

"Yeah." I should become a speechwriter I have such a way with words. God. A babbling infant is more articulate than I. "So, you're going to school?"

"No, I was working full time, trying to save some money, but I got laid off. How do you like that? Victim of a poorly run Internet company. It was fun until the venture capital ran out. So now my girlfriend is supporting me. Able Technologies is keeping a roof over my head once again."

"I think there is a part to this story that I'm not getting," Owen says.

"Rick's dad . . . " I begin.

"My father got the ax from Able back in the '90s. It was D-S Technologies back then, but it was the same company. He was unemployed for ten months. Couldn't find any work, nothing. My mom got a waitressing job, but it wasn't enough to pay the mortgage. We lost the car first, then the house. My dad figured he was worth more dead than alive, what with life insurance. So he staged an accident, drove into a ravine. The insurance company determined that the death wasn't an accident. One big business considers my dad's life worth nothing, why wouldn't another big business?"

"I'm sorry, Rick . . . " I say.

"Hey, I'm sorry about your dad, man, but it's not like Helaina is responsible," Owen says.

"I'm not saying it's her fault. Just trying to strike up a friendly conversation about the role of business in society."

"If you want to hate my father, take a number and get in line."

"I suppose you're right. To be successful, you make a few enemies along the way. It was good to see you again, Helaina. Nice to meet you, Owen. I'll see you around."

I watch Rick as he walks away and feel jittery and breathless. Maybe because, in a strange way, I do feel responsible for what happened to his dad and to his life. "Do you want to get going?" I ask.

"Do you?"

"Yeah, I guess. If you do."

We say our good-byes and walk out to the car. I click my seatbelt into place with trembling hands.

"Your friends seem cool." Owen turns the ignition on.

"I love them, although they are completely different than my starving-artist friends in New York. I think you'd like my New York friends. My roommate Kendra is an actress and my other roommate, Lynne, is a writer. They're awesome."

"How do your starving-artist friends feel about your father being Gary Denner?"

"They don't know who my father is. I go by my mother's maiden name in New York. I don't talk about my family. When the subject of money comes up, I don't say anything. I try not to go crazy buying stuff, but I don't lie exactly either. Well, I say I got an inheritance from my grandparents, which is true."

"Why don't you just tell them?"

"Because I hate the Dillon Frasiers of the world kissing up to me. And it's like . . . " I think for a moment, trying to figure out how to express what I want to say. "My dad is constantly being given awards and getting asked to speak at colleges and stuff, and he thinks it's because he's so great and people love him. He never seems to notice that these organizations that honor him with these awards are the same ones that he's given money to or that are trying to get him to give money. I don't want guys to date me because they're hoping my dad can get them a job after college or something. I don't want people to hang out with me because they're hoping my dad can fund their film or play or whatever."

"People knowing who your dad is might open doors."

"I don't want to be a Tori Spelling. I want to get movies made because I'm good at what I do. I've got a lot to learn. I mean, I'm not saying I'm going to do the whole starving-artist thing until I'm discovered; I know that being my dad's daughter has lots of advantages and I'm not going to be stupid and just ignore opportunities that come my way . . . I don't know, I'm talking out my ass. I have no idea what I'm saying."

Owen pulls into my driveway and parks the car.

"You want to come in?" I ask.

"Sure."

As soon as he says yes, I realize it's not what I want at all. Shit. I just invited him out of politeness, out of habit, like when someone asks you how you are and no matter how crappy you feel, you just say, "Fine thanks." Seeing Rick Harwell unnerved me.

Owen follows me inside. He shakes his head as he surveys my enormous room. "Wow, I just can't get over this place."

"I know. Three of my apartments in New York could fit into here. And even if we had a team of maids cleaning that place, it could never look like this. It has a more or less permanent grunge."

"Why do you live in a grungy apartment? Wouldn't your dad get you something chic and pricey?"

"He actually bought me a penthouse, but I ended up deciding I didn't want to live there. I wanted a different kind of college life. The week before school started, Mom and I flew out to New York to help me get settled in. I wanted to check out the area on my own. As I walked around and saw people in saris and turbans and dreadlocks, I decided I didn't want to be another rich-girl clone; I wanted to figure out my own path. I didn't want people to think of me as another wealthy girl from the suburbs. I wanted to find friends who only cared about who I was, not who my father was. College was a new world. Why shouldn't I start a different life?"

Owen nods. "That makes sense. Most college students rebel by drinking too much. Your way is much more original."

"Oh, I drink way too much, too," I assure him. "Anyway, I walked around the School of Arts trying not to look like the star-struck freshman that I was. I stumbled upon the community bulletin board and read the posted messages, and one of the flyers said, 'Roommate wanted to live with two only somewhat crazy actor-writer types. Female preferred.' The idea of living with crazy artistic types was exactly what I wanted, so I called them on my cell. Kendra answered and said I could come over. I took a cab to their place and walked up the three flights of stairs to get to the apartment, and I was just appalled by the squalor. The stairwell was brutally hot and it smelled of stale urine and body odor. Then Kendra opened the door with this big smile. She was wearing a faded gray t-shirt and frayed jeans, but she's just one of those beautiful women who can look stunning in sackcloth. Kendra told me she was a waitress slash actress, and that her roommate, Lynne, was a copywriter slash unpublished novelist. I didn't really think she'd know who my dad was, but I introduced myself as Helaina Merrill and told her I was a film student, and she was like, 'It'll be perfect, Lynne can write the screenplays, I'll be the big star, and you can direct.' There was something about her that was really . . . I don't know how to describe it. Kendra is just the kind of person you can't help but be drawn to. There was no air-conditioning, and they'd set up an elaborate network of fans that made all this noise but had little effect against the heat. So even though the apartment was cramped, ugly, and falling apart, right away I wanted to live there. I told them I'd move in the next day. Dad ended up renting out the apartment he'd bought me and made a killing."

"I think that's cool that you're comfortable in both worlds." He smiles at me, and then he stands and walks over to my bookshelf. "You have quite a library here. I take it you like to read?"

"I love stories. It's fun to try on other people's lives for a couple hours."

Owen sits on the edge of my bed and regards me thoughtfully. "If you wrote the story of your life, how would you change it?"

I chew on my lip for a moment, thinking. It's a big question. "I think I've been pretty lucky with my life for the most part, but of course if I could, I'd rewind these last couple years and spend a lot more time with Mom. I miss her." Out of nowhere, my voice gets husky and tears pool in my eyes. I feel like I've been hanging on pretty well, but every now and then I'm reminded that I am caught at the epicenter of an emotional hurricane. It's exhausting.

I crawl next to him on the bed. He hugs me. His body feels good—warm, strong, muscular—but I tense, waiting for the hug to become a grope. The thought of that right now disgusts me. But it doesn't come. He just holds me. The warmth of him, the sound of his steady breath, it's the elixir I need.

I cry quietly.

"It's okay," he said. "It's okay to feel the pain. It's the only way you'll get through it."

My roommate Kendra basically told me the same thing. "Own the pain," she'd said. Right now, though, as hot tears run down my face and my nose gets all unsexily blubbery, I try to feel the pain, but I don't feel anything. It's like the tears know I'm sad and are acting out and my mind and heart aren't able to catch up or even fully know what's going on.

Owen holds me tighter. We fall asleep that way. When I wake up, I think, for the first time in two months, that maybe someday things will be okay again.

Chapter 7

Gilda's profile of my Dad comes out this morning, so when I get to work, I pull up her newspaper's homepage to see what she wrote.

THE KING OF INFORMATION SERVICES
By Gilda Lee, *The New York Citizen*

Gary Denner is the kind of man alumni profiles are made of. He's handsome, successful, and very, very rich.

He comes from a modest background. His father was a marketing executive who did well enough to own a car and a nice house, but he couldn't begin to imagine the wealth that his son would one day come to know—dozens of cars, mansions, villas across the world, and endless trips around the globe.

"I never planned on becoming a CEO," Denner said.

My jaw clenches with anger, but I force myself to keep reading. I read every last word, and by the time I get to the end, I feel ill. Seasick almost, as if I've been tossed around on turbulent waves of angry ocean. Not only does the damned article not skewer my father even once, it deifies him.

"Hey." I look up. Owen is standing there, smiling kindly. "What are you doing?"

I shake my head. I'm afraid if I try to speak, I'll burst into tears.

"I was thinking—" Owen begins, but his words are cut off when Polly charges up to our desk, interrupting us.

"Clothes make such a difference," she announces.

"What?" I ask.

"I'm wearing this new outfit today and I just feel so fabulous. I feel confident, I feel pretty, I feel ready to take on the world. It just shows you how important clothes really are. Anyway, we're going to have an editorial meeting in about five minutes, would you like to join us, Helaina? It might be educational."

I don't know, I have so much to do I'm not sure if I can pull myself away. "Sure."

I follow Polly into the boardroom. Jill hands out black-and-white copies of the galleys of the next issue. There are eight people in the meeting. Jill and Amanda, the two ad sales people, the two designers, Polly, and me, of course. The first part of the meeting blazes by while Amanda and Jill cover what articles they have completed, what articles are almost ready, what photographs they already have and what photographs they are waiting for.

"I've just about finished writing the 'Who, What, When, Wear' column—" Jill says.

"What do you mean? I thought Claudia wrote that?" I ask.

"Claudia chats with Jill each month about pressing fashion issues, and Jill writes up the piece," Polly interjects.

"Then why is Claudia's name on there?" I ask.

"Because your aunt was a famous actress and she's still very beautiful at forty-four, which is a target age of our key demographic," Jill says. "Claudia has more name recognition, more celebrity."

I mouth "oh" and Jill keeps talking about the upcoming issue. The stories for this issue include the "Best of Denver's Doctors"—doctors for cancer treatment, ob-gyn, plastic surgery, etc.; a piece about a local start-up company that has been seeing impressive revenues; and a feature on team-building activities in Colorado, profiling one woman's horse ranch in particular.

One of the designers, a young guy with an earring and a goatee, reports that all of the ads but one are laid out for the July issue, and about 30 percent of the pages are done. They are just waiting to find out what the cover story is going to be.

"I think we should put the horse ranch article on the cover. We could have a nice view of the mountains behind Linda," Polly says. "I've been to Linda's ranch. It's gorgeous."

The way Polly uses only her first name makes me suspect that Linda is a friend of Polly's or some kind of business associate. I think about what Owen said about this being a four-color PR outlet.

Jill gives Amanda a look, but Amanda doesn't see it. I watch Amanda as she clenches her jaw, closes her eyes, and rolls her head a couple times as if she's got a sore neck.

Polly keeps talking about how nice it is to get away from the office, how important team building is, how she wishes the staff members had more time and the magazine more money so they could do such activities together, and how getting out into nature is the perfect place to regroup. Then she launches into some story about this trip she took river rafting and how she was so rejuvenated when she got back she was really able to be more productive at work, and this doctor that was on this trip with her . . .

Amanda looks at her watch. It's obvious that there are a few times when she is about to say something, about to try and interrupt, but it looks like she is waiting for Polly to take a breath, and that's the problem, Polly never does.

People start shifting uncomfortably in their chairs the way I used to when I was bored in church or when it was the last few minutes of the school day and I couldn't wait for the bell to ring.

Finally she pauses, just for a moment, and Amanda seizes the opportunity to jump in.

"I think you've got a good idea there, going with Linda on the cover. If it's okay, before we make any decisions, I just want to toss out a few things to discuss, you know, just play devil's advocate for a minute or two. As you know, Polly, historically we've done our 'Best of Denver's Doctors' on the cover, and just to let Helaina know since she's new, the reason we do that is because we're the only publication that provides this kind of un-biased information about the Denver area to our readers. It's basically like getting a personal recommendation be-cause the way we collect the information is by polling readers and a cross-section of locals. Our readers tend to be wealthy baby boomers, predominantly women, so the info on plastic surgeons and, God forbid, cancer special-ists, is important to them. It's not like a hot read, but a lot of people buy our magazine and use it like you would any reference book, you know? I mean if you have cancer, do you want to find your doctor out of the Yellow Pages? Of course not. Some of our past 'Best of Denver's Doctors' have been among our best-selling issues."

"That's true," Polly interrupts. "We do reader polls all the time to gauge what people like, why people were attracted to some issues more than others, and you know what we found out about why the 'Best of Denver's Doctors' was such a hit? Our divorced, middle-aged female readers were hoping to find divorced, middle-aged doctors to marry!"

"Anyway, we don't have to decide the cover right away," Amanda says. "We've got a few more days to think it over. We do need to discuss . . . "

"I think we should go with the 'Best of Denver's Doctors' on the cover," Polly says. "Like I said, last year's issue was one of the best-selling issues of all time."

Like *she* said? I thought Amanda said that. I look at Amanda, who has just a hint of a smile on her lips.

"I agree with that," Amanda says. "Any other opinions?"

"Good choice," Jill agrees.

"Which doctor's picture are we putting on the cover?" the Goatee Guy asks.

"The cutest one," Amanda says. She looks through a stack of pictures she has in a folder and pulls out a few promising choices. "Polly, what do you think?"

All three choices are middle-aged men, two white, one black. Polly taps her index finger beneath one of the pictures, one of the white men. Amanda and Jill nod in agreement.

A few more business issues are discussed, and then the meeting adjourns. I walk out of the room in a daze. I'm the last person to leave, behind Amanda, and I'm so out of it I step on the back of her heel.

"Sorry!"

"No problem. Hey, are you okay?"

"That was the most surreal experience," I say.

She laughs. "Welcome to the real world."

I return to my desk and report to Owen about how the meeting went. He just chuckles. "That sounds about right. So, you want to catch that movie tonight?"

"I'd like that." I would, but there is a part of me that wonders *why* he wants to hang out with me. Don't get me wrong, this isn't a crisis of self-esteem, it's just that he's only known me in my psychomourning mode. I'm not sure that I was ever a girl who could be lauded for my steady emotions, but I'm not usually quite such a basket case either.

"Owen, why do you like me?" The question pops out entirely of its own accord without my permission, yet another instance of my newly acquired disease of Dating Tourette's revealing itself.

"I like you because you are beautiful, you're smart, you're complicated, and you like weird movies."

"I never realized being complicated and liking weird movies were attractive qualities."

"You're interesting, that's my point, that's what I like. Why do you like me?"

"Who said I did, Mr. Presumptuous?"

"You're going to the movies with me. I think that means you like me."

"That, or else I'm just really bored."

He laughs. "I'll take my chances."

Chapter 8

When I get home, the house is silent. I call out, "Hello?" but no one answers. I start to head toward my room, and as I walk by my father's study, I stop. He would kill me if he caught me going through his things, but I vowed to Mom (her memory, anyway) that I would check things out. Trembling slightly and glancing around, I push the door open.

The room is empty. Dad's desk is total chaos, littered with loose stamps and pens, opened envelopes, sticky notes, and scraps of paper with phone numbers and cryptic messages in my father's cramped handwriting. Maria is allowed to vacuum and dust in here, but she's not allowed to touch Dad's desk.

On the desk there's a ledger with lots of numbers that mean nothing to me and piles of files stuffed with loose sheets of paper. I'm about to pick up the first file when I hear my father's voice coming toward the study. My heart does a backflip and I quietly put the file back, close the desk drawer, climb under the desk, and pull the chair in as far as I can.

I hear the study door close. He could sit down at his desk at any moment. He's in here with me, just a few feet away. I feel as nervous as a refugee hiding from an invading army. I know my behavior is ridiculous—so what if Dad finds me? It's not like he's going to have me carted off to jail. But I'm scared anyway.

I hear my father's voice in that falsetto salesman's tone of his, "Steve, Steve, it sounds like you're suggesting something underhanded is going on here. I can assure you that is not the case, nothing of the sort is—" he laughs.

"It's complicated perhaps, but not overly so. Have you spoken to our CFO, Bill Hansen? He's the best person to talk to about how we present our financial statements—"

"Of *course*, well, I mean, I'm certainly familiar with them, but Hansen would just be the better person to explain the details. You know, Hansen won *Fortune*'s CFO of the Year award two years ago for his creative—

"What are you suggesting?" Dad's tone abruptly changes from placating to defensive. "Well, it sounds to me like you're suggesting that 'creative' means 'unethical.' Steve, I believe—

"No, *you're* not listening to *me*. Our financial statements are not oblique. We have nothing to hide. We're in a complex economy, but we've never had any analyst complain about our earnings statements—

"Those are just rumors, unsubstantiated rumors. No, no, there is no truth to that at all. Absolutely not! I'm not going to take this from a reporter who makes maybe $60,000 a year and couldn't possibly begin to understand how to balance a billion-dollar budget. I believe our conversation is over." I hear a beep—Dad turning his cell phone off, I guess—then something crash against the wall. The cell phone, maybe, or something that had been sitting on the desk.

"Shit," Dad mutters, smashing his hand against the desk. I shudder as if he had hit me.

My father is less than a foot away from me. Though I

can't see him, I can picture him leaning over the desk, his head in his hands. I don't want him to find me right now. I don't want to get in his path. I've seen him blow up like this. It would be like facing a bull in the ring without any red cape to divert his attention from me. If he knew I just overheard this conversation—whatever it was that I heard—he'd kill me.

I hold my breath, try not to inhale, itch, cough, sneeze. I try to disappear. Twenty seconds pass, thirty, but it feels like twenty minutes, half an hour. Finally, finally, I hear my father swear, open the study door, and slam it closed behind him. I push the chair out and get up slowly. Though probably only five minutes have passed, I'd apparently clenched my muscles so taut they've cramped.

I can't open the door to see if Dad is out there. If he's sitting in the dining room—I can picture him pouring himself a drink right now—he'd hear me if I tried to climb out the window. Shit. What if he comes back in here? Should I hide under the desk again? For how long? What if he comes back in here and sits at his desk?

This is ridiculous. I can't hide in here all day. I just need to suck it up and risk it, just open the door and walk out of here. His study is the place he gravitates to most when he's home. I catch my breath and go to open the door when I hear a car pulling out of the driveway. I run over to the window and peek out. The car is Dad's Mercedes. Thank God. I race out of the study and up to my room.

I pace around my room, trying to figure out what it was that I just heard. He was talking to a reporter. He sounded angry and defensive. Does he have something to hide? Maybe he's embezzling or something. Is it serious? I'm mad at Dad, but it's not like I want him to go to jail.

I don't know how long I'm lost in my tumble of

thoughts, but at some point I glance at the clock and think to myself, "What day is it?" It takes my brain a few seconds to remember. Great. I have dementia at the age of twenty. As soon as I remember the day of the week, I remember that I have a date to get ready for. I try to push the thoughts of what I overheard out of my head. I'll worry about it later.

Owen picks me up and we go to a movie at the Mayan, one of the art theaters in Denver, then go across the street for drinks and dinner.

"So, when do I get to read some of your poetry?" I ask after the waitress sets down our beers.

"Actually, there's going to be a slam poetry night at the Mercury Café pretty soon. I was thinking about performing something. Want to go?"

"Sure." I'm not usually a fan of regular poetry readings, but I like slam poetry. Since it's judged, poets aren't allowed to be boring, and I like the way it mixes performance art, theater, and poetry into one.

I take a sip of my beer and try to think of something else to say. I think about asking him what he thought of the movie, but that seems so cliché. Fortunately, Owen keeps the conversation going. "So, tell me everything about yourself."

"Where should I start?"

"Tell me how you got interested in film."

"Claudia's phenomenal acting."

He laughs. "Yeah, right. I've seen *Becoming*. More cheese than a Kraft factory."

"That's pretty typical of '80s movies though. They don't trust the audience to understand anything. Like if they want to show that time has passed, they have the calendar flip pages or the clock hand rotate. Or if they want to show that a guy is interested in a girl, they go into slow motion as she tosses her hair around or whatever and sultry music is pumped in. The camera swings back from the guy's wide eyes to the woman and then back to the guy, then back to the girl. They just beat you over the head with it."

"You haven't answered my question yet."

I take a sip of my beer. "In high school, Dad bought me a video camera, and I joined the video yearbook committee. I actually got class credit for it, and all we did was go around videotaping interviews with students, the usual footage of football games, school dances, school plays, that sort of thing. I had a lot of fun. Then my senior year, I wanted an easy class, so I took drama, and it turned out that I really enjoyed it. I liked writing too and decided film was the best way to combine all my interests."

"What kind of movies do you want to make?"

"To be honest, right now I'm not really sure. I tend to like arty films simply because I like movies that don't assume that the audience is filled with lobotomized robots with brain damage that are unable to think for themselves. I also really like British films just because I like movies where the actors look like real people, not movie stars. I think American actresses are so beautiful it's distracting. Sometimes when I'm watching an American movie I can't concentrate on the story line because I'm too busy wondering how much surgery a woman must have had to look so young even though she's in her forties or whatever. But I'm not a total movie snob. I like some blockbuster movies as long as they're well done. Anyway, that's my story. How about you, how'd you become a poet?"

"My dad was an editor and publisher and my mom was

a writer. My mom and I read thousands of books together when I was a kid. We were constantly going to the bookstore or library. I learned that I thought better when I got words organized on the page. When I felt unhappy or confused, the only way I could make sense of how I felt was to write it down."

The waitress brings our food. I have a vegetable-and-black-bean soft taco; Owen has a chicken sandwich and fries. I'm putting sour cream on my taco when I notice two large, hulking men enter the bar. The bigger guy is so creepy looking I shiver involuntarily. He has dark eyebrows that come to a point, two triangles above malevolent icicle-blue eyes.

Owen is busy getting ketchup on his plate and doesn't notice my reaction. He eats a fry, and then, looking up at me, says, "Okay, my turn. Have you ever been in love?"

"Ooh, moving right on to the hard questions."

"I don't mess around."

"Clearly. Well, I dated a guy for a while in high school. I thought it was love, but now I realize I was just delirious with excitement about the idea of being in love and the prospect of getting laid. I mean we had fun together, but it was really just kind of a joke. I've dated a couple guys since then, nothing serious."

Dan and I met because we were both on the video-yearbook committee together. Dan was good looking and he constantly told me how pretty and talented I was. The attention was intoxicating. Plus, my girlfriends were all having sex and I felt like it was time for me to cast off the burdensome armor of virginity, too. It was surprisingly easy to convince myself that I was falling in love with Dan. I needed to believe that lie so I could feel all right about sleeping with him. We dated throughout our senior year, sleeping together whenever his parents or my parents were gone. And when we went our separate ways for college, I can't say that I was heartbroken. Dan was a nice enough guy. It wasn't his fault I worked so hard to erect emotional barriers so no one could really work his way into my heart.

I take a bite of my taco and wonder why what I just said feels like a lie. Maybe Owen is asking so he knows how likely I am to give him an STD or something, in which case I'm not exactly giving him the whole story. But I don't want to tell him I've slept with three guys since Dan and I broke up—all three very stupid one-night stands. How can I explain my sexual schizophrenia? Sometimes I feel like you should only have sex when you're in love or at least in a semiserious relationship, and other times, like after I've been hanging out with Hannah, I feel like I should just experiment and have fun and not worry about who I sleep with and under what conditions. Then I wake up the next morning with a hangover and regrets. Suddenly, instead of seeing the world like Hannah does, I see it from Marni or Kendra's point of view. Marni has been with the same guy since high school. Kendra has slept with three guys, and they were all serious, long-term relationships. She doesn't believe in messing around, not even a little harmless necking with a cute stranger in a dark bar after a few drinks. How can I explain to Owen that for me, having sex with a guy is a convoluted mathematical formula: take how long you've known a guy (in days), multiplied by the number of dates you've gone on, times the number of hours you've spent talking on the phone. You also have to consider how many guys you've slept with ever, and how long the relationship lasts. If you sleep with someone on a first date, but end up marrying that person, for example, it was okay to sleep with him so soon. It's very tricky. You don't learn this stuff in school, you learn it by what your friends, the movies, and magazines say and what they don't say. It's exhausting trying to keep it all straight.

"How about you?"

"There was a woman I dated for a couple years in college." Owen looks at the foam clinging to the sides of his half-finished pint. He brings the glass to his lips and takes a long swallow. "She was a talented poet, very beautiful, but she'd gone through some really bad stuff in her life, and it messed her up. She drank a lot, did a lot of drugs, she got herself into a lot of debt. She actually left me."

"I'm so sorry." I don't like the idea of Owen having to feel pain ever. I know it's not possible, but I want it just the same. At the same time, I feel a strange pang of jealousy toward his ex. I wonder what would happen if she suddenly wanted to get back together with him. Would he hook up with her again?

This is ridiculous. Why am I even thinking like this?

"It's all right. It was for the best. And poets need pain, right? Okay, my turn. Do you believe in the death penalty?" he asks.

"What is this, twenty questions?"

"How else do you get to know a person?"

"I don't know, you hang out with them, learn stuff about them a little at a time."

The waitress comes by and clears our plates. We order another round of beer.

"You'll be leaving for New York and I'll be leaving for Iowa at the end of the summer. We have to speed things up."

"Okay. Well, no, I don't. I think prison is a crueler punishment than the death penalty, so if we really want to punish the dregs of humanity, life sentences are the way to go. For one thing, poor people and people of color disproportionately get the death penalty, so it's racist and classist, and for another thing, we're always putting people to death for crimes it turns out they didn't commit— that's just crazy. But mostly I just think the death penalty is too good for some people. I'd rather die than live in jail, getting raped and beaten up and eating crap food and never getting to travel, being locked up in a tiny cage. It sounds like a living hell."

Of course I'd thought about taking my own life a few drunken nights since Mom died despite living in total comfort, extravagant wealth, and complete freedom. The pain I felt for Mom's death was so intense, I'd thought about slitting my wrists a couple of fleeting times. I so desperately wanted to stop the ferocious ache I felt, the loss simply seemed too great. I can hardly be objective about capital punishment's use as retribution when I myself had thought about the sweet escape death offered.

"You wouldn't say that if it happened to you. There's nothing more horrible than death."

"I disagree. Once you're dead, you don't feel pain anymore. That sounds like a pretty good deal to me. I mean in movies, you're supposed to be all happy when the good guy shoots the bad guy a couple times and the bad guy dies a quick, painless death. Slow torture, shame, humiliation . . . that's so much worse, and thus a better retribution."

"Yikes. Remind me not to piss you off."

I smile. "How about you, do you believe in the death penalty?"

"No, but not because I think we should slowly torture people by letting them rot in prison."

Owen agrees with me about the racist and classist issues—he says the death penalty in its current incarnation is just a modern, legal version of lynching. Then he starts telling me about his views on the drug war and how our laws make it virtually impossible for convicts to make a successful transition into society upon their release. He sounds like he knows what he's talking about.

Our conversation jumps around to lighter topics back to weightier ones back to lighter ones again.

I look up and see an old lady enter the restaurant with the help of a man in his fifties—I'm assuming it's her son.

"What are you looking at?" Owen asks me.

"That lady reminds me of an old woman I used to do volunteer work for in high school."

"What kind of volunteer work?"

I take my eyes off the old woman and meet Owen's gaze. "Mostly what I did was drive elderly people to doctors' appointments. The people I worked for were too old or too sick to drive."

"That's interesting."

"What is?"

"That you volunteered for old people. I would have pegged you for someone who spent your time buying shoes at the mall or having fun with your friends."

"I do believe I've just been insulted."

"Sorry, that came out wrong. But you know what I mean."

"Yeah, I do. And most of the time I *was* partying and shopping. My mom volunteered a lot, so I guess I take after her in some ways. I guess I've always felt like . . . well, I'm unsure what my feelings are about Heaven, right? So I've always believed that just in case there is no such thing as Heaven, I need to really make what time I do have on earth count."

"I think that's a great outlook."

"Maybe. Seeing all those old people made me sort of afraid to get old myself. It really does not look like any fun. There was this one old lady that I helped out: The very first thing I saw when I first met her was her naked butt. I opened the door to her apartment and there it was: old lady butt as far as the eye could see. I don't know if you've ever seen an eighty-eight-year-old's butt, but it isn't pretty."

He laughs.

Owen's and my attention is diverted by the sound of loud voices over at the bar. There is an obviously drunk girl barely able to stay on the stool. The two big guys I saw come in earlier are standing next to her.

"Go away!" she says again, loudly and angrily.

"Come on, sweetheart," says the bigger guy. "We just want to make sure you get home safely."

"Leave me alone," the girl says. She's thin, with long dark hair. She might be pretty if she didn't have that glassy, vacant look in her eyes. I think she's high as well as drunk. There is an eerie pallor in her complexion.

Before I know what's happening, Owen has leapt up from the table. "Is there a problem here?"

Owen, are you insane? Those two guys could clobber you! One of them is only a couple inches taller than he is, but the other has a good five inches and sixty pounds on him.

"There's no problem here. You gotta problem?" the bigger guy asks.

"Miss, do you know these two guys?"

"No! Fuck, no!"

"Come on, sweetheart, that's not true," smaller guy says.

"What's her name?" Owen asks them.

"What's it to fucking you?"

I stand and go over to them. "Hi," I say to the girl. "Are you okay? Are these guys bothering you?"

"Yes!"

"Do you need a ride home or anything?" I ask.

"No! I'm fine."

"How are you going to get home?" Owen asks her.

"Fuck off," bigger guy says, pushing Owen back a foot or two. Owen gives him an irritated glance.

My heart is pounding. There aren't many people in the bar left except for a couple of the staff, none of whom I see at the moment.

The girl shrugs in response to Owen's question.

"We'd be happy to give you a ride," I say.

The girl looks at me, then at the two guys. She nods. "Yeah, okay."

"Fuck you! We're taking her home."

"How do you know her?" Owen asks.

"We met her tonight. So?"

"Owen," I say, "I'm going to throw some money on the table."

He nods. "I'll meet you outside."

"Owen will take you to the car," I explain to the girl. "I'll be right there."

The girl looks at Owen. Her expression is confused, but she decides that Owen and I seem the safer bet. Owen helps her off the stool. She nearly falls but as she goes down Owen grabs her arm before she hits the ground.

"Don't you do that. Don't you fucking do that," bigger guy says.

I hurl a handful of twenties on the table. Owen is already walking out the door with the girl. I watch the two guys follow them outside. Shit! Shit! I don't want to go out there. Should I call the police? But there is no way they'd get here in time. Fuck you, Owen, for getting us into this. We're going to get the shit kicked out of us.

I exhale. If I go out there, maybe that will diffuse the tension. I don't want to be brave, honestly, but if stupid

Owen is going to risk it, I'm not sure I have any other choice.

I push the door open and look down the sidewalk. Our car is only a couple blocks down the street. Owen can't go very fast because the girl is so unsteady on her feet he's practically carrying her. The two guys walk just behind them, and that's when I realize that they are just as scared as we are. They could have taken Owen by now if they were going to do anything. Still, my heart is pounding and my breath is jagged as I hurry past them.

"Where the fuck you think you're going?" one says.

I ignore him and help Owen get the girl in the front seat and buckle her in.

"Get in the car," Owen orders.

"I'm not leaving you!"

Owen closes the door and for the moment, he and I are just standing there, facing the two guys who are maybe ten feet away. "That was a very stupid fucking thing to do," bigger guy says.

Owen laughs. He actually laughs! "Have a good night, guys." And with that, he calmly walks over to the driver's side. I don't need any more encouragement. I dive in the backseat and quickly lock my door and make sure the girl's door is locked, too. Owen starts the car at the same moment the bigger guy pounds on my window with the side of his fist. I jump in my seat, thinking for a moment that he's going to break the window. The guy's face is inches away from mine, and his facial features are so prominent they look like a caricature of a Halloween pumpkin carved into a lurid expression.

Owen pulls away and I watch the two guys standing there trying to look menacing, when in fact, they are totally impotent now.

I exhale and slump down in my seat. Owen asks the

girl where she lives. She makes a confused expression, and then tells him the names of two intersecting streets that aren't too far from here.

I'm still trying to get my pulse and breath back to normal when we get to the intersection.

"Which building?" Owen asks her. He slows the car to a crawl; fortunately the traffic is light at this time of the night.

She looks around. She doesn't say anything. I'm beginning to worry she doesn't have a clue *where* she lives when abruptly she taps on the window. "There. I live there. That's where I live."

Owen parks the car. Together he and I help her walk to the entrance of her apartment building. We get her to the door, but she doesn't make a move to open it.

"Do you have the keys?" I ask gently.

She gives me a curious look, as if trying to remember if she knows me. "Keys," she says at last. "Yeah." She roots through her purse and digs them out. She starts looking at each one, squinting at them. Finally she attempts to put one in the lock and drops the whole set on the ground.

Owen reaches down, picks them up, and starts trying the keys himself. He gets the right one on the third try.

"What apartment are you in?" I ask.

Again, she studies me for a moment. "It's 102."

Thank God, she's on the first floor.

We awkwardly stumble inside and down the hall. Owen again tries the keys. This time he gets it right the first time. The girl staggers inside to the couch. Owen locks the lower lock—the one in the doorknob—so that he can lock the door behind us and sets her keys down just inside her door. He pulls the door closed as we leave.

I exhale again. "Shit."

He smiles, looking tired and relieved.

We walk back out to the car. "How the hell did you know those guys weren't going to slaughter you?" I ask.

"I didn't. If they had been drunk I would have been a lot more worried because drunk people do idiotic things. Most guys, though, don't really want to fight."

We click our seatbelts on and he pulls out.

"Have you ever gotten into a bar fight before?"

"No. Once a friend of mine at a bar almost got into a fight, and me and my other friend ran to his side. The guy who wanted to fight took one look at us and backed off. I think if you look like you're ready to fight, you rarely actually have to do it."

"Damn. I'm really glad I'm not a guy."

"You were pretty smooth out there tonight, too."

"No, I was a basket case. I just figured if I was at your side, that girl might figure we were safe."

"That takes bravery."

"It sure didn't feel that way."

"That's what bravery is. Doing something even though you're scared to."

"I guess."

We drive the next fifteen minutes or so home in silence.

He pulls into my driveway. "I guess I should get to bed soon so I can wake up bright and early for another day at the office, now that I'm a working girl and all," I say.

"Work is a real novelty for you, isn't it?"

"I guess. I don't need to work. I have an inheritance from Mom and my grandparents."

"Do you get money from your dad?"

"If I wanted or needed it, he would have his secretary give it to me. But since I ended up living in the dumpy place I live in, I really don't need much. The inheritance

I got from Mom covers my tuition and living expenses. I'd rather not rely on Dad."

"You're only twenty years old. You're still in college. A lot of college kids still have their parents pay their way. My parents covered my undergrad degree."

"Maybe. It's not like I'm living under a bridge or anything. I'm doing okay."

"If you're so rich, why don't you have your own car?" he asks.

"I had a BMW in high school, but we sold it when I left for school. Dad gets bored with cars really quick so he's always selling old ones, and by old I mean like a year old, and buying new ones. Anyway, it's not like you need a car in New York. Nobody I know there has a car. Plus, Dad owns like six, so when I'm home I borrow one. It's crazy, when I drive some of my Dad's cars, people, both guys and girls, honk and wave at me. Or I'll be getting in the car and people will stop and start asking me all these questions and heaping on the compliments. It's like driving an expensive car makes me some kind of celebrity."

"Really? That seems kind of weird."

"Some of the cars are worth as much as $250,000. Don't you find that impressive?"

"I guess not."

"What does impress you about a person?"

"Honesty. Trustworthiness. Loyalty."

"You never wanted to be rich?"

"Money's nice, I'm not saying it's not. I don't want to be broke, but no, I don't need to be rich."

The thing is, I believe him. I believe that he's not after me for my money, and it's a relief. When I dated my high school boyfriend, Dan, I always worried that at least part of his attraction to me was my father's money and connections. I didn't have anything concrete to base my worry on, but when you have money, you always have to wonder if people like you for you or for your bank account.

His gaze is intense. I can't figure out what his smile means. Do I amuse him? Am I some sort of novelty to him? Is he going to go home and write poems about a flaky rich girl? He leans toward me, touches my neck with the tips of his fingers, and pulls me closer for a kiss. The kiss is nice, but I feel nervous and stupid and confused. I can't handle this. I pull away, tell him I had a nice time and I'll see him tomorrow at work. I open the door and am about to dash inside when he says, "Did I say something wrong?"

"No, no, not at all."

"I'll see you tomorrow at work."

"See you tomorrow."

Inside, I'm struck by how quiet it is. It's two o'clock in the morning, so of course it would be quiet, but I get this strange feeling I'm all alone. I go to the kitchen to get a glass of water and see the note Claudia hung on the refrigerator with a magnet.

Helaina,
Your father has a business trip in California
this weekend and I have a fashion show in New
York to attend. We'll see you Sunday night.
—Claudia

The note reminds me of all the Christmas gifts and birthday cards I got that were signed "Love Mom and Dad" in Mom's handwriting.

And yeah, right, they both just happened to have business trips this weekend. They're probably at some spa in California drinking champagne and fucking each other raw.

But this is my chance; I have the place to myself. I can finally check things out.

I race upstairs to the master bedroom and push the door open. This is where Mom slept for the last few years of their marriage. Dad usually slept in the guest bedroom at the end of the hall. The only time they slept together was when we had guests staying over. It was always very important that everyone thought their marriage was a happy one.

I used to spend hours in here with Mom. I used to sit on the bed and watch her get ready for parties. She'd be wearing her slip and sitting at the vanity table putting on her makeup. On nights when Dad was out of town Mom and I used to snuggle up on the bed together and watch movies. I realize I never really noticed what the room looked like before. The whole room is done in shades of pale blue—the walls, the silk canopy bed, the plush carpet. The icy color makes the room seem unwelcoming and cold in a way I never noticed.

After the funeral, I left without going through Mom's things. I couldn't even think about it. But now I wonder if Claudia has just taken all of Mom's stuff. I don't need emeralds or gold necklaces or fur coats, but I sure as hell don't want Claudia to have them.

I open the closet. It's filled with clothes and shoes. I close the door and walk over to her dresser and open her jewelry box, which is still filled with glittering jewelry. The vanity table is still covered with makeup and brushes and perfume. But I can't tell if the clothes, makeup, and jewelry are Mom's or Claudia's. There are only two pieces of Mom's jewelry that I remember distinctly, and I don't see either of them. I don't see her wedding ring or the firestone-opal pendant that her friend brought her back from Australia. She was probably wearing those when she died and was cremated in them. She wore the firestone opal almost every day. It was a beautiful necklace. A striking orange color with milky undertones, it always reminded me of a psychic's crystal ball. Her wedding ring was distinctive, too. Dad had had two more karats added to it on their tenth anniversary, and two years later he had a third diamond band soldered onto the rest. When he gave it to her over dinner—we were on a cruise through the Caribbean at the time to celebrate their anniversary—I saw the slightest flicker of disappointment pass across her face before she smiled and thanked him.

Not that the gift had been a surprise. She'd known he was going to do something to the ring when he'd asked to borrow it two weeks before the trip.

"Please don't change it, I like it just the way it is," she'd protested when he'd asked for it.

"I'm just going to have it cleaned."

"It's already so big. It gets caught on everything."

"Just a cleaning, I promise," he'd sworn. Then when he'd given her the larger ring, she just thanked him politely, though I could tell she didn't mean it.

Dad only stayed for half of the six-day trip. When we docked on an island for a day of shopping, he left and flew home early to get back to work, citing an emergency. One evening after he'd gone, when it was just me and Mom, I asked her if she liked the ring. The way it reflected light was stunning, blinding as a disco ball.

"I liked it better before actually," she said. "It's a little much. It gets caught on things."

"Is something wrong, Mom?"

"No."

"I can tell something's wrong. What is it?"

She sighed. "It's just that . . . hon, when you give a gift to someone, you should think about what they would want. Not about what you would want or what you wish they would want. Sometimes your Dad gives gifts not because they are something I want but because it's something he wants."

"Why would he want you to have a big diamond ring?"

"He wants his wife to have it so her ring will be bigger than other executives' wives."

I loved when she talked to me like that, like I was an adult and not just a kid. And I understood what she meant, mostly.

Dad's closets are full, which suggests he's sleeping in here again. I go through the door to the adjoining room that Mom used both as her studio and her study. The walls are lined with books, both Mom's fiction and art books and Dad's business books. Mom's desk faces the window. There are two recliners and a couch where Mom used to like to curl up and read. There used to be an easel where Mom worked, but that and all the canvasses and other supplies are no longer there. This is where Mom went to be alone, to plan dinner parties, to make sure the household accounts were in order. It was also where she would paint. She never tried to sell her work as far as I know. She hung a couple of pieces in our house; I have no idea what happened to the rest.

It's not until I walk through the bedroom, bathroom, and study for a second time that I notice what is different. All of the pictures Mom had of me and her and of her and Dad from their wedding are gone. I can't imagine Dad taking the time to round up the pictures and get rid of them. It must have been Claudia. She probably threw them away so she didn't have to compete with Mom's memory. Or maybe so she didn't have to face her own guilty conscience by having to look into the eyes of the sister she betrayed.

I try to think back to Christmas, try to remember which room Claudia had been staying in, but I can't remember. My guess is that she stayed in the guest bedroom on the other side of the house, so that's where I go.

There are a few women's suits hanging in the closet, a few sweaters on the shelf. There are no underwear or socks in any of the drawers.

There are five other guest bedrooms, and I check each of them, and none show any signs of Claudia staying in them, which means Dad and Claudia must be sleeping together in the master bedroom.

How could I not have noticed this before?

I go back to Mom's study/studio and sit down at the desk and begin opening the drawers. There is a stack of folders with a brochure titled "The Secret to Success: Every Detail Counts." It's a brochure for Claudia's company, Prima Facie. There's a picture of Claudia in there, plus her business card. I pull the stack of folders out, but there is nothing under them. I put them back and open the other drawer. There are envelopes, tape, a ruler, a few empty notebooks, a day planner. I open the top drawer on the other side. There are pens in a shallow basket, thank you cards, a box of tacks, a box of staples, a stapler. There is nothing of Mom's at all. Claudia must have taken the desk over after Mom died, wiping out any traces this had ever belonged to my mother. It's too neat, though. It doesn't look like a desk she actually works at.

I look around the room. I look more closely at the laptop sitting on the desk and realize it's not my mother's. She had a dark gray HP; this is a light gray Mac. I boot the computer up and a box pops up. It prompts the user name "merrillc" and asks for a password. I type "becoming" and get right in. She is *so* predictable. Still basking in the glory twenty years after the fact.

I open up her Internet browser and check the history of the websites she's visited: vogue.com, glamour.com, forbes.com, entertainmentweekly.com, wallstreetjournal. com, nytimes.com, fortune.com. It's hard for me to think of Claudia as someone who reads the *Wall Street Journal*, but it's not like it's some scintillating discovery.

I randomly open folders. She's got an Excel file of contact names and two contracts for consulting projects. I find a folder titled Accounts Payable, and open it.

Harper, Ann: August 12–13, 16 hours @ $200 an hour = $3,200
Kennedy, Douglas H.: December 14, 10 hours @ $200 an hour = $2,000
Lowe, Elizabeth P.: February 23, 40 hours @ $200 an hour = $8,000

This can't be all the business she's gotten. After paying taxes, with the extra-hefty tax you pay when you're self-employed—Kendra and Lynne, who do acting jobs and freelance writing gigs, respectively, bitch about it all the time—she'd be clearing about $7,000 a year. Hardly a lavish income.

I look through all the other files but all I find are a few Word documents with choppy ideas for "Who, What, When, Wear" columns: Out: Stripes. In: Plaid. Out: Paying too much for a passing fad. In: Classic good taste.

I turn off the computer and look through the drawers again. I pull out the day planner and flip through it. There is very little here. *Haircut w/Eric. Nails with Sara. LC deadline. Meet with Liz Lowe.* According to the day planner and the accounts receivable, Claudia's business is hardly lucrative. Is it just a front for something? Like what? Does she actually try to drum up business? Did she lose her enthusiasm for being a small business owner when she realized that as a rich man's mistress, she'd never have to work again?

I put the day planner back in the drawer and push it closed, then open it again. I open the other top drawer. The one on the right with the pens and stapler seems shallower than the one on the left. It *is* shallower—by at least an inch or two. I pull the right drawer out, take everything out, feel around, and push gently on the bottom of it. Nothing. I reach beneath the drawer, feel around the bottom of it, and trace the edge with my fingers. I feel a square of metal about the size of a character on a keyboard. I press on it and it gives. The "bottom" of the drawer flips open to reveal another bottom and a blue-leather journal the size of a paperback. My heart races. Claudia's journal. This will tell me what I need to know. I don't know what that is, or what I'll do with the information once I have it, but I feel certain I've found what I've been looking for.

I open it and catch my breath. The handwriting is my mother's.

My heart is pounding as I put the drawer bottom back in, put the pens, stapler, and tacks back in the drawer, and take the diary back to my room. I crawl under the covers and open the diary to the first page with shaking hands.

May 15, 2005
Anna says writing things down can help. I don't see how writing is different than talking about it, and I've been talking with Anna twice a week for the last year, and things don't seem to be getting any better. In fact, Anna

doubled my dose of Celexa two weeks ago. She keeps assuring me that it's one of the milder of the antidepressants, but still, this doesn't feel like progress. Worse is how she toys with me regarding the Xanax. I understand that it's addictive, but sleep comes so quickly. There is none of that endless tossing and turning I've become so very used to. Just sweet, painless oblivion in minutes—I adore it. She'll only give me enough to take every other night. It's been two weeks since I got the prescription renewed and I've taken one every night—at this rate I'll be out at the end of the month. But instead of pacing myself, I'm thinking things like whether I can go to a new doctor and see if I can get him to get me a prescription—if I pay for it out of pocket instead of going through the insurance company, is there a database that would know multiple doctors are writing multiple copies of the same prescription? Or maybe I can buy more on the Internet or in Mexico or from some shady doctor. Crazy thoughts I'm having, but that's what depression does to you, it makes you crazy.

So I'm trying this writing therapy thing. I'll try anything. I'm so sick of feeling like this. I feel so very lonely. I feel like I have no one I can turn to.

I'd hoped that in inviting Claudia to live with us, I'd finally get to know my sister after all these years. I'd hoped we could become friends. But she's been here for three months, and she remains as elusive as ever.

She's trying to start her own consulting company. She is constantly asking Gary for tips and suggestions. She embraces his ideas enthusiastically, and Gary laps up the attention. Of course, we all like getting attention. It's been years since Gary adored me, but I guess we're even because it's been a long time since I felt that way about him, too.

I always wanted the kind of sister who was my best

friend. Someone who I could go out and have fun with. All these years, she's only told me only the sketchiest details about her life. I never met any of her boyfriends. I didn't see how she was doing her hair. I didn't know what books she was reading. I wanted to hear about the three pounds she'd lost that week or the new shoes she'd bought. I wanted to know what was going on in her life, who she was dating and how he kissed. I wanted to know the tiniest details and all I got were broad strokes, vague glimpses.

Now that she lives with me, I see how she styles her hair and the new shoes she buys, but she's emotionally as distant as ever. She never tells me what she thinks or how she feels. She keeps herself hidden during the day most of the time. At night, I make it a point to seek her out and ask her about her day. She reports insignificant events, never casting judgment or stating an opinion. I'll try to ask her about her plans for the company, to get some idea of her goals and ambitions, but all she gives me are monosyllabic answers.

It's entirely different when Gary is around. When he's here she's animated and talkative. She laughs and jokes around.

One thing we don't have to talk about anymore is money. Now that she has her own credit cards and her own "income" (allowance would be a more appropriate term, but we have to keep up appearances here), she doesn't have to go through the groveling that we'd both become so accustomed to and we both hated so much.

Her credit card bills go right to Gary's accountant, who quietly pays them. Claudia worked that out right away. She didn't want me to be able to see how she spends our money. But what does she think, I don't see the new clothes, the new shoes, the expensive haircuts?

I don't care about the money. Well, I do and I don't.

We have the money, certainly. It just seems like if you help somebody out, they'd be grateful. They'd say, "Thanks sis, let's catch a movie together, let's get some lunch."

She has so much anger toward me, so much jealousy. She's always been jealous of me, always, ever since we were little girls. I got to stay up later, I got to go on sleep-overs before she could, I got to date and drive and get a job at the Dairy Queen before she could. I know I've been blessed in many ways. I wish Claudia could find it in her-self to look past my good fortune and care about me as I do her.

May 21, 2005
I think Claudia is eager to get a man in her life. She walks around wearing blouses with plunging necklines, skimpy bikinis, and nearly translucent pajamas (without a bra). Most of the time, the only people here are me, her, and Maria. Sometimes Gary comes home with a colleague or by himself. Whenever that happens, I feel embarrassed for her. I expect her to put on a robe or something, but she shows no signs of being uncomfortable. It must be all the years she spent living in LA as an actress. I think actresses are more comfortable with their bodies than other women.

I feel like I have no one to talk to except for Anna, and I pay her to listen to me talk. Somehow I can't talk to Dana or Barb or Christine about how I'm feeling. I know they are supposed to be my friends, but I don't feel that I can really count on them or trust them. Isn't that awful? I just keep thinking about things like what nasty, horrible things they said about Becky Donovan after her latest round of plastic surgery, about how she was trying desper-ately to keep her husband interested in her when everyone knows he's cheating on her with at least two different women twenty years her junior. It's almost as if they think that by saying enough cruel things about Becky, we can avoid her fate when secretly I think we all identify with her pain and her ineffectual attempts to keep from looking her age.

It's exhausting always trying to pretend like my life is perfect, but it seems the safest thing.

Right now I feel like I've had three double shots of espresso. I feel so nervous. I feel anxious, and I have no idea why.

Anna wants me to spend time each day counting my blessings. It's true I have much to be thankful for. I have a beautiful, smart, talented daughter who is filled with spirit. Her spiritedness means she can be a bit of a spitfire at times, but I think the reason we sometimes get on each other's nerves is that because ultimately, we're really a lot alike.

May 26, 2005
Claudia has been telling me I should take a trip to a spa and get away for a while. She tells me again and again that I should take some time to get away and relax. My daughter is away at school, Maria and Paul take care of the cooking and cleaning, I don't have a day job, all I have to do is show up to events every now and then looking pretty. What exactly does Claudia think is so stressful in my life that I need to get away from it all?

I suggested that we go together and have a weekend of sisterly bonding. She said she was too busy with her consulting business. It's not that I don't believe her, but it doesn't add up. I never see her working. I never see her making phone calls or sending out direct mail pieces. She works out for two to three hours a day, then she sits by the pool for a few hours. She spends her evenings drinking cocktails on the veranda and reading magazines. It's pretty clear to me that whatever it is that's holding her back it's not her rigorous work schedule.

Helaina called me today. God that kid cracks me up. She told me about how she stepped on a piece of glass that got lodged so deep she couldn't get it out herself and she needed to go to the hospital. That's not the funny part of the story, of course. Once Helaina assured me her foot was fine, it was just going to be a little sore for a few days, she told me about the hours she had to wait to get to see a doctor. She was stuck on a gurney in the middle of the hallway waiting for a room to free up, trapped next to a homeless woman who wouldn't stop talking about her ongoing battle with drug addiction and her myriad diseases including diabetes, arthritis, and cancer that was now in remission. Helaina talked about how she was unable to flee the pungent odor of urine emanating from the woman who rambled on and on and simply wouldn't shut up. Helaina did an impersonation of the woman saying, "Sho I do coke and PCP. Dare's so much vi-lence in dis worl, dat's why I do drugs." Helaina's dry account of her day just cracked me up. Her phone call really cheered me.

I suppose a better mother would be horrified to hear about her daughter chatting with a homeless drug addict in a hospital, but instead, I feel proud of Helaina. So many of her friends can't imagine a life without privilege. Her friends Hannah and Marni are nice enough girls but they talk about their clothes and shoes and cars as though it was their right to own anything and everything they want and they can't imagine a world in which teenagers don't drive hundred-thousand-dollar cars. Though Helaina can't remember a time when we weren't wealthy, she can "keep it real," as they say. (I think that's how it goes.) She's a down to earth person. I think that's what I love most about her, and with Helaina, there is a lot to love.

I wipe the tears from my eyes when I read those words. I remember how hard I made Mom laugh with my story about my day-in-the-hospital woes. I wish I'd called her every day. Maybe that would have helped her keep her spirits up.

June 1, 2005

I could barely get myself out of bed today. The sleeping pills make me so groggy that I simply must drink coffee in the morning to wake up, even though I'm not supposed to.

After my coffee, I went to work out as usual. Anna keeps touting the mental as well as physical benefits of working out, but I just went through the motions of my usual routine.

At least it killed a couple of hours of my day. That's all life has become: Units of twenty-four hours that I have to somehow get through.

I can't believe I used to run an advertising agency. I used to manage a dozen artists, writers, and project managers while placating demanding clients. I used to be able to raise a daughter and manage a business, and now it's all I can do to fix myself a cup of coffee or remember the last time I've eaten.

I came home, showered, ate a lunch of vegetables and skinless chicken, and went to the art museum. That's always my favorite part of the day, the hours I spend at the museum. Even though it's only a volunteer position, it's gratifying taking people around and telling them about the pieces, helping them get a deeper appreciation and understanding of what they are looking at. I feel comforted when I'm surrounded by all that beauty. Nothing captures the spirit of a person or a place like when it's interpreted through the eyes of a talented artist.

Dinner was lettuce and vegetables decadently sprinkled

with sunflower seeds and honey mustard dressing. I ate alone, as usual. Claudia appeared out of nowhere just as I was finishing. Tonight she was wearing a loose silk tank top without a bra and silk pajama bottoms that clung to her body leaving little to the imagination. Gary came home at eight—early for him—and was able to appreciate the view. He didn't even try to mask the fact that he was ogling her as I sat just a few feet away.

But did I say anything? No, I just left the room, poured myself a drink, locked myself in my study, and started writing. I just don't have the energy to fight anymore.

I have to tell Claudia she has to leave. As soon as I work up the energy I'll do it.

My heart is racing right now as I think about Claudia and Gary in the other room. I'm fighting back tears. But I'm through fighting.

If Claudia wants him so bad, she can have him. Everyone else has.

The first time I found out he was cheating on me was the hardest. His teary-eyed, twenty-two-year-old marketing coordinator at my door and telling me that they really loved each other. He'd left her because of me, but I didn't understand, just because I was married to him didn't mean they weren't meant for each other. It was destiny, didn't I see that?

After she left, I screamed and cried and threw things. He promised he wouldn't do it again. I chose to believe him. I was eight months pregnant. What else could I do?

It was the most painful thing I'd ever experienced. I loved him so much, more than I ever knew possible. But when you love someone so much, your ability to be hurt becomes that much more intense as well. It was so much harder because our marriage was so new. Not even a year old. And I was fat and pregnant with Helaina. I felt so ugly and so tired and so ill.

I wonder if the reason I didn't have more children was because I couldn't take the way Gary looked at me when I was pregnant, the disgust in his eyes when he looked at my enormous belly and swollen face. I couldn't bare his disapproval at the way my breasts sagged after she was born. So I had the surgery to get my breasts lifted and took care never to get pregnant again.

What we go through to feel pretty! What lengths we go to to try to keep our husbands from straying. There is nothing more painful than the betrayal of a spouse sleeping with another woman. Nothing more clearly states, "you are not enough. Not beautiful enough, not smart enough, not charming enough to keep my attention."

I didn't know for sure about any other women until Helaina was twelve. Again he told me he'd end it and again I decided to believe him. I didn't want Helaina to have to go through an ugly divorce. I worried that Gary would lie about his finances and somehow Helaina and I would have ended up living paycheck to paycheck. I lived my life in fear. I made all my decisions out of fear. Fear that I wouldn't get a good job. Fear that Helaina wouldn't have every possible opportunity if we lost the house. I didn't even fight to see if Gary would pay child support. I was too afraid I'd lose everything.

Things weren't always like this with Gary. When we were dating . . . our engagement . . . even when Helaina was still little, he was so charming and fun to be with. He made me feel like the most special woman in the world. Then when his business started taking off, it was like he became addicted to work and the power that came with it.

I knew Dad cheated on Mom, but I didn't realize it had begun in the very first year of their marriage. No wonder she became a faded version of herself over time, like a photo left in the rain.

August 13, 2005
It's happened. I can tell by the way they've been looking at each other, the perpetual smile on Claudia's face, it's like the two of them are closer to each other than I could ever be to either of them, like they know the secret password, the secret code for happiness, and I'm left outside, looking in.

I skip about thirty pages ahead to November.

November 5, 2005
It's been months since I've been able to sleep without a sleeping pill, Xanax, several drinks, or more often a combination of all of the above.
I'm not supposed to be drinking while taking the antidepressant, but I did it a few times when I couldn't sleep, and I didn't die or have a seizure, so I figure, why not?
The Celexa is helping me from feeling the lowest lows, but it also keeps out the highs. It's like instead of having a life of ups and downs, my life has flatlined.

November 18, 2005
I told Gary today that I'm going to tell Claudia she can't stay here anymore. He said if I do, he'll drag me through a very painful, very public divorce. He said it with such anger, as if he were finally able to get back at me after all these years. Get back at me for what is what I want to know. All I've done is support him, help his career, be there for him, look good for him, put a smile on my face, and pretend to be happy.
And anyway, he's bluffing. It wouldn't be good for his career to go through a nasty divorce. In a way, a divorce would be an absolute dream. I would get enough money that I could live comfortably until I die. I could go on trips with Helaina, travel the world, take art and writing

classes, maybe even meet someone new, someone who cared about me and not just his career.

So why am I still here? Why am I paralyzed with shock and pain? I've known our marriage was a sham for years. Even when Helaina was little, I suspected that Gary wasn't spending the nights in his hotel room when he was off on business alone. All those fawning interns and middle managers were happy to help him pass the time.

I didn't used to be so scared, so terrified of my own shadow. Ten years ago, I would have thrown pans and glasses and statues across the room if I found out my sister was sleeping with my husband. Now I'm just lurking around my own house like a guest, pretending like nothing is wrong. No wonder Gary fell out of love with me.

I've been spending hours every day at the health club working out. It's gratifying, watching the pounds melt away. I feel like at least I have control over something.

February 14, 2006
It's Valentine's Day, and Gary is away on "business." Claudia just happens to be away on "business" as well. I know they are together.

February 16, 2006
I went to the beautician's today, and as I was walking to the back to get my hair shampooed, I felt as if all eyes were on me. And not in a, oh-look-at-that-lovely-glamorous-woman sort of look, a feeling I could never get enough of. There was something smug in their gaze, just the slightest hint of a grin on their lips.

As Eric washed and massaged my hair and scalp, I couldn't relax like I normally do. I was sure I could hear a rumbling of rude comments, even with my hearing clouded by the rush of water.

I felt suddenly anxious, like I'd gotten up on stage for a singing competition and belted out a wretched number, totally oblivious that my voice was an atonal screech.

Eric and I walked back to his station. Eric was gossiping away, telling me what he no doubt thought was a very funny story about how Erma Schmitz walked in to her daughter's house to find her teenage grandson baking cookies. She thought it was so sweet that he was just hanging around the house baking, and when a batch came out of the oven, she insisted on trying one. She couldn't understand his resistance.

The punch line had something to do with there being pot in the cookies I think, but I wasn't paying close attention. I was too busy focusing on Dana Sinha. By looking in my mirror I could see her reflection in her mirror as the beautician styled her hair. She's thirty-two. Sometimes I forget that no matter how well you take care of yourself, there is no substitute for youth.

When Dana's hair was done, she stopped by my chair.

"Hi Ellen, it's so good to see you."

There was something in her tone, and the way she looked at me, that made it clear she knew a secret about me. But what?

That's when I realized she knows about Claudia and Gary. Everyone does. Everyone knows that my husband is cheating on me with my own sister, and I'm letting her live under my roof, giving her money even.

Getting through the haircut without losing my composure took everything I had.

Before I left, Eric whispered that he had something to tell me. He said he wasn't sure that telling me was the right thing to do, but he hoped it was. I couldn't speak. I just looked at him as he told me Claudia and Gary were sleeping together.

"Are you okay?" he asked.

I shook my head, barely managing to rein in the tears. I gave Eric his usual tip, staggered out to the car, and cried harder than I have in years.

This hurts so much. I'm so humiliated. How can I ever show my face around here again? I'm sure people wouldn't be surprised to learn that Gary had cheated, but he'd always done it at a distance before, never with my sister, never with a woman who lived under our own roof.

For so long, all I cared about was keeping up appearances. In my friends' eyes, I had a wonderful life, and I let that be enough. I haven't been happy in my marriage for years, but I always took solace in the fact that other people thought we were happy. Now I don't even have that.

I flip through the pages. The last entry is on March 17, the day my mother died.

March 17, 2006

I'm going to visit Rita at the vineyard for the weekend. I have to get away. I can't take this pain anymore. Even after a double dose of Celexa, a Xanax, and a stiff Bloody Mary, the pain is unbearable. A few days away is just what I need. Hell, maybe a few weeks away, months, years even.

And that's it. The final entry. It doesn't prove that my mother killed herself by driving off the cliff on purpose, but it certainly offers a reason why she didn't make the turn. Xanax and alcohol before a road trip on an icy mountain road. Dad and Claudia didn't drive my mother off the cliff, but they may as well have. Mom couldn't shut out thoughts of her husband and her sister betraying her and ruining her reputation. Gossip, that cruel poison to the ear, had killed my mother.

I close the book and look at the clock. It's six in the morning; time to get up. I make myself a double cappuccino and get to work early. When Owen gets there, I tell him that Dad and Claudia are gone so we have the place to ourselves for the weekend. I don't tell him about the journal.

All day I think about Mom and Claudia and Dad. It's so unfair. I hate that this is the way the world works, that the greedy people without consciences feed off the kind souls like my mother, like vultures that gain their strength from the dead.

I keep thinking about the things my mother wrote, *In their eyes, I had a wonderful life, and I let that be enough . . . I didn't used to be so scared, so terrified of my own shadow . . . In their eyes, I had a wonderful life, and I let that be enough.* Thoughts of my mother, Claudia, and Dad crowd my head like a staticy TV I can't shut up. It just keeps getting louder and louder.

How can I quiet the noise? Revenge? That's hardly my style. I want Dad and Claudia to learn from their behavior. What means enough to them to get them to change their ways? What do they care about most? Wealth and prestige. What could I possibly do to damage either?

Chapter 9

The next day, my thoughts tumble confusedly through my mind from the moment I wake up in the morning. I don't feel healthy physically or spiritually right now. I wish Kendra was here with me or I was with her in New York. Kendra is big into detoxifying teas and supplements. She has about a million different kinds of vitamins and if Lynne or I ever come down with a cold, Kendra whips up glasses of Emergen-C and spirulina.

Another thing Kendra is into is candles. I like candles, both the smell and the calming flickering of the flames, but personally I doubt the claims that a few scented candles can transform your mood. Can a candle really infuse you with feelings of serenity and well-being? Can bergamot really energize you? Does lavender really relax you? Is ylang-ylang really an aphrodisiac? Right now, though, I think I'm desperate enough to try anything. It couldn't hurt, anyway. I resolve to go to a health food store and stock up on teas and supplements and aromatherapy candles just as soon as I get some energy.

Wrapped in my towel, my hair still wet but combed into some semblance of order, I rifle through my underwear drawer. Most of my underwear could be described as sassy rather than sexy. I have lots of bright colors and silly leopard-skin silk undies that are like a private joke to myself. It makes me think of some bachelor who thinks he's so hot because he's got a faux animal-print bedspread or something.

I slip on a pair of black silk bikinis. I've lost so much weight the underwear pooches up a little like a partially filled balloon. Very sexy.

It's been a while since I cared about what I look like in underwear, but I realize that at some point Owen may see me in them, and I don't want to look like an air mattress that's only filled halfway. I'll try to remember to buy more, but my brain is so scattered. I want to just be a normal twenty-year-old who goes shopping for clothes and has a romance with a cute guy. I don't want to worry about death and betrayal.

Although I would never admit it to anyone, mostly because it would make me indebted to Claudia and I'm determined not to like her (fortunately, most of the time she makes this very easy), I'm grateful to have a job. Though I don't have enough work to keep me busy, I do have Owen to talk to. If I were home alone with my thoughts, well, let's just say I'm crazy enough as it is.

Though some might think I've been partying a little hard lately, things were worse back at school. I woke up far too many mornings puking up something in a radioactive shade of green. I'm pretty sure on those mornings my apartment qualified to be a government Superfund hazardous waste site.

When Owen gets to work he says, "You don't look good."

"Thanks."

"I mean you seem unhappy. Let me take you out tonight and try to cheer you up."

I nod. "Okay."

"What should we do?"

"Work on attaining serenity and inner peace?"

"Good plan. Any suggestions how we might go about that?"

"Not a one. You?"

Owen thinks a moment. "I know. I read in the paper the other day about this tea garden restaurant thing that just opened up. There's supposed to be a serenity pond there."

"What is a serenity pond?"

"A regular pond I think, but when you design with feng shui in mind, water is supposed to calm your nerves or something."

"So you're thinking that if we're near something serene, we too will become serene, like through osmosis?"

"Hey, give me a break. It's the best I could do on short notice."

"It sounds fun, but I have a question and I want you to answer honestly. Do you even drink tea?"

"I drink iced tea every now and then. Does that count?"

"If you don't drink tea, why would you offer to take me to a tea garden? Why not a beer garden?"

"A beer garden sounds pretty good, too. But I'm trying to woo you here. I'm trying to impress you. I want you to think I'm a great guy."

"You're not?"

"I am. Just not really in a tea-drinking sort of way. Anyway, this place is supposed to serve fresh desserts and baked goods so I can always get a sugar buzz while you're sipping your way to enlightenment."

"Actually, a tea party sounds pretty fun."

"Did you have tea parties as a little girl?"

"No. I didn't have Barbie dolls either. I had lots of stuffed animals and a complete obsession with the entire line of Strawberry Shortcake dolls and books and toys."

"I've never even heard of Strawberry Shortcake."

"Well then, you, my friend, are missing out. My mother did drag me to a tea party once, though, when I was a teenager. A friend of hers opened up this restaurant that hosted high teas in the afternoon. I thought it was the queerest thing I'd ever heard of and I put up a big fuss trying to get out of it, but Mom won. It actually turned out to be a ton of fun. Once they put a plate of cookies and cakes in front of me, I started warming up to the idea right away. And my roommate Kendra is always forcing cups of tea down my throat so I've sort of been forced to start liking it. Kendra completely believes in any claims made on the side of a tea box. I swear if some tea claimed it could make you rich and famous, she would drink it and just sit there waiting to be offered the lead in a blockbuster movie."

After work, Owen takes me to the tea garden. It reminds me of a restaurant in New York because it's long and narrow; it's not a giant box like most places out West. The employees are all tragically hip Asians in their early twenties. There are three women and one guy and they all have the coolest haircuts and clothes—they all must have been fashion models back in Tokyo or something. They wear see-through plastic aprons. The restaurant itself has exposed brick walls and block-shaped wood tables and chairs. There's a wait when we get there so we put our names on the list and stand in the entryway that is far too tiny for the two of us, let alone the four other groups who are also in line. My guess is that the review in the paper got everyone in Denver excited to check the place out.

From the crowded waiting area I can see the serenity pond that Owen told me about. It is actually very calming. Water burbles out gently from an unseen jet. Pebbles cover the base of the pool and flower petals float delicately along the top. Three goldfish, one of which is black, swim peacefully around in circles.

As we wait, my throat gets increasingly dry and thirsty. We have to wait forty-five minutes because there simply aren't that many tables.

At last we are shown to a small table. We peruse the menus and quickly decide to share the scones, one apricot and one almond.

"This looks good," I say, pointing to the description of the chai tea. It contains things like ginger root and fennel root, which, if I remember correctly from Kendra's enthusiastic discussions on the cure-all effects of tea, are supposed to be good for digestion.

"I've never had chai."

"I think you might like it. It's a spiced tea that's brewed with milk. It's big in Indian restaurants."

"Should we share a pot?"

"Sure."

We close our menus and wait eagerly for a waiter to stop by. We don't talk; we're too busy trying to get a waiter's attention, but we may as well be invisible. There are four waiters and only ten or so tables. And yes, I'm counting. You'd think they would be incredibly attentive but no. I can't even think of anything to talk about with Owen because I'm too thirsty. I'm much too focused on watching the waiters slowly attend to other tables as I long for someone to stop by with glasses of water. The more time passes, the more annoyed and unserene I become. Can you die of dehydration in the middle of a tea shop? What an ironic death that would be . . .

Eventually a woman with shiny black hair stops at our table with glasses of water the size of contact lenses. I drain my teardrop of water in less than an instant and ask her for a refill, and then we order.

Now that our order is in, I relax and look at Owen. "This place is really cute," I say.

"I think it's important to try new things. I tend to always go to the same few restaurants all the time. I find something I like and go back again and again."

"I do the exact same thing! I live in a city that has about a million restaurants, and yet I go to the same three ones night after night."

"I've never been to New York."

"You've never been to New York! My God, that's criminal. How do you know you want to move there after graduation?"

"That's where all the publishing houses are. There are a few places in California, too, but most of those are for computer manuals and magazines. I don't have much interest in computers. I like e-mail and I like the Internet, but I genuinely don't care to know how the technology works or what new innovative products there are."

"You're not a gadget guy?"

"Not really."

The waitress returns with a small carafe of water. I have to refill my cup about eighty times before I can get enough fluid in me to hydrate myself, but at least my thirst is gone. Plus, it keeps me occupied as I salivate over thoughts of a scone and tea. I skipped lunch today and I feel hungry. My appetite has been so messed up lately I gratefully welcome feelings of hunger.

We've been sitting and talking for half an hour by the time the waitress brings us our scones.

"Finally," I say. "How long does it take to plunk down

two scones and a dollop of jam and a dollop of clotted cream? I mean really."

I wait patiently for her to come back with our tea since you clearly can't have a scone without tea. But she doesn't come back with our tea. Instead, she goes and waits on another table.

We wait. And wait. The scones taunt us, begging to be eaten. *Don't do it!* I tell myself. *Hold strong! Hold out for the tea.* I think about telling Owen about the diary, and then decide not to. Thoughts of it are heavy on my mind, but I want to enjoy myself.

At last the tea arrives. It's brought in a bowl with two spoons. The cups we're given look like something either created by a three-year-old or a drunk potter who dropped the wet clay and shoved the mashed creation to harden in the kiln anyway. It doesn't even occur to me that we're supposed to spoon the tea into our cups. I take the bowl and attempt to pour the tea into his cup. I succeed in getting most of the tea into Owen's cup, but a distressing amount of it goes slopping onto the table and running down the table toward his lap. Owen's jeans are only saved because of his lightning-fast reflexes—he snatches his napkin and laps up the runaway tea just before it spills over the edge.

"I think we're supposed to spoon the tea out."

"Oh," I say. "But that's going to take forever."

"Tea is a process. That's what the article I read said."

"Process schmocess, what a waste of time. Why didn't they just bring us a pitcher or a teapot? Spooning the tea," I shake my head at the ridiculousness of it all but begin laboriously filling my cup one spoonful at a time.

We split the two small scones in half so we each get a taste of both kinds. I spread the clotted cream on thickly and cover that with a generous coat of raspberry jam.

The sweet, milky tea offers a perfect complement to our small treat and I feel very happy and content until Owen and I each get to our last few bites of scone only to run out of jam. I ask the waitress for more. She nods and I assume she'll scoop up a spoonful and come right back. But she doesn't.

To pass the time I complain again about the silliness of bringing tea in a bowl. "It's like the chopstick. Have you ever heard the *Seinfeld* bit about the chopstick?"

"I don't think so."

"Jerry's like, 'Ya gotta admire the Chinese . . . they've seen the fork, and they're still going with the chopstick."

Owen snickers.

"I mean there are lots of great things Easterners have contributed. Acupuncture, Chinese food, fortune cookies . . . but the chopstick, I don't know."

I pretend to be talking with Owen, but really I'm glancing up every three seconds to see where the hell our waitress could be with a little more jelly. How long does it take to fetch a little jam, I ask you?

My day's scheduled acquisition of inner peace has been shot to hell all because of a dollop of jam. How can a person attain enlightenment without a proper jam-to-scone ratio?

The waitress walks by and I flag her down. "Um, hi, do you think we could get a little more jam?"

"I asked the kitchen but they're all backed up. It should be ready soon."

"Oh. Thanks." When the waitress leaves I shake my head and say, "Apparently there is some complex hierarchy in the kitchen in which only the grand chefs are allowed to disperse the jam rations."

At last she returns with enough jam to cover about seventy-eight loaves of bread. We finish our scones and tea and after waiting a comparatively brief fifteen minutes for our check, we pay the bill.

Owen comes back to my place and we hang out by the swimming pool until Owen says he's hungry for dinner. We make a dinner of red wine, brie and bread, strawberries, and grapes. We talk and drink more wine and at around ten I suggest we go to bed.

I didn't necessarily mean to sleep. Not necessarily. I take off my shorts and pull off my bra through my sleeve à la *Flashdance*, stripping down to a t-shirt and underwear. Owen takes my cue and strips to his boxers. We lay in the dark kissing and hugging. I wait for his hand to wander to my breast, my ass, or my thigh, but it never strays from my back or arm, where he strokes me lightly, his fingers warm against my skin.

"Do you like me?" I ask. I'm whispering, but in the dark, quiet room, it sounds like a shout.

He laughs. "Of course. Why?"

"It's just, it's just that most guys would have tried something by now."

"What makes you think I'm like most guys?"

"Absolutely nothing."

"Don't think I don't want to. I want to. I really want to. You've been through a lot recently, I just want to be sure you're ready."

"Cool," I say. I rest my head on his chest and hold him until I fall asleep in his arms.

We spend Saturday morning suntanning by the swimming pool. In the pool house I make a fresh batch of piña coladas and bring them out in goblet-shaped plastic cups. I give Owen a long, licentious kiss before settling down onto my own chaise lounge.

I lean back, close my eyes, and relax in the warmth of the sun.

"You seem to be doing a lot better today," Owen says. I realize that I'm smiling. "I am. I have a lot of things I'm trying to figure out."

"Yeah?"

"Yeah, you know, it's just, I have all these memories, you know, and now that I know what I know, the pieces are just coming together."

"I have no idea what you're talking about."

"Like I think about this one time when I was twelve and my mom was mad at my dad for missing my recital, they were arguing, and suddenly Mom reached up to Dad's neck with her index and middle finger like this"—I demonstrate with my hand to his neck—"and when she pulled away, her fingertips had this waxy, reddish-pink stuff on them, and she started yelling at him about how *this* was more important than his daughter's recital? She was shaking her fingers at him like it was evidence, and at the time all I could think was, 'What is that stuff?' I didn't realize it was lipstick. I was just a dumb kid. And all those arguments they had over the years when I'd hear phrases like, 'Where were you?' and 'Who is she?' I had no idea who or what they were talking about, and now I do."

"How do you feel about it?"

"I don't know how I feel. Mom knew he cheated on her since she was pregnant with me. I think she stayed with him because she thought it was what was best for me, but . . . " Ugh. I'm so sick of thinking about this stuff. I want to think about something else.

The pool is twinkling beneath the sun. The huge, beautifully landscaped yard is a work of art in botany. I'm twenty years old and should just be able to enjoy all of this.

I look over at Owen, who is lying on a chaise lounge next to me in his baggy hunter green swimming trunks.

His arms and face are tan, but his chest clearly hasn't seen much sun this summer. He's got a sexy, broad chest and a flat stomach that glistens with a thin sheen of sweat. I'm wearing a bikini, suntan oil, and nothing else.

It's weird to me that Owen hasn't tried to have sex yet. Is it just because he's a gentleman or is he the only twenty-four-year-old on the planet who genuinely puts his respect for women above his own crushing drive for sex? At school, I'm used to guys asking me a couple questions about myself and they think that's all the courtship we need before they attempt to probe my mouth with their tongues while pawing at my breasts. Clearly Owen isn't that barbarically inept, but still . . .

Oh, I know what it is. He's afraid that I'm too fragile. I hate people thinking I'm weak. But what's worse is that I do, in fact, feel emotionally weak right now. I used to think I was a pretty strong person with my own ideas and goals. I thought I was a woman who didn't take shit from anyone or anything. Now, I don't seem to know anything about who I am.

I stand up. I straddle him and announce, "I'm ready."

He gives me a quizzical look.

"You said you didn't want to have sex until I'm ready. I'm ready," I say. I curl my index finger into a follow-me gesture.

"Are you sure about this?"

"I'm sure."

He doesn't make a move. He just studies me.

"What? You don't like aggressive women?"

He laughs. "Trust me, I like aggressive women just fine." With that he stands. I take his hand and we walk inside, up the stairs to my room. I close and lock the door behind us and turn to him. He wraps his arms around me and puts his lips on mine. We are both a little sweaty; I smell of coconut from the sunscreen. We kiss gently for a few moments, then Owen tries to inch us over to the bed. We both laugh at this awkward, sideways sort of crab-walk. We fall on the bed in a tumble of giggles. Then I sit up and face him. I put my hand behind my back where my bikini is tied. I pause a moment for effect. Owen catches his breath, his gaze drifting from my breasts to my eyes. I pull the bikini string languidly and let the top fall. Owen breathes more rapidly, his gaze drinking me in.

"Oh God," he says, pulling me beside him on the bed.

As we kiss and touch and make love, I try not to think about anything except how this feels, how Owen smells, the sensations my body is experiencing. I try to just listen to the sound of our breath and moans and our bodies against each other. I still feel this low-grade ache inside me, this guilt and sorrow, so I fuck Owen harder, as if to jar the bad feelings out of me. It doesn't totally work, but it helps a little, at least for the moment.

"You didn't come, did you?" he asks as we lay in each other's arms, naked and even more sweaty than when we began.

"I don't think so. But don't worry. It isn't you. I've never had one."

"I'm not worried. I love a challenge. It will happen."

I smile. I think he's right. If anyone could help me get over whatever emotional or physical barrier that's keeping me from having an orgasm, I think Owen can.

We emerge from my bedroom hours later, ravenous with hunger. Owen has pulled on some shorts and, to my dismay, a t-shirt.

"But I want to ogle your body," I protest.

"What if someone comes in?"

"Everyone is gone for the weekend."

"Including all the maids and everything?"

"Fine, wear a stupid shirt."

He follows me to the kitchen.

"I will now attempt to dazzle you with my culinary skills," Owen says, looking through the refrigerator. "Of course, you employ a professional cook, so I probably won't be able to impress you that much."

"You'd be surprised. I never cook at school. I might heat up some pasta or make myself some salad or something, but that's about it."

"You don't like to cook?"

"No. I'm not very good at it either. I'm not sure if I don't like to cook because I'm not good at it or if I'm not good at it because I don't like to do it. I have very few talents, actually."

Owen looks at me. "I've just spent three hours being on the receiving end of your many talents, and I can attest that you're very talented indeed."

"Oh shut up!" I give him a light punch in the arm.

"I've never cooked for a vegetarian before. I don't know how good I'll be with tofu."

"We have soy chicken patties. You can cook them like they're real chicken."

"Do they taste like chicken?"

"Not exactly. They taste like a nonviolent protein alternative."

"Yeah, that sounds *great*. Very promising."

"Hey babe, don't knock it till you've tried it."

Owen makes risotto with sun-dried tomatoes and asparagus and grills up a couple faux chicken patties. I get a couple of bottles of red wine from the cellar as he makes dinner. (I chop and clean the asparagus and occasionally help him find a spice or pot that he's looking for, but that's about the extent of my assistance.) I sit on a stool at the counter, drink wine, and watch him work. My body feels tingly and supersensitive as I flash on images of the time we just spent together.

When our dinner is ready, we sit across from each other. We can't stop smiling.

"This risotto is incredible," I say truthfully.

"Thank you. I can make about three things well and this is one of them. This 'chicken' is pretty good, too."

"See, you have to be open to new experiences."

We spend almost all of the next day in bed, only getting up to get something to eat or drink. Owen is a considerate lover, slow and sensual. He doesn't rush like my ex-boyfriend, Dan, did. He touches me like a blind man who has never touched a woman's body, as if it were the most astonishing sensation he's ever experienced.

We lie beside each other and talk, sharing random anecdotes about our lives. His favorite Christmas ever: when he and Laura woke up to find a toboggan under the tree and the whole family spent the day racing down a mountain together. My favorite Christmas memory: spending Christmas Eve making cookies with Mom and singing our heads off along with a rock-and-roll Christmas carol CD. His least favorite state in the union: Nebraska. Mine: any state that's not New York (Colorado is okay too, I concede, but only for skiing and visiting friends before quickly returning to New York).

I like everything about Owen's body. I like his smell, his muscular thighs, his smile. I like the way he catches his breath when I kiss him on the neck, just behind his ear.

Then, out of nowhere, I start to feel anxious like I'd left for a long trip and can't remember whether I'd turned the iron off. Then I realize I'm anxious because Dad and Claudia are coming home soon.

"Let's go out," I announce suddenly, springing out of bed.

"Out where?"

"I don't care. Out. Let's meet some friends for dinner or something."

"It's only four."

"We can get drinks first." I call Marni.

"Hello?"

"Marni, do you want to get some dinner or something?"

"Sure. Jake is back in town. He can come, right?"

"Of course. Where should we meet?" I ask.

"What are you in the mood for?" Marni asks.

"I don't know. You decide."

"How about Vesta's?"

"Okay. I'll see you in an hour or so."

I call Hannah next and she says she and Todd will meet us there, too.

We shower and get dressed and are just about to leave when we run straight into Dad and Claudia—who just happen to be arriving home at the exact same time.

"Hello!" Claudia coos. "How was your weekend?"

"Good, really good," I say. I feel like I've just shoplifted something and run straight into a cop. Why do I feel so nervous and guilty?

"We got a call from Polly on our way home from the airport. She wants us all to come over to dinner tomorrow night. She has some big news to share with us," Claudia says.

"She wants me there?" I wonder if everyone knows about me and Owen. I don't see why it would matter if they did, but me being his girlfriend—if that's in fact what I am—is the only reason I can think of that Polly would invite me to dinner with the rest of them.

"She wants the whole family there."

I flinch at the word "family." I look at Owen. He gives me a shrug, like "sure, whatever." I tell Claudia we'll both be there.

When we get to the restaurant, Hannah and Todd are already waiting for us on the couch near the entrance.

"Hello. Hello. Hello," I trill.

Hannah stands to hug me. "Darhlin,'" she says, "you look marvelous." She pulls away to inspect my efforts at tanning. "Spending some time in the sun I see." She leans in and whispers in my ear, "And, judging by that smile on your face, you've been spending some time out of it as well."

"Maybe." I smile harder.

Owen and I join Hannah and Todd on the couch to wait for Marni and Jake. "So, Todd, how are things in the accounting world?" I ask.

Hannah gives me a pointed look that Todd can't see. I remember how she said she couldn't stand listening to him talk about work. Oops. Just trying to be polite.

"Things are going well. Able is a leading company in Colorado. I'm proud to be working for them, even part time."

He sounds like he's trying to interview for a job. It's funny how people think I have some sort of sway over what goes on at Able or what my father does. Fortunately Marni and Jake arrive at just that moment. We exchange hugs and greetings, and then the six of us are shown to our table. We order a couple of bottles of wine to start out and a few appetizers.

"So Jake, how was Europe?" I ask him.

"Awesome."

Marni pouts. "I wish I could have gone with him."

"Why didn't you?" I ask.

"I wanted to do the volunteer work," she says with a shrug.

What I think is that she has her entire life to volunteer, but you only get so many chances to travel through Europe with your lover.

"So tell us all about it," I say.

Jake starts to tell us about the castles he saw in Ireland when Todd interjects, "When I went to Ireland, all I saw were the insides of pubs."

We smile, and then return our attention to Jake. "We went to the Aran Islands next. I'm telling you, I'm not sure I've ever seen anything so beautiful. It's like—"

"Didn't you think Dublin was a blast?" Todd says.

"Wha . . . oh, yes. Anyway . . . " Jake continues to tell his story in fits and starts between Todd's interjections. I get the feeling that Todd thinks it's very important that we all know that he's been to Ireland, even though he's only seen Dublin while Jake got two weeks to do a lap around the country.

"I have to go to the bathroom," Marni announces. "Helaina?"

"Might as well."

I follow her to the bathroom.

"I find Todd a little insufferable," she says.

"To say the least."

"So, did you and Owen . . . you know?"

I nod. She squeals and claps her hands. "And?"

"And, it was wonderful."

"And?"

I know she's asking me if I've had an orgasm yet. "No, not yet."

"Soon."

I nod.

"Do you think you love him?"

"Oh . . . oh, God, Marni, I don't know. I like him. But love?"

"You're so indecisive. You know you are or you know you aren't."

I open the bathroom door and peek out to take a look at Owen. "But how do you know you know?"

"Trust me, you know."

But I don't know. I'm not sure of anything.

Chapter 10

The next night, I drive with Dad and Claudia down to Polly's house, which is in a subdivision in Highlands Ranch. Highlands Ranch is allegedly just south of Denver, but it seems to take about a hundred years to get there. Maybe it's because I feel trapped, being in the car with Dad and Claudia.

"These houses all look the same," Claudia says scornfully.

We're in a subdivision. What does she expect?

"It looks like we're driving through an SUV dealership there are so many of them parked on the road," Dad says.

Claudia roars with laughter and pats my father's arm appreciatively. "You're so funny! You're *hilarious*!"

My father smiles.

Dad is driving his Porsche. He points out all the features to me. I nod and listen attentively, but for the most part, I don't have a clue what he's talking about.

I feel a tremendous sense of relief when we get there. I practically sprint to Owen's side and immediately feel safer.

It's just the five of us since Laura is in Europe somewhere doing something financial and corporate. Polly makes martinis for Dad and Claudia. I have a glass of wine and sit next to Owen on the couch.

"This is a huge place for two people," I observe. "One, really, since you're mostly away at school."

"Dad and Polly moved here a few years ago, after Laura and I were away at college. I don't know how she keeps it up by herself. I mean Dad had a decent life insurance policy, but it has to be getting low by now."

Polly calls us around to the table. A mixed green salad with raspberry vinaigrette is placed at each setting. Polly stands at the head of the table and clinks her fork against her wine glass to quiet the talking.

"The reason I asked you all over tonight is that I have a wonderful announcement to make," Polly says. "*Local Color* is up for an award from the Western Region Magazine Association, which is the most prestigious publishing association in this part of the United States."

"That's great, Polly. Congrats. What's the award for?" Owen asks.

She continues talking as if she hadn't heard him. "All the local travel, trade, and entertainment magazines are included, and believe me, there are hundreds. And out of all these publications, we're up for best new entertainment column for Claudia's 'Who, What, When, Wear' column!"

Claudia shrieks and claps her hands. Dad kisses Claudia on the cheek and tells her congratulations. I feel like I've been punched in the stomach.

Everyone is talking around me, but I don't hear what they are saying. This isn't really that big a deal, right? Who's ever heard of the Western Region Magazine Association? It's not like she's getting a Pulitzer.

I drain my glass of wine and pour myself another.

This is not the way the world is supposed to work. What about "what goes around comes around"? When is Claudia going to get hers?

People pass me plates. I take a roll, some rice, some veggies, and skip the chicken, but I can't eat even the small portions I've taken. I finish my second glass of wine in a long sip. I haven't eaten anything for seven hours and I can already feel a buzz.

Owen leans close to me and whispers, "Are you okay?"

"She doesn't even write the column."

"I know it's been hard on you, them sleeping together."

That's all this is, isn't it? A philandering husband, an absent father, a mistress who doesn't care who she uses to get want she wants. It's not such a unique story. Why does this hurt so much? Maybe because everyone is going on about their lives like Mom never existed, like her life didn't matter.

And so what if my dad makes me feel like shit about myself? A lot of dads are like that. I let him do it to me. It's so easy to believe the shitty things he says about me. I can leave for New York tomorrow. I never have to see them again.

I'd miss Owen, though. I don't know if this is a fling or just something to help me get my mind off my mother, but I don't want it to end yet if I can help it.

I pour myself more wine, finishing off the bottle.

"That went fast," Polly says.

"Don't you think you're drinking that a little quickly?" Claudia asks me.

"You've got to be kidding me. This from somebody who lost her career because of her drinking problem?" Oh shit.

Claudia looks at me; her gaze hardens with fury.

"Apologize to your aunt," Dad says.

I do feel bad about what I said, but I don't know what to say. I'm too angry for "sorry."

So I say nothing. I push my chair away from the table, and I'm about to race outside when I realize I didn't drive, so I can't leave. I'm trapped. Fuck.

I run upstairs. Owen follows. He catches up to me in the upstairs hallway. "Helaina? Helaina!"

"Which room is yours?"

He opens one of the doors to reveal an austere room. It has a bed, desk, and dresser. There are no decorations on the walls, just stacks and stacks of books. I lock the door behind us. Owen and I sit on the edge of the bed.

"What was that about?"

"I don't know." I'm so embarrassed. Why can't I pull my shit together already? "I can't think about it right now. I'm so tired. I'm just dog tired. Have you ever been tired in your muscles and your bones and your whole being?"

"Why don't you get some rest? Maybe some music will relax you." He has a boom box on the floor next to his bed. When he gets up off the bed, I slip right off the edge onto the floor. Even though I'm in a crappy mood, I start laughing.

From my vantage point on the floor, I see a little black-and-white cat who'd sought refuge under the bed.

"Oh, come here, kitty, kitty, kitty," I say. "Which one is this?"

Owen looks under the bed. "That's Salinger."

"Where's Calliope?"

"She's probably in the closet. That's her favorite place to sleep."

We both look up at the same time and sure enough, a long-haired gray cat that looks cloud-soft is resting comfortably on a pile of sweatshirts on the shelf above where Owen hangs his shirts.

"They're so cute. How old are they?"

"Let's see, Laura got them the year before she left for college so that'd make them about nine."

"I thought they were yours."

"They're mine now, but they were Laura's first. She left them behind when she went to school." Owen helps me back up onto the bed. "Just get a little rest."

"Don't leave me."

"I won't." He lies down beside me. I can't identify the music that's playing, Beethoven maybe? Something soothing anyway.

I try to calm down. I hear Owen leave, closing the door behind him. But I'm too restless, so I get up and go downstairs. The voices are coming from the kitchen.

"I'm worried about her. She's been drinking a lot lately," Owen says.

"Of course she's upset, her mother just died. Helaina has always been an emotional person, just like her mother. She'll be fine," Dad says.

"He might be right, Gary. She has been acting extremely angry," Claudia says. "She's been excessively depressed and antisocial. She's been through a lot I know, but she's taking this harder than most people. This may be the sign of a bigger problem. I know a place she could go in New England to rest. It's one of the best facilities in the country. The doctors can give her something that can calm her down and make her feel better."

They are talking about me like I'm some mental patient.

I push the doors open. Four sets of eyes turn to look at me. "It's true, I've been depressed these last few months, but I have a good reason—my mother just died. I don't need to be thrown in a mental hospital. I just need time to mourn. Hell, if anyone's acting weird it's you guys. Claudia, your sister died. Your only sibling is gone. It would be normal for you to be upset. Dad, your wife of twenty-one years is dead, and it doesn't seem like you care at all."

"Of course I'm devastated. I just don't need to make everyone around me as miserable as I am," Claudia says.

"Yeah, I forgot about what a great actress you are. Very noble of you how you keep up such a strong front." I turn to Owen. "I thought I could trust you." I brush past him, bumping him hard. He follows me into the living room. I want to storm out of here, but I remember again that I didn't bring a car.

"I'm just worried about you. I know you're upset, but nothing is going to be made better by doing what you're doing," Owen says.

"My mother just fucking died. What am I supposed to do?"

"Helaina, I know about pain. My mother killed herself when I was nine years old. She'd been manic depressive her entire life. I have aunts and uncles on both sides of my family that suffered from depression, I know something about this. I know that if you keep hiding from your pain, you're never going to work through it."

"Look, I'm trying, okay? Please give me a ride home. I can't be here anymore."

"Yeah, sure, of course."

I don't talk for the first twenty minutes of the way. Why do I do stupid shit like this, go crazy and lash out? This isn't going to solve anything. I wish I could erase this night from Owen's mind, Dad's mind, Claudia's mind, Polly's mind. My own memory. Dad already thinks I'm a total screwup, anyway, this just confirms it.

"Owen," I say at last. "I know I've been acting out lately, but you should have come to me if you were worried."

"They're your family."

"Dad and Claudia are family only by blood. In the sense that family is there for you and cares about you, they're not that kind of family. I can't even tell you how many plays Dad missed, how many recitals and graduations and awards ceremonies he wasn't there for. He always promised to be there and never managed to make it. Work always came first. I spent my whole life trying to impress him."

Owen pulls into the driveway, looking contrite.

"I know that I haven't been eating well or taking care of myself. I know I need to get my body healthy and I will. Right now I just don't really have the strength to take care of myself." I sigh and look out the window. "Do you want to come inside?"

"Are you sure you want me to?"

"I'm still mad at you, but I don't want to be alone tonight."

"Okay, yes."

Inside, Owen sits in my desk chair, his head back, his eyes closed, his hand massaging his forehead like he has a headache.

"I want to show you something," I say.

He opens his eyes. I hand him Mom's diary. "It's Mom's. I found it a few days ago. I want you to read it. I think it'll help you understand my feelings toward Dad and Claudia."

He nods. "I will."

"Come here."

He comes over to the bed and we lie down, our arms wrapped around each other. Though I'm still angry with him, I cling to him, my life raft on a stormy sea.

Chapter 11

Owen must have left at some point in the night because when I wake the next morning he's not there. When I see him at the office in the morning, I don't even realize I'm scowling until he asks me what's wrong.

"I woke up in a dangerously foul mood this morning, that's all."

"You look tired."

"Good morning to you, too."

I turn on my computer and pretend to work. After several minutes, a pop-up box announces, "You have new mail. Would you like to read it now?" I click yes. The e-mail is from Owen. The subject line says "e-poetry. Don't hold this against me when I'm named poet laureate."

You know you're going the wrong way
Living life half-awake
Hand hovering over the break
Considering, seeking courage

Slow down, slow down
Turnaround
There is still time
To go the other way

His silly poem makes me mad, but a few seconds later I get another e-mail that improves my mood.

Subject: e-poetry, part two

Why do I care?

Because you don't play dumb
You have opinions

Because of the way your smile spreads slowly
First just a hint at the corner of your mouth
Then across your entire face
Like a flower opening to full bloom

Because your eyes are like a kaleidoscope
Chameleon in their color
But honest in their gaze

Because if I'm going to be bored all day at my job
There's nothing I'd rather stare at for eight hours
    than you

I can't help it, even though I'm mad at him, I smile. "Forgive me?"

"Get back to work, mister. We don't pay you to write sweet nothings to your girlfriend." I reread the first poem. I *am* living my life half-awake. "Slow down, slow down/turnaround/there is still time/to go the other way."

"Rhyming poetry? Couldn't you get kicked out of the writer's workshop for that?"

"Definitely. I'm like a politician with a fifteen-year-old girlfriend. You could bring me down. I'm trusting you."

"You just better be nice."

"But of course."

As we work, I remember again the hours we spent talking and laughing and making love. Our entire world over the weekend was basically my bed. I had many hours to study the light sprinkling of brown hairs on his chest and arms and legs. Remembering the way he smiled at me and teased me with his words and touches . . . well, all I can say is that I hope there isn't anyone who can read minds, at least not around here.

At lunch, Owen says he has to run a few errands. I feel snubbed for a moment, and then realize I'm overreacting. We've been going to lunch together most days, taking as long as we can over sandwiches that I can never eat more of than a few bites. But I know it's not fair of me to begrudge him an hour on his own.

Since I don't have Owen to go out to lunch with, I decide to skip it. I used to have a ravenous appetite. I remember when I was dating Dan there were times when I would eat more than him despite the fact he was seven inches taller than me and about sixty pounds heavier. These days I can't do much more than push my food around on my plate.

The afternoon passes slowly. I've already finished my reviews for the month. I asked Amanda if there was anything else I could help out with and I managed to get about two days' worth of work typing in the calendar of upcoming events, but now I'm out of work again and bored. Still, I end up staying at the office long after it's technically time to go home.

I don't want to go home and face Dad and Claudia. I'm afraid they're going to be waiting for me with some kind of intervention.

When I get home from work, no one is there. There is, however, a package addressed to me. I take it upstairs to my room where I go straight to my minirefrigerator to make myself a vodka martini when I remember that I promised Owen I'd cut down on my drinking.

I take a pair of scissors and open the box. In it is a card from Owen. There is also peach detox tea, two candles—one vanilla and one rainforest mist—and various health supplements, including a big bottle of vitamin C, a bottle of multivitamins, and ingestible aloe vera, which is apparently supposed to be good for your immune system. What I think is best of all, however, is that in the box he included several colorful squares of word confetti—construction paper he cut up into inch-long squares, each with a word like "Health," "Peace," "Happiness," "Love," "Strength," "Courage," "Balance," and "Truth," written in his clear cursive handwriting.

His card reads,

> *Helaina, I know you are going through a difficult time right now, but even though I've only known you a short time, I can see that you have the inner strength to get through this. Take it easy. Relax. Take care of yourself the best you can. There are a lot of people who want to see you feeling healthy and happy again.*
> *—Owen*

I'm so touched that tears well in my eyes. I don't know if anyone has ever given me such a thoughtful gift before.

I call Owen. "I got your care package. Thank you. I think it may be the sweetest gift I've ever gotten."

"You're welcome."

"It's weird because I was just thinking about how I needed some tea and how I should buy some candles. It's like you read my mind."

"I just want you to be happy."

"Hey, you want to catch a movie?"

"I'd love to."

It's an escape, but not a chemical one. That seems like promise.

At work the next day, Polly calls us all to the boardroom and announces that she's decided to hell with it, we're going on a team-building retreat on Friday.

"We need the break. We need to get away from it all and regroup," she says.

Amanda looks genuinely horrified. "*This* Friday? Polly, we're behind schedule as it is. Can't we take a day off after we've gotten this issue to the printer next week, when we have a little wiggle room in our schedules?"

"Linda had a cancellation, that's why she was able to get us in so quickly. Our schedules are always hectic. We just need to *make* the time. Friday morning, eight AM, we'll meet here and the bus will drive us up to the mountains. It'll be great!"

Polly charges out of the room and several people follow her. Owen, Amanda, Jill, Goatee Guy, and I linger.

"Great," Amanda says. "I already had to come in to the office Saturday; now I'll have to come in on Sunday as well. If I'd wanted to work 80-hour weeks I would have gone to work for a good magazine in New York and at least get paid what I was worth. My husband is going to divorce me; my kids are going to hate me. Christ, I just can't miss another soccer game."

"Team building!" Jill adds. "What a load of crap. I see you people every single day, and no offense you guys, but if I need to get away from the office, I'd like to spend the time with my family, not you people."

On Friday morning, the staff gathers in the parking lot

as we've been told to. We linger in loose circles, grumbling quietly amongst ourselves and cradling cups of Starbucks in our hands. We all wear layers of flannel wrapped around our waists, preparing for cooler weather up on the mountain.

The bus pulls up a few minutes late and we climb in like schoolchildren. It takes two-and-a-half hours to get to the ranch. Most of us are still so tired we don't talk much more than the occasional mumbled exchange to our seatmate. Owen and I sit next to each other, Jill and Amanda sit together, the sales people sit together, and Polly sits by herself. So far, we aren't doing a great job of building interdepartmental spirit.

When we get to Linda's ranch, we are required to sign waivers written in distressingly small typeface. I've never been one to read the fine print, but I think the gist of it is that if we fall on our heads and crack our skulls open, it's our own damn fault so we shouldn't even think about suing Pine Creek Ranch.

We are divided into three teams. Disappointingly, Owen isn't on mine. Jill and Amanda are separated, the sales people are separated, and the art and production people are separated. Pretty sneaky if you ask me.

Our team's guide is a burly woman with a gruff voice and bad attitude. She explains that we are going to have a Global Positioning System (GPS) tracking/horseshoe scavenger hunt/horse riding adventure. Various horseshoes are hidden across several acres of mountainous land, and we're allegedly going to find them using the GPS device. The gadget is about the size of a walkie-talkie. You punch in a few numbers and it gives you the coordinates for where the next horseshoe is. Then another member of the team uses these coordinates and looks at a compass to point us in the right direction. I'd like to point out that we're supposed to hold this device while riding the horses. Excuse me, I want to ask, but when you're doing everything you can to avoid being hurtled to your death from atop a treacherously huge animal, don't you think you should use every limb you have to hang on?

My horse's name is Shadow. As we wait for the games to begin, I look down from my perch atop Shadow at the muddy ground, which seems a very, very long way away.

"Is there anyone here who hasn't ridden a horse before?" Burly Guide Woman asks.

"Yes, well, I mean I have, but only once, but I was twelve and it was at a birthday party and it was a really long time ago," I squeak.

Burly Guide woman grunts and says dismissively, "You'll be fine."

There are five members on my team, and the guide pulls two of them aside and explains how to use the GPS device and compass. Apparently these people will then pull two of us aside for the next round and explain to us how to use them, and by following each other around and guiding each other, we'll all become a unified, productive team, several parts working together as one.

We find the first horseshoe without hazard. Goatee Guy passes the GPS device to me and tells me how to use it. It's all up to me now to guide my teammates to the next horseshoe. Holding the compass with one hand, I feel even more perilously situated. I guide the team partway to our destination when, for no apparent reason, Shadow takes off as though he thought we'd just entered the Kentucky Derby. With my one hand, I tug futilely at the reins. "Stop! Stop!" I shriek, but he fails to heed my pleas and continues to race on. My heart thunders painfully and I envision a future spent in a wheelchair as a quadriplegic. I knew a guy in a wheelchair who couldn't use the bathroom on his own and had to use a catheter and go around with a bag of his own urine. You don't appreciate simple things in life like being able to use a toilet until you're blazing along a rocky mountain trail atop a psychotic horse that wants you dead.

Finally, my yanking at the reins works—either that or Shadow just tires out—and we come to a stop. The female guide, brimming over with condescension, comes riding up next to me to scold me. "Don't let him run off like that!" she chides. Excuse me, don't *let* him run off? I don't believe he asked my opinion in the matter. As she continues to disparage my ability to handle the animal, all I can think is, "Hey look, lady, let's review the facts. I work at an *office*. I'm not auditioning for a job as a *wrangler*. I don't believe I mention the ability to charge a 1,000-pound steed through treacherous terrain anywhere on my resume."

After we find the horseshoe, I pass the GPS device on to another teammate, and we continue on to the next horseshoe. Two things quickly become apparent. One is that my horse, though named Shadow, should be named The Flatulator. Number two is that Amanda's horse can't get enough of Shadow's noxious emissions. Amanda's Candy Stripe is adamant about sticking her snout right into The Flatulator's rump, and with every jarring step we take, The Flatulator toots, steady as a rap rhythm: toot, toot, ta-toot too. Toot, toot, ta-toot too. While embarrassing for me— surely a most egregious failing in equestrian decorum to be unable to keep my horse from hurtling such effluvium into the atmosphere—I fear the situation is far worse for Amanda, who is in The Flatulator's direct line of fire.

While the air is becoming a more toxic miasma with every step we take, at least we're able to find the next two horseshoes without any horses jetting off toward Alaska or anyone experiencing grievous bodily harm. Then it's my turn to take the electronic compass and Amanda takes over the GPS device. She gives me the coordinates and I punch them into the electronic compass.

"To the right!" I call, a regular modern Magellan. The compass says we are 0.6 miles away from the target site. For a few leisurely moments, I have time to just absorb the beauty around me, to appreciate the fresh mountain air, and think that maybe this isn't so bad after all.

Then the guide asks if we want to pick up the pace a bit.

My cries of "No! No!" are drowned out by my team-mates' enthusiastic Yes's! Excuse me, but when did my mild-mannered coworkers become fearless mountain-charging cavalry?

As soon as the other horses begin racing off—Burly Guide Woman claims we are merely trotting, but I'm skinny and let me tell you, the only word that comes to mind is *sportsbra*, as in, dear God in Heaven, why didn't I wear a sportsbra to this barbaric event?—I look at the compass and see that suddenly we're 1.8 miles away from our destination. How did we get farther away?

"Um, we need to turn and go that way," I tell my team.

They follow my lead for several minutes.

"Are you sure about this?" Burly Guide Woman asks. I'm telling you, I strongly suspect this woman eats nails for breakfast and kills small animals for sport.

"Um, no."

"What number is in the upper left-hand corner of the screen?"

There's a number in the upper left-hand corner of the screen? Three. Uh-oh. Apparently when we went hurtling through the mountains at the speed of light and I was being tossed around like a snow globe in a hurricane, I hit the button on the compass and it gave me the coordinates for the third horseshoe we tracked down when we're on the sixth and last.

I sheepishly explain what happened and Burly Guide Woman glares at me like I'm some team-building day terrorist. She helps me get back to the right coordinates and we find the final horseshoe at last. My mistake, however, cost us valuable time and we're the last team to return to camp, meaning we're the giant losers of the day, a fact that Burly Guide Woman seems to take as a personal affront.

In summary: What my coworkers have learned about me today is that I'm an untrustworthy flake with no leadership skills whatsoever. That's just great. That's just *super duper*.

But at least the dangerous scavenger hunt of doom is over. I'm supremely relieved to get off my four-legged death machine. Horses are beautiful, but I prefer to appreciate their beauty from a distance rather than close-up. I don't have an ounce of cowboy in my blood.

"Did you have fun?" Owen asks me.

"Except for almost getting killed, it was a great time. Just *great*."

Chapter 12

I come home to find Claudia sitting at the dining room table playing bridge with Barb, Dana, and Christine, my mother's friends who she always used to play bridge with. Claudia is sitting where Mom used to sit.

"Hi Helaina, honey," Claudia says. "We were just talking about redoing the downstairs bathroom. I was thinking of doing the floor in a black-and-white pattern, sort of retro '50s. What do you think?"

I shrug. Why is she talking about redecorating as if this were her house to decorate? Why are these women playing bridge with Claudia? Was that all my mother was to these women, an exchangeable fourth for a card game?

"Isn't it exciting about the TV show?" Barb asks.

"What TV show?"

"I haven't had a chance to tell her yet," Claudia says. "After that article about me in *Redbook*, I got a call from an agent."

"What article?"

"Didn't you know? I'm on the cover of this month's *Redbook*. Anyway, they're interested in having me star in a sitcom. It would be about an actress who's . . . a little past her prime, shall we say, but still struggling to make it as an actress. As a result she does crazy gigs like doing a commercial wearing a chicken suit, that kind of thing. It sounds like it will be really funny. And they want to have a different formerly popular actress do a cameo on each episode. You know, like someone who had a hit show fifteen years ago but nobody's heard from since."

"Isn't that exciting?" Barb asks again.

"I'll fly out to tape the pilot in September. They'll launch it midseason in February, right in time for sweeps. I'm trying not to get my hopes up too high, but it's just so exciting to get the chance to act again."

My mouth goes dry. "Congratulations, Claudia."

"There's a copy of the magazine on the coffee table if you're interested."

"Yeah, sure."

My hands shake as I open the magazine and turn to the right page.

ACTRESS FINDS NEW LIFE AS BUSINESSWOMAN

Success didn't come overnight for Claudia Merrill, but failure seemed to.

Merrill played a series of small roles in movies and on TV shows in her late teens and early twenties. In 1986, when she was just twenty-four years old, she got her break. Merrill played the lead role in *Becoming,* which was an instant box-office hit. For a time, Merrill was on top of the world.

Fate wasn't through with her yet. Just when it seemed she would win the game, her game got rained out.

In a series of unfortunate choices by Merrill and her manager, April Cooney, her next three movies bombed. Producers worried that Merrill no longer had what it took to attract audiences. On top of all that, her husband left her—with considerable debt.

When the movie roles stopped coming in, Claudia Merrill was so despondent, she actually considered suicide.

"I'd spent my whole life as an actress, and one day the money had run out, I couldn't get any work, my husband had left me, and I felt like my life was over. It's very hard to be an actress in your thirties. The roles dry up; Hollywood doesn't want to have anything to do with you."

But Merrill didn't give up. After years of struggling, Merrill found a new role for herself. That of a successful businesswoman. It's her best role yet.

Merrill launched her own business, Prima Facie, more than a year ago. The consulting company helps businessmen and women dress for success.

"Studies have shown that good-looking people tend to achieve more success more quickly than homely people. Whether you like it or not, what you wear and how you look play a part in whether you'll make that sale or get that promotion. But most people don't know which colors and styles flatter them. That's where I come in. I typically work with a person between one day and one week. I start by going to their office and getting an idea of their office culture. The industry they're in and their location in the country both play a part in my recommendations. I wouldn't tell people to dress conservatively for a job at a creative ad agency in New York, for example— it would alienate them from their coworkers. Their boss would think they didn't have the creativity to come up with new ideas. Similarly, I wouldn't tell a woman in a marketing job in Denver to wear high heels. The West is much more relaxed than the East. A woman who wore heels would be perceived as someone who was too into her appearance, too frilly, not down-to-earth. It's all about perception."

Once she gets an idea of her client's job, she goes through their wardrobe with them, tells them what to keep and what to get rid of. Then they go shopping for new clothes, new shoes, and/or new accessories. "I'll give them advice on how to cut their hair. I'll help women buy the right makeup for their coloring. I can't turn a toad into a prince, but I can come darn close. Plus, busy businesspeople can't keep up with all the fashion magazines. I can. For some clients, I'll meet with them once a year to help them update their wardrobe and keep them up with the times."

In addition to her consulting business, Claudia is a fashion columnist for the upscale Denver-based magazine *Local Color*. Moreover, Claudia is a board member of Able Technologies, one of the biggest telecommunications companies in the world . . .

You have got to be kidding me. She's on the board? That's ridiculous. She has no business experience. How the hell did she get on the board?

Oh my God—Dad. Dad must have given her a spot. It doesn't make sense. The board is comprised of hugely successful businesspeople—entrepreneurs with MBAs and years of experience who help the company make strategic decisions. To include an unemployed actress in that group is ludicrous.

I can't finish the article. I put the magazine down.

"That's great, Claudia." I feel like the earth underneath me is being ripped open; I'm on unsteady ground. "I should go upstairs and clean up." I feel like a marionette—someone is making my mouth open and close and forcing words to come out, but I have nothing whatsoever to do with it.

I try to walk across the room and up the stairs on legs that have no bones or muscles, unsteady as Silly Putty.

I get to my bed and focus on breathing in and out, in and out. I can't be here in this house with her.

Trembling, I pick up the phone and call Owen.

"Hey Owen, are you busy?"

"I'm just hanging out."

"I need to get out. I really need to get out and be distracted. Will you go dancing with me?"

"I'd love to. Is something wrong?"

I exhale. "I'll tell you about it when I see you."

"Fair enough. I'll pick you up in an hour or so."

"Sounds good. See you then."

I spend the next hour alternately primping and pacing. I sit down at my desk, put eyeliner on, then jump up. I walk over to my closet, then change my mind and head toward my jewelry box on the dresser, put my watch and some earrings on, and then go to my closet again, but I forget what it was I wanted to get.

I can't believe Dad would put her on the board of directors. That's worse than just fucking her. It means he takes her seriously.

I sit at my desk feeling confused and impotent. I want to *do* something. But what?

It takes me a moment to identify the noise as a knock. "Helaina?" It's Maria.

"Huh? Um, yes?"

"Owen is here."

"Oh. Thanks."

Feeling dazed, I pick up my purse. I go down the stairs quickly. As soon as I see Owen, my heart feels lighter.

"Hey gorgeous."

"Hi."

"So, where would you like to go?"

"I don't care. You tell me. What's your favorite place to go dancing?"

He thinks a moment. "Would you like to go to the Epic or to Turnsol?"

"I don't care. You choose."

"Uh, woman, you're impossible."

He takes me to Turnsol. It's still early, so there aren't many people there, but I don't care that Owen and I are the only ones on the dance floor. He doesn't seem to care either. Even though I'm totally sober, I go nuts, and I'm sweating within just a few minutes.

Owen is a good dancer. "You're a man of many talents," I tell him.

"What?" he yells.

"You're a good dancer!" I shout, enunciating clearly so he can read my lips. "I love guys that aren't too uptight to shake their thang on the dance floor!"

I'm not sure if he understands everything I said, but he nods and smiles.

Little by little, the dance floor fills up.

I can't remember the last time I went dancing without a buzz. In fact, I don't know if I've ever gone dancing stone cold sober. I like it. I like being alert enough to be able to watch the people around me.

Owen and I stop a few times to cool off and drink bottle after bottle of water, but except for ten-minute breaks here and there, we dance our asses off until one in the morning. I alternate between closing my eyes and losing myself in the anonymity of the mass of swaying bodies, my body moving with the sensual throbbing music, and watching the people around me. The good dancers. The awkward ones. The people who are trying too hard to look different or sexy.

* * *

Even though I'm exhausted and sweaty, when we get home, I act like some psycho porn chick, tearing Owen's clothes off and pushing him on the bed.

Afterward, when we've caught our breath, I say, "Here's my dilemma, I'm sweaty and smelly and want to shower but I'm also exhausted and I don't have the energy to move."

"Yeah, I wish somebody would brush my teeth for me."

We don't move. I continue lying in his arms, my head on his chest, and within minutes I'm asleep.

I wake up before he does. He looks so angelic when he sleeps.

I wish I could have introduced Mom to him. She would have really liked him. I wish I could go meet Mom for coffee this morning, maybe get some breakfast with her. I'd like to talk to her about Owen. I'd like to ask Mom if she thinks I should stay in Denver and risk the psychic trauma Dad and Claudia seem to inflict, or go back to New York and maybe lose Owen.

How am I supposed to get married without a mom? Who is going to calm me down when I get too stressed out before I walk down the aisle? Who will help me pick out a dress? If Hannah and Marni go bridal-dress shopping with me, I know I'll end up in some high-fashion avant-garde thing that will probably fall off halfway through the ceremony. If I go with Kendra or Lynne, I'll end up looking like some hippy child in inexpensive muslin hanging off me in a loose cloud of fabric. Mom would be the only one who wouldn't talk me out of what I wanted but would instead make me feel like I was making the right decision.

I want Mom to be there when my first movie gets made. I want to ask her what she thinks the weather might do. I want my mom back.

Chapter 13

I almost manage to push the awards ceremony from my mind until the morning of it, when I wake up abruptly and remember that it's tonight. I feel anxious, my pulse racing so hard it hurts. Part of me wants to just skip it, but part of me thinks the event will present me with some kind of opportunity, though I don't know what.

I envision going to the ceremony and casually tripping Claudia as she gets up to accept the award. I'll do it so casually and deftly, no one will know it's intentional. I imagine slipping psychedelic drugs into her wine glass and watching her make some crazy acceptance speech in front of hundreds of people. I know these are silly thoughts and I'll never actually act on them, but I want to do *something*.

Owen picks up on my anxiety as soon as I get to the office.

"What's wrong? You seem nervous," he says.

"I think I just had too much coffee this morning. It made me a little jittery. What is it? Why are you looking at me like that?"

"I read the journal," Owen says.

"What did you think?"

"I think your father and Claudia treated your mother poorly. I think your mom lost her way at some point. She stopped believing in herself."

"No thanks to Dad and Claudia."

"How well do you know your father and Claudia? I think they didn't intentionally try to hurt your mother. I think that's just the way they are."

"So because they're manipulative and self-absorbed by nature, we're supposed to let them off the hook?"

"I just think you should try to see things from their perspective."

"Sorry, I'm too busy seeing things from Mom's perspective."

"Are you mad at me?"

"No. I just think you should let me be angry."

"If you let the negative emotions run wild for too long, they'll destroy you."

"I need more time." I stand up.

"Where are you going?" he asks.

"I need more coffee. I haven't been sleeping well lately."

"I can't imagine why," he jokes. But I'm annoyed with him and don't laugh.

In the kitchen, there are four people hanging out, talking about the ceremony tonight. Goatee Guy puts one hand palm up horizontally, as if holding the base of the award, and one hand slightly cupped as if holding the body of the award.

"I would just like to thank the staff of *Local Color*, who made this possible, particularly Jill Henderson, who actually wrote the column."

There are more jokes, but I can tell that no one (except me) really minds if she wins because any publicity will be good for the magazine.

I go back to my desk, but I don't really have any work to do. I e-mail my friends in New York, visit every movie site and online news source I can think of, and look at the clock about every eleven seconds.

I decide to look up the addresses of places I can send my movie. My original enthusiasm for sending the movie to film festivals sort of died after I showed it to Dad. I don't want to humiliate myself with the movers and shakers of the film industry, but on the other hand, if I don't try, I'm never going to make a name for myself. I figure it can't hurt to collect the names and addresses of some production companies so I can send it out if I ever work up the courage.

After work, I realize that I have nothing to wear to the awards banquet—nothing that fits me anyway. I could just wear something that will swim on me, but I think it's important to look good tonight. I need whatever confidence I can muster.

I go to the boutiques in an upscale neighborhood in Denver and take a stab at what size I think I am these days and make my way to the dressing room. Even a size down from what I normally wear, the dress fits me like a muumuu. How much weight have I lost? I've got to start eating again. I'm disappearing. Anyway, thank God for the Wonderbra.

I get dressed again and leave the dressing room. I select several dresses in a range of smaller sizes since I haven't a clue what fits me these days. I find a black silk dress. It's an original design by Niki Dresden, a Denver designer who sells her work exclusively through tiny boutiques like this one. The dress is almost too pretty to wear. I just want to gaze adoringly at it and stroke its softness reverently, but I try it on anyway. It reveals my back, shoulders, and arms and gives the illusion of cleavage. It's classic and casually elegant. I feel pretty in the dress (except for my bony bird arms that are a little too Calista Flockhart-like) so I buy it along with ridiculously expensive black nylons. I have the perfect black high-heeled shoes that I bought under Hannah's influence over Christmas break and have never worn.

When Owen picks me up, he tells me over and over again how gorgeous I look.

"That's the hundredth time you've told me that. All these compliments are going to go to my head," I say, though I'm flattered by his comments.

Dad and Claudia have already left. Owen gets Maria to take our picture. She takes almost an entire twenty-four-shot roll of film.

"I feel like I'm going to my prom. Enough already!" I say.

"Nobody at school is going to believe I dated such a stunningly beautiful rich girl, I want proof," Owen says. "Now say 'cheese.'"

We finally leave and get to the hotel ballroom where the ceremony is being held. The ballroom is decorated in ornate red-and-gold accents with a tremendous vaulted ceiling and several large chandeliers that look capable of killing a few dozen people should one ever fall from where it dangles from the ceiling overhead.

There are twenty minutes left of the cocktail hour. I get Owen and myself each a cocktail, then make my way over to the table that we've been assigned to. It's practically on the opposite end of the room from the table where Dad, Claudia, and Polly are sitting. Owen is making idle conversation with an older couple sitting at the table with us. There's something about this room that makes it hard to breathe. The very vastness of it somehow makes me feel claustrophobic.

"Owen, I'm going to go outside for a minute and get some fresh air."

He nods. "Okay."

I go outside to the patio. It's dark out. The sky is thick with stars twinkling like the chandeliers inside. A well-dressed, middle-aged man comes out on the patio beside me.

"Good evening."

"Hi."

"I'm Wayne Hammond."

"It's nice to meet you," I extend my hand. "I'm Helaina—" I don't know which last name to use. He may know "Merrill" from Claudia. He'll definitely know the name "Denner." So instead I say, "I'm interning at *Local Color* this summer, writing film reviews, doing the calendar items, that sort of thing."

"Oh, how do you like it?"

"I don't know. I guess I'm learning a lot about how the real world works."

"Like what?"

"Like how incompetent management is."

"Oh?"

"Like my boss, she comes in late and leaves early. She doesn't really know what's going on. Every time she does try to manage something, it's worse than it would have been without her. From what I can tell, she only got where she was by marrying the guy who ran everything. She has two really great senior editors though; they keep things running smoothly despite her. They are really great. Overworked and underpaid though, I can tell you that much. Plus, I think Polly's editorial policy is really keeping the magazine from going as far as it could go. She keeps everything so fluffy. I really think the magazine could reach a wider audience if it were a little more edgy. It's got all the depth of a piece of gauze."

"Interesting," he says.

"Yeah, and then there is the fly problem. It's disgusting. We've called maintenance and all they've done is leave some fly strips so we can watch hordes of flies die slow, horrible deaths. All I can say is that I'm glad I'm an intern and this is not my real life."

Someone gets onstage and asks if we can all find our seats. I tell Wayne it was nice meeting him and return to my table way out in the boonies. The MC, a tall man in his early fifties, starts announcing the awards for the different categories: feature writing, news reporting, best local in-depth investigation. On and on it goes until they get to best column. There are five people up for the award. When he says "Claudia Merrill" and she stands up and gives a little Miss America wave, I want to scream. Then when he announces the winner, and it's Claudia Merrill, and she goes up to the stage wearing my mother's jewels and an expensive dress paid for by my father and she expresses her gratitude to Gary Denner for all his help, to Polly Kirkland for giving her this opportunity, and to about a zillion other people—though not my mother—I don't think I can keep it together anymore. I want to stand up and shout, "She's a phony! She doesn't even write it!"

For a second I imagine doing it, really doing it. I can imagine the audience's horrified expressions. But they wouldn't think less of Claudia, they would just think I was some maladjusted youth, bitter about my mother's death and jealous of my aunt's success.

"Are you okay?" Owen asks me in a whisper.

"I am so fucking sick of everyone asking me that all the time!"

"Guess that answers my question."

"Can we please leave?"

"Now?"

"Please?"

"I really should stay until the awards are over—say congrats to Polly and Claudia."

"I'll wait for you in the car." I push my chair away from the table, and with a sigh, Owen follows.

When we get home, I tell Owen that I'd rather he didn't come in, I'd rather be alone. I get into my room and fall onto my bed with my clothes still on, tears streaming down my face.

When I wake in the morning, I have a few moments of not remembering why it is I feel like I'm trapped in a dark cloud. Then I remember. I lie in bed frowning, wishing there was something I could do to honor my mother. Everyone has been acting like she never existed. But what could I . . . I'm not good at anything. What have I done with my life? I've made one decent short film . . .

It hits me . . . a vague thought. Could I make a movie about her? I sit up. Maybe I could write a screenplay. Maybe it'll be called *The Executive's Wife*. It will show the world what an amazing woman my mother was and what kind of people Dad and Claudia really are. It won't be a documentary or anything; I'll pretend that it's fiction, but the movie reviewers, the journalists, and the public will all know who my father is. They'll know that my mother died under mysterious circumstances and that Claudia lived with us, and they'll speculate that it's based on my true life story. Rumors will abound, and the world will finally know what Claudia Merrill is really like.

I take out a notebook and a pen. Where to start? Shit. I can't think straight.

What's it going to be about? Maybe it can be like *The First Wives' Club*. Women everywhere will identify with the conniving husband, the friend/sister who betrays them, the sacrifices made that went unnoticed. People will laugh, they'll cry. It won't be an artsy film. It can't be. It needs to get to the broadest possible audience. This won't be my Academy Award winner. It doesn't have to be.

For now I just need to figure out how to start the damn thing. I grab one of my books on scriptwriting. I read about thirty pages, then I take my notebook and write, "Fade in."

I write random stabs of dialogue for a couple of hours. I have no illusion that this is going to be easy or that my first draft (or even tenth or twentieth) will be any good, but I have to start somewhere.

Chapter 14

Marni calls me that afternoon and asks me if I want to get together with her and Hannah for a cocktail.

"Where's Jake?"

"He has a birthday party with some friends of his."

"Ah," I say. I've always thought Jake was a nice enough guy, but he's the type that doesn't say a word until he really gets to know you. Marni has told me that he's very funny and talkative, but only with her. I guess I believe her, but sometimes I think it's like Marni went off and started dating an imaginary friend, someone she can see and know but nobody else can.

"Let's meet at the Tin Man at four."

"Sounds good." I return the phone to its cradle. It'll be good for me to get out and hang out with friends—it will help inspire my art, surely.

When I get to the bar, Hannah is already there reading a newspaper.

"Hi." I sit down across from her. Behind Hannah there is an older woman sitting with a cup of tea, but otherwise the bar is pretty dead at this time of day.

"What are you doing?" I ask.

"Have you heard that Lana Garnand has been accused of murdering her husband?" she asks. Lana is a former actress like Claudia, and about Claudia's same age.

"And," Hannah says, "according to an article in the *Enquirer*, Lana is a necrophiliac."

"The *Enquirer* is known for being a source of reliable journalism, so I'm sure we should take the accusations very seriously."

"Listen to this. It says, 'After being the victim of molestation as a child, Lana prefers to have intercourse with someone she can control. According to Dr. Vance Hardwig—'"

"Dr. Vance Hardwig? Are you kidding me? What kind of name is that? Where does somebody—"

"The complete subjugation of a corpse can be a turn-on for some. Notorious necrophiliac Leilah Wendall, author of the book *Necromantic*—"

"Ah! Ah! Stop! I can't take it anymore. Gross, gross, gross."

"My point is—"

"To torture me, obviously."

"That if Lana really is a necrophiliac, then maybe that's why she killed her husband. She *is* eccentric after all."

I look at the kindly old woman who is sitting next to me, looking at us in wide-eyed horror. I offer a cheerful smile and return my attention back to Hannah.

"That is the worst motivation for a murder I have ever heard."

"There are lots of killers who keep the bodies around to have sex with the corpses. Ed Gein, the guy the movie *Psycho* is based on, Ed Kemper, Ted Bundy, that Russian cannibal guy—"

"Yeah, yeah, okay, I get it."

Hannah goes back to reading from the paper. "'Her career began when she was seventeen with the popular 1975 sitcom *The New Kid in Town*. After *The New Kid* went off the air in 1980, Garnard drifted, taking small roles here and there. She went bankrupt in 1984, then

she made the news several times in rapid succession in
'85, first when she was found wandering in a suburb of
LA naked—it was later determined she was high on co-
caine—and then when she wrapped her car around a phone
booth and was subsequently put into rehab. Not a peep
was heard from her until 1990, when she landed a role in
the indie film *What We Forget*, which garnered her a best
supporting actress nomination. The Oscar buzz briefly
revitalized her career, and she landed a few walk-on parts
in TV shows and another small role in a critically acclaimed
movie. For the next several years she became a tabloid favorite second only to Michael Jackson for her eccentrici-
ties. She collects funereal art—'"

"What does that mean?"

"It's stuff like gravestones, urns, figurines. But it's also,
you know, a cemetery from Victorian times is different
than a modern European cemetery. It's just an appreciation for Victorian cemeteries as opposed to say, Victorian
architecture."

"Hence the necrophilia accusations."

"Hmm."

I feel a little guilty talking about this woman we don't
even know, but at the same time, it's kind of fun. Lana is
beautiful and rich and at least mildly famous. Who knows,
her PR people probably made up the necrophilia charges
as a way to get her name back in the papers and revitalize
her career. Even though I think the charges are probably
baseless, it's fun toying with the idea that she's so eccentric. It also makes me think about Claudia—maybe getting fame young and then falling from the spotlight does
something to you.

"Hi guys, sorry I'm late." Marni dumps her Kate
Spade bag on the table and takes a seat. "What have I
missed? What's up with you guys?"

Hannah folds up the newspaper she was reading, already bored with today's gossip. I tell them about Claudia winning the award and getting offered the TV role.

"No!" Marni and Hannah hiss in unison, showing just the level of outrage I was looking for. "That's so unfair."

"Tell me about it."

I love that they both dislike Claudia on principle, though they've never met her. It's important to have friends who take your side no matter what. I can't stand friends who encourage you to look at things from the other person's perspective. I mean really. Sometimes you just need to be pissed off.

We order a round of Bushwhackers, a deceptively innocuous drink—they are fruity and sweet and come with little umbrellas. They slide down our throats like Kool-Aid.

About three sips into it we're about ready to pass out, and that's when two unbelievably good-looking guys come up to us and introduce themselves.

"I'm Chris, this is Kai."

I look over my shoulder to try to find the women they actually mean to be talking to. I think Hannah is used to getting hit on by good-looking guys, but I usually just have to fend off the typical sleazebags who use a spaghetti-against-a-wall approach to dating: they throw a bunch of bad come-ons out there and see what sticks, so when a real-life cutie approaches, I have trouble believing his sights are set on me.

When I work at it, which isn't often, and certainly not at this moment, I can pull off "sultry." This requires lots of eyeliner and mascara and heaps of red lipstick. Usually, though, I don't wear a lot of makeup. My hairstyle could best be described as wild-animal-tortured-into-submission until I step away from the bathroom, and then it's like a dog that climbs right up onto the couch as soon as its owner leaves—it knows what it's supposed to do but isn't about to do it. I'm no natural beauty, that's all I'm saying.

Kai is a Nordic blond, which is not my usual type, but as Chris begins chatting up Hannah, Kai slides in next to me and tells me he works in restaurant sales. They buy us another round of drinks.

As I talk to him, I start missing Owen. Kai is cute, but he's just not Owen, that's all there is to it. I'm blurry from the alcohol, so when he crushes his lips against mine, my reaction time is delayed and it takes me a few elongated seconds to pull away. Immediately my heart hammers and I look around the bar, suddenly fearful that someone who knows Owen saw me and is going to tell him what happened. This is how my whole life has been lately—I've been walking around in a fog, fuzzy and ineffectual. I don't seem to be in control of any part of my life.

"Kai," I say, pushing him away. "I'm seeing someone. I just really came here tonight to hang out with my girl-friends."

He smiles. "Sorry. I'll leave you alone. Chris, you ready?"

Chris looks up from where he was staring into Hannah's eyes. "Your boyfriends never have to know."

"She's right, we just came out for a girls' night out," Hannah says without a trace of regret.

"If you change your minds, here's my card. Call me." Chris flicks a business card on the table as agilely as a magician with a deck of playing cards.

"Well, they were cute," Marni says, watching them go.

I shrug. "You didn't like Chris?" I ask Hannah.

"Look at them." She nods in their direction. They are already talking to two other girls. "They're players. Total players."

It's odd—my feelings are actually hurt that they are

hitting on new women. Even though I'm dating someone else and all we exchanged was a drunken conversation and a few hazy kisses, I want to believe in love at first sight, attraction, and commitment. This idea that sex can be so random and shallow hurts somehow. Maybe, I realize, that's why the whole thing with Dad and Claudia hurts so much—they aren't letting me believe that lust and attraction and love are things that can last for twenty years in a marriage. I really want to believe that.

"Have you guys ever tried anal sex?" Hannah asks.

"No. Ouch. Have you?" Marni asks.

"I tried it once. It hurt. It wasn't that fun."

They look at me. "No way."

"My feeling is, why? There's another perfectly good entryway right there," Marnie says.

"You said it, sistah," I agree.

"You know, I've been thinking I might actually want to settle down." Hannah digs around her purse for a cigarette.

"What? You?" I'm flabbergasted. I put my hands in "L" shapes beneath my face as if to frame it. "This is the expression I make when I'm doubtful." I raise my eyebrow. "If you ever wanted to know what I look like when I'm having trouble believing something, this is what it looks like."

"Seriously, Han, she's got a point."

"Well, here's the thing. You know I've slept with my share of guys."

"Mmm-mmm," Marni and I say in unison, nodding our heads.

"And with each guy you do the 'What do you like?' 'What do you not like?' series of questions when you're naked in bed. I'm having trouble keeping things straight. Like, my ex loved to have his balls licked. Todd squeals and wriggles every time I forget that his balls are ticklish. That's not the effect you want to have on someone in bed. I just want to be with someone long enough that I can remember whether he likes his balls licked or not."

We laugh and take another sip of our drinks. The conversation goes on like this for much of the night. You know, deeply insightful queries about the mysteries of human sexuality, that sort of thing. Every now and then I glance over at Kai and Chris. They were a part of our lives for less than fifteen minutes, but something about the exchange niggles at me. Their come-on reminds me of the way "courtship" works on spring break. In real life, you might get a hug on the first date, a kiss on the second, and maybe sex on the third at the very soonest. Even with a one-night stand you usually spend the whole night talking with someone before you decide to head back to their place. But on spring break, the mating ritual is sped up like a flower on a time-elapse video, where you see it go from sprout to full bloom in about ten seconds: guys will come up to you, ask you your name and where you're from, then they try to shove their tongues down your throats, as if the answers to those two questions proved so insightful you now have a meaningful relationship and can commence with groping and sex.

When I see Kai and Chris leave with the women they've been chatting up for the last hour, something inside me feels hollow. I take another sip of my drink. I am grateful for the blurry peace it brings, even if it is only temporary.

Chapter 15

Office coffee is a special kind of hell. This is what I'm thinking as I pour myself a needed but unwanted cup, trying to stir in the sad-looking powdered creamer that is nothing like real milk. Its only resemblance is that it, too, makes my coffee a little lighter, and for that reason alone I stir it in. I look up to Owen whose face is twisted in a frantic expression.

"Did you hear?"

"Hear what?"

"Polly was fired. Amanda and Jill have both been given big raises and have been promoted to coeditors-in-chief."

"You're kidding? Why? What happened?"

"One of the owners of the publishing group, Wayne Hammond—"

"Wayne Hammond?"

"Yeah, he said they wanted to run a tighter ship here and he wasn't happy with her work. Which is so weird, considering the magazine just won an award. Anyway, I feel terrible for Polly. I know she wasn't the best editor-in-chief, but I didn't want her to get fired. There is no way in hell she's going to get another job around here as an editor. I mean maybe a copy editor or an entry-level journalist, but nothing that will let her continue living like she's been living. She's going to have to sell the house. She'll never be able to make those payments. She's effectively been blackballed around here. Even if she moved, I don't think she'll get the references she'd need to get a decent job."

"Oh my God."

"Jill likes you and me, so I think she'll let us stay on to the end of the summer, but there are no guarantees." He shakes his head. "Are you okay? You look pale."

"Uh . . . I'm just really surprised." Holy shit. What have I done? How could I have gotten this woman fired? What is she going to do?

"I know, me too. They called her in early this morning, then the board met with Jill and Amanda. I mean this all happened just like an hour ago."

Jill walks into the kitchen. "Hi guys. I guess you've heard?" We nod. "How's your stepmom doing?" she asks Owen.

"I don't know. I haven't seen her. I heard through the grapevine this morning."

"We're going to get everyone together for a meeting at 10:30 in the boardroom."

Owen nods. "Well congrats, Jill, you deserve it."

"Thanks. Are you going to be okay?"

"I'm surprised, but I'll be fine when the shock wears off."

Owen and I go back to our desks. "How are you? You seem really upset," he says.

"I feel bad for your stepmom, that's all," I say. What if Owen finds out it was me who got Polly fired? If I don't tell him, it's the same thing as lying. But if he does find out, will he break up with me? He's the one good thing that's happened to me in a long time. I don't know if I love him, but I love the way he looks, smells, makes me laugh, the way I feel when I'm around him—I can't lose him.

· At the staff meeting, the mood is more stunned than happy. Even though Polly wasn't a popular boss, it's hard to celebrate her getting fired—it makes people think about how expendable and insecure their own jobs are.

Amanda leads the meeting. She says that like everyone else, she was stunned by what happened this morning. "Things haven't been perfect around here, and there is definitely room for improvement, but we're in a good position. Winning the award Friday night . . . "—someone in the back groans—"will only help our efforts to grow and increase profitability. I don't want you to think that Polly being let go is the start of a mass layoff. Nothing could be further from the truth. We're going to hire another writer, we'll hire another editor, and when the fall comes and we lose Owen and Helaina, we'll hire two more interns to keep the workload reasonable. In terms of revenue and work flow, we're in a very good position."

The next day at work, my first question to Owen is how Polly is.

"Not good." Owen sits down and boots up his computer. "You don't look all that great. Are you okay?"

"I had some trouble sleeping last night." I didn't get any sleep at all. I know I have to do something to help Polly, but I'm not sure what I can do. "She'll be okay, though, right?"

"Eventually. It'll take some time."

"You know I could loan her some money . . . "

"Helaina, that's nice of you, but really, she'll figure things out."

Nothing changes for the next couple of days at the office in terms of Owen and me getting any work. We're just as bored as usual. The boredom seems an especially cruel punishment because it leaves me plenty of time to kick myself for talking badly about Polly behind her back. Why is it so difficult being a decent human being? Is it this hard for everyone?

I try to think of ways I can help Polly. My first idea is to stage some sort of fake lottery or sweepstakes and just send a check large enough to cover a year's worth of salary for her, but then I dismiss the idea as ludicrous. The only way to help her would be to get her a new job. I do have some contacts in New York. I've met lots of publishers and journalists through various events and parties. In high school Mom and Dad often took me to New York for social functions with society types, and I've been to a few parties with Gilda, who knows just about everyone who is anyone. As soon as she introduces me to someone in the publishing industry as Gary Denner's daughter, that person wants to be my best friend. Maybe it's time I used the fact that Gary Denner is my father to pull some strings.

"Helaina?"

"Hmm?" I look up to see Jill standing over me.

"Amanda would like to see you in her office."

"Oh sure." I stand and as soon as I begin walking I know, I just *know* that Amanda knows it was me who got Polly fired. Shit.

"Thanks for coming, Helaina. Have a seat." I do. "Jill and I have spent the last two days brainstorming for the next issue. We've been charged with making *Local Color* more 'edgy.' Do you think you could handle a heavier workload?"

What? She's giving me more work? Does she really not know about Polly? "Uh, sure."

"Good. I think both you and Owen are talented writers, and I'd like to broaden your beats. You'll split the entertainment beat. I'm going to assign you three profiles. I'd like them to be about eight hundred words each. We can run them at any time, but I'd like you to get right on this one." She hands me a news release. "A producer is going to start shooting a sitcom that will be filmed in Denver. I want you to find out about him, the show, why they chose Denver, and what the challenges are of being one of the few TV shows not shot in LA, Vancouver, or New York. Do some research, get your questions ready, then call him at the number here." She taps the release I'm holding. "Think you're up to it?"

"Yeah, sure."

She gives me some info on a local band and local restaurant she wants reviewed, and then I return to my desk. The rest of the day flies by, and I couldn't be happier. Owen also gets several assignments, and we spend our afternoon in a hum of activity.

Thursday morning I'm sitting at the kitchen table drinking my latte and eating a bowl of cereal when Dad blazes through the kitchen. He's carrying his briefcase and has a sport coat slung over his shoulder.

"Hi honey," he says. He hangs his coat over a chair and pours himself a cup of coffee.

"Going on a trip?"

"San Francisco. I'll be back Monday."

"Does Claudia have a business trip this weekend?"

He shakes his head. "Not that I know of."

I sip my latte. "How are you doing, Dad?"

"What do you mean?"

"I'm just wondering how you're doing, how things are going."

"The stock market isn't doing as well as it was. I mean it was bound to happen, but it gets investors and bankers edgy."

"That's not really what I . . . "

"It was good talking to you. I have to get going. I'll see you Monday." He gives me a perfunctory kiss on the forehead and rushes out.

Thanks for asking me how I'm doing, how my job is going, how things are going with Owen.

Let it go. Breathe. Just let it go . . .

With Dad gone, I invite everybody over Friday night after work. It's about eleven PM and the gang's all here: Hannah and Todd, Marni and Jake, me and Owen. We're sitting in the hot tub, drinking Cosmopolitans.

"I'm hungry," Hannah says.

"Let's order pizza," Marni suggests.

"Good idea, I'll order a veggielover's. What do you carnivores want?" I ask.

"Sausage," Todd offers. "And Canadian bacon and pepperoni."

"Should I order a defibrillator to go with that?"

"I think Jake and I will stick to cheese. Maybe some tomatoes and mushrooms if you guys like them," Marni says.

"I'm not a big fan of sausage," Owen says, "but I could go with a plain pepperoni."

"Have you ever had headcheese?" Hannah asks no one in particular.

"What is headcheese?" Marni asks.

I decide I've had my fill of hot tubbing, so I climb out, towel off, and slip on my short terry cloth robe. In the background, I hear Todd defining headcheese, and the conversation turns to a discussion of the relative merits of liver pâté and caviar.

I brought my video camera out here earlier, figuring I should take some footage to help me remember the days of Owen and Hannah and Marni and being twenty and drinking far too many Cosmopolitans. I imagine showing scenes of it at Hannah or Marni's wedding, how amusing everyone will find it, what a hit it will be.

I turn the camera on and walk around the hot tub.

"Six friends, one hot tub, an endless supply of vodka. What *will* the night bring?" I ask.

"The next Steven Spielberg at work," Todd says.

"I was thinking more like Ang Lee or David Mamet," I say.

"And we can say we knew you when," Hannah says.

I turn the camera to Marni and Jake. "So tell us, Marn, when did you know it was true love?"

"He was the only Jewish guy in the school; I had no other choice." He tickles her and she giggles.

"I think I knew before we ever even went out on our first date," she says. "We kept trying to get together for dinner and a movie but something always came up—my grandmother died and I had to go to the funeral in Wisconsin, he sprained his ankle and had to go to the hospital—all this crazy stuff, so for two weeks, we just talked on the phone, trying to figure out when we could get together, and we'd always talk for hours and hours, we never ran out of things to talk about. I just knew I'd found my soul mate."

"Soul mate, schmole mate. What about pizza? I thought we were going to order pizza," Hannah says.

I'm about to tell her not to worry, I'll order some pizza, when the horrible sound of crashing metal thunders through the air. We turn in the direction the noise is coming from—the garage. The front of Dad's Mercedes is crumpled accordion-like into the corner of the garage.

"Holy shit."

"Jesus."

"What happened?"

I can't see the driver from here, so I run through the yard to the driveway.

It's Claudia! She backs up, straightens out, then pulls in again.

"Holy shit," I say again.

Owen, Marni, Todd, Jake, and Hannah come up behind me, wrapped in towels and dripping wet.

"It's Claudia," I tell them. "Come on." We run inside through the kitchen door and run to the pantry. I close the door behind us.

"Shhh!" I order. The Record button on my video camera is still on. I peer through the camera lens through the slits of the pantry door. Claudia staggers in, weaving drunkenly.

"She's fucking tanked," I whisper. She drops the keys on the counter; they slip off onto the floor. Claudia doesn't pick them up—she just stumbles through the kitchen doors into the living room. I get the whole thing on tape.

I can't wait till Dad gets home. I won't need to exact any revenge on Claudia after all. Dad will take care of it for me.

Chapter 16

Dad is supposed to get home today, so I come home from work ready to hear Dad unleash his wrath on Claudia. At around 8:30 or 9:00, I'm in my room, trying to read a book when Dad pounds on my bedroom door and asks, "May I come in?" in a tone that sounds more like, "Open this goddamn door."

I unlock the door and Dad storms in. His face is red, his jaws are clenched. He walks across the room, pivots abruptly, looks at me, then looks away, paces again.

"I'm so disappointed in you. I'm furious with you."

I wonder if Dad has found out about the car yet, or if this is about Polly losing her job or something.

"What's going on?"

"Don't give me that. Don't pretend like you don't know what this is about."

"I'm sorry, I seriously don't know what this is about."

"You had to take the Mercedes. You know that car means more to me than all of the others put together. And then you go and drink. Drinking and driving, great idea, Helaina."

"Dad, it wasn't me. I had friends over Friday night. I have five witnesses who can vouch for the fact that it wasn't me, it was Claudia."

"That's very interesting. Claudia told me you were responsible."

"You're kidding." But there is no sign he is kidding. His face is hardened. "I swear, it wasn't me. It was Claudia."

"I'm afraid I don't believe you."

"You're kidding, right?"

"You've been stealing bottles of wine from the cellar, you've been drinking uncontrollably lately—I'm actually surprised something like this didn't happen sooner."

"I didn't realize I wasn't allowed to take the wine. Am I allowed to take food out of the refrigerator, or is that stealing too?"

"Don't be flip with me. I've let this go on for too long. I'm sending you to a rehab clinic. If that doesn't work . . . " he shakes his head. He's not looking at me, he's looking at the floor as if that's where he can find the answer to how to deal with a hellion like me. "I'll have to get tough."

"Tougher than sending me to rehab? What, you'll send me to a Turkish prison or something? Dad, this is so crazy, I didn't even crash the car, Claudia did."

"I know you don't like Claudia, you've been rude to her all summer. She's an important part of my life and I won't let you continue to treat her this way. I'm going to have my assistant look into rehab programs and I'll get back to you. This is for your own good."

I let out this sort of choked laugh. I can't help it, this whole thing is so surreal. "I'll be waiting with bated breath."

Dad storms out, slamming the door behind him.

Unbelievable. Unbefuckinglievable. The tears come out in a rush, extravagant sobs. What a jackass. I can't believe him. I didn't even . . .

The video! I forgot about the video.

I consider charging out to the living room or wherever Dad is and showing him the video, but I can't go out
there when I'm a tear-stained hysteric. I have to calm
down.

I can't believe he believes Claudia over me. Yes, I can.
Claudia provides a useful service to him; I'm just a useless
mooch.

The first sign of trouble in my life and his solution is
to send me off to rehab.

Wait, Dad can't do this to me, can he? I'm an adult.
Still, that he'd want to, just like that. Get rid of me, ship
me off.

I have never felt such anger toward my father. Right
now, I hate him, I really hate him. I'll go back to New
York. I'll never speak to him again. Not like he'd even
notice.

No. Even better: if he is embezzling, I'll find the evidence myself. I'll go through his books. I'll turn the evidence in to the cops or the FBI or whoever and I'll help
send him to prison myself.

I get to work early the next morning to use the Internet.
I have a computer and high-speed Internet access at home,
of course, but Dad probably has that software that can
track every move I make.

The first thing I do is search on the Web for "Claudia
Merrill" and get dozens of hits. I begin reading. Some of
the information is very interesting indeed.

I dig through my purse to find Gilda's business card,
and I send her an e-mail that begins, "Remember how
you owe me one? Well I've got a favor that I think you
might really enjoy doing." I copy some text from some of

the Web sites I visited and copy some additional URLs in there. Gilda's a smart girl—she'll be able to fill in the blanks.

Next I go to Able Technologies' Web site and read the marketing junk, the executive bios, the company history, the investor relations information.

COMPANY HISTORY

Able Technologies, Inc. was founded by Gary Denner and Charles Sinha as D-S Technologies, an information services and communications company headquartered in Boston, Mass.

When D-S moved its corporate headquarters to Denver, Colo., they announced it was changing its name to Able Technologies. In recent years, the company has substantially increased the emphasis it places on and the resources devoted to its communications and information services business. With the acquisition of Avec Communications, Able solidified its position as one of the leading providers of information services in the world.

"Do you know anything about the stock market?" I ask Owen when he gets in.

"Some. Why?"

"How does it work? How do you know what stock to buy and why some stock is worth more than others?"

"A lot of stuff goes into it, but typically what happens is that financial analysts review earnings statements and sales and industry reports, and then make projections and recommendations based on that."

"Couldn't a company lie and say it was doing better than it was to boost the stock price?"

"Well, yes and no. There is some room for creativity,

but they are legally bound to report their expenses and income. There is some leeway for how and when they claim those costs or profits. Like let's say Microsoft sells $250 worth of software. They'll only claim they made $175 now, saying they'll have to offer tech support for the product later and will be out expenses then. They're trying to pretend like they make less money each year than they do so it looks like they're not a monopoly."

I spend the next several hours reading *Fortune* and *BusinessWeek*, going through several months' worth of old columns and articles that talk about Able stock and the telecommunications industry in general.

"Owen, I'm going to take a lunch break. Maybe a long one. I need to clear my head," I say.

"Want some company?"

"If it's okay with you, I'd really like to be alone right now."

"Of course."

I drive over to Able Technologies headquarters. I know that if something is going on, I'll find it in the finance and accounting department, so that's the department I head for.

Finance is located on the twelfth floor. I know this because I came here just about every year in high school for Career Development Day. An ebullient HR person would show us around and talk about different career options and what degrees and internships to get to succeed in our chosen field. Different people from different departments would get up and talk about their jobs and how much they loved them.

I watch the men in their white shirts and ties, the women in their suits or skirts and sweaters hustling along. All of them appear to be in a very big hurry.

What do I think I'm going to do? March up to some

empty computer and hack into the mainframe? I don't actually even know what a mainframe is—I just heard the word in a movie. I need to find Todd.

I'm not wandering for long before I see him.

"Hey, how's it going?" I ask.

"Hey, you. What's up? What are you doing here?"

"You're not going to believe this, but I actually came here to talk to you."

"Yeah, right."

"No, really. I was hoping you could help me with something. I'm thinking about changing majors, maybe becoming a business major, finance or something."

"Yeah, *right*."

"Well, okay, the truth is, I'm doing research for a movie script I'm writing."

"Why don't you talk to your dad?"

"Trying to get a hold of my dad for more than three seconds is like trying to build a perpetual motion machine. He's a very busy man. It's never going to happen. You're young, you're cool, I figure you can help me find what I need."

"I'll see what I can do. What are you looking for?"

"Well, you're getting ready for the um, is it called the investor financial statement or something?"

"Earnings statement?"

"Yeah, right, that."

He taps at a thick stack of papers on his desk. "Yeah, I know all about that. Wish I didn't."

"So those are pretty complicated?"

"Not if you know what you're looking for."

"Well, I guess that's what my question is. If I were an investor, how would I know what to look for? Hey, you know, would you mind going to lunch with me? My treat. I printed off some financial statements from Able's Web site, and it would be so awesome if you could help me go through them, answer some questions for me."

"Sure. No problem." He smiles.

We go downstairs and get into my car. As I drive to a restaurant, I ask him again what investors look for in an earnings statement.

"Well, usually investors don't know enough about that sort of thing to read an earnings statement. Investors read publications like the *Wall Street Journal* and read what journalists have written based on financial analysts' reports."

Todd looks so smug and pleased with himself I wonder for a moment if he thinks I'm flirting with him or something.

"I'm very happy with Owen you know," I say, with no transition.

"What?"

"I just want you to know, I'm not asking you to lunch because I'm interested in you. I just need to understand how this works."

"I didn't think you had any ulterior motive."

"Okay," I say, still a little unsure.

I park and the two of us walk into the restaurant. It's a fancy place, dimly lit with red tablecloths and flickering candles.

After we place our orders, I say, "I read these articles about how Able keeps racking up debt buying up fiberoptic lines and that they have all this negative cash flow, but their stock prices just keep going up. I don't get it."

Todd laughs. "I can't tell you the specifics of Able's finances, but I can give you some generalized basics on how this stuff works."

"Fine, I'll take it."

Two hours and two martinis later, Todd has answered

a lot of my questions and given me a crash course in investment. I still have a lot more questions than answers, there is so much I don't know, but for what I need, I don't have to be an expert. I just need to help point an actual expert in the right direction.

After dropping Todd off, I return to the office and pull up fortune.com. After a little digging, I find a columnist who recently wrote a scathing article about a company's overvalued stock price. I click on the hyperlink to Steve Tyson's e-mail address. Then I realize I can't exactly e-mail him from my own account, so I go to Yahoo and create a new one: concernedinsider432@yahoo.com.

I use the subject line "Just how much are Able's stocks really worth?" In the body of the e-mail I type, "For the last three years, Able Technologies has reported record growth. They've seen their stock shares soar. Much of this is based on their trading portfolio, since their cash flow from operations was last reported to be negative $1.3 billion. Plus, they've continued to rack up debt to build hundreds of miles of fiber-optic cable and they haven't received any return on investment yet. Able has been accused of having extremely complex earnings reports, yet analysts have continually given them the benefit of the doubt. But maybe they shouldn't. Ask yourself how Able's stock has managed to stay so strong despite a slowing economy. And ask yourself why, if Able's doing so well, CEO Gary Denner has sold more than $35 million in stock this year alone."

I send the e-mail and stare at the screen as if it will enable me to divine whether Steve Tyson will even read the e-mail or do anything about it and if he does, whether it will have any impact on Dad or Able.

"It's after five," Owen says.

"What?"

"It's after five. Aren't you going to go home?"

I smile. "I don't know. I may be carted off to rehab if I go home."

"What? Why? It seems like you've hardly been drinking lately."

"Rehab isn't to help me, it's to punish me. Claudia told Dad that I was the one who totaled the Mercedes and he believed her."

"How could Claudia lie about that?"

"Because she knew Dad would believe her. And she was right. Even though her struggles with alcohol have been written about in major magazines, he chose to believe her."

"There are five witnesses who can vouch it wasn't you."

"I told him that and he said you guys were my friends and would lie for me."

"You have it on videotape."

"Yeah, but when he was accusing me I was so flustered I forgot about it."

"That's rough, Helaina, I'm sorry. You can stay at my place until your Dad calms down."

"He won't calm down about this. When I got that two-inch scratch on his car when I was in high school, he acted like I'd intentionally cut off all his limbs and set him on fire, like I deliberately set out to hurt him. It's so dumb because he's got insurance and even if he didn't, no matter how expensive the car is, it's still chump change to him. Anyway, if he wanted to find me, your place would be the first place he'd look." *If he wanted to find me.* Would he actually take the time to look? "You know, maybe staying with you would be a good idea. Let's stop by my place so I can pick up some clothes. Dad won't be home from work yet, so I should be safe."

We go home and I open the door just a crack like I'm some amateur spy or something. I don't see anything so I wave Owen in and we sneak upstairs, quiet as we can be.

I pack up at least two weeks' worth of clothes, shoes, bras, and underwear. When we get to Owen's house, he unlocks the front door and holds it open for me. I stop abruptly in the doorway, struck by the sight of Polly, who is sitting in a chair looking like a heavily sedated mental patient, starring distractedly at the wall. She's pale and her hair is greasy. She's wearing a silk robe with bright flowers on it over black leggings and a University of Colorado sweatshirt. My body fills with leaden dread, the heavy burden of guilt.

"Ahem," Owen says jokingly behind me, urging me forward since I'm blocking his way.

I step inside. "Hi Polly, how are you?"

She looks at me for a moment before she registers who I am. "I'll be okay."

"It's good to see you."

"Helaina is going to be staying with us for a few days. I'll make the three of us some dinner," Owen says. I follow Owen up the stairs to his room.

"She looks terrible," I say.

"She'll be okay. She's just in shock. We talked the other night; I think she's going to put the house on the market. She'll find a smaller place somewhere, but I don't think she'll stay in Colorado. It's going to be tough for her to find a job around here. She's dealing with a lot of changes at once. It's going to take a while to get over."

After we drop my bags off in Owen's room, he suggests we go downstairs and make dinner.

I'm too much of a chickenshit to face Polly, but I don't see what other choice I have. Should I tell Owen the truth that it was me who got her fired, even if it was unintentional? But what good could that possibly do?

Owen and I go into the kitchen and Owen begins opening and closing cupboards. "I'm not really sure what we have that's vegetarian. Actually, we don't have much carnivorian, for that matter either. We might need to go to the store."

"Carnivorian? Is that a word? I think I may have to report you to the vocabulary police."

"Please don't. I'll be good."

"Promise?"

He looks at me with mock sincerity and nods.

"All right. You're off the hook this time."

Owen opens the freezer. "Here we go. We have mushroom ravioli and some french bread."

He pulls out a loaf of bread from the freezer and I inspect it curiously. "Frozen garlic bread? Wow. I thought my roommates and I were the laziest cooks in the universe. This is a new low."

"They put so much butter on it, it tastes even better than fresh bread. You can actually feel your arteries closing a little more with every bite."

"Sounds like I'm in for a treat."

When dinner is ready, we bring some to the nearly catatonic Polly, who pushes the food around with her fork.

"I'm going to lose the house," she mutters. "I only have enough savings to get me through the next two months."

"Polly, we won't let you lose the house," I say. "I can

loan you money. And I'm sure Dad and Claudia will help you after all you've done for Claudia and me."

"The gas bill will be about two hundred. Cable is fifty-four. The phone will be . . . " she keeps muttering a list of numbers. "What if I can't sell the house? What if I *do* sell the house? Where will I go?"

My assurances that I won't let anything happen to her go unheard. I think about the phone calls I made to my contacts in New York. Please let something come of it. *Please.*

E xcept for the guilt that I feel every time I see Polly, staying at Owen's is great. We drive into work together, come home and make dinner together, hang out in his room watching videos or reading or writing. I'm still puttering along trying to work on my screenplay. I'm afraid that rather than being the Monet-caliber tribute I would like it to be, it will be something more along the lines of Toddler With Finger Paints—lots of points for intention and effort but not much for execution. Still, I know it's going to take years to work on my craft. The harder I work now, the less time it will take me to get to the point where I no longer suck.

I keep waiting to get carted off in a straitjacket in a paddy wagon, but days go by and I don't hear anything from Dad or Claudia. For all they know, I could be dead, not that they'd mind. Dad probably didn't have the time to bother figuring out how to get me locked up. He'd probably rather I just kill myself with alcohol.

I read fortune.com every day and read the print version each week, but I don't see anything about Able from Steve Tyson or anyone else.

On Thursday Dad's secretary calls me at work and says

that my father would like me to attend a dinner at our house tomorrow night. I'm free to invite Owen and it's very important that I be there.

"It's at seven. So you'll be there?"

My first thought is that it's an intervention. But then why would Debbie tell me it's okay to invite Owen as my date? They would just invite him themselves. And who would they invite to an intervention? That's when it hits me: this dinner isn't about me. They are going to invite Dad's friends and colleagues and Mom's friends that Claudia commandeered for her own and they are going to announce that they are getting married.

"Yeah, I can be there," I say at last.

Chapter 17

There are about twenty people at the party. All of the bigwigs from Dad's office are here. Claudia's agent, Dennis, flew out from California with his saline-enhanced girlfriend, Monica, on his arm. Monica is all faux-platinum hair; pearly pink lipstick; ghetto-talon nails; leopard-print clothes; and breasts as rock hard, plastic, and synthetic as Barbie's. I would be very surprised if "stripper" hadn't appeared on her resume at some point in her career.

Barb and Dana and Christine are here with their husbands. Polly is noticeably absent. Now that she's no longer an editor-in-chief of a magazine, she's no longer needed. There are several other couples here who I don't recognize.

Claudia has hired extra staff for the night, and they go around passing out hors d'oeuvres and keeping wine glasses full. We mill about the great room, standing around plucking appetizers off trays and sipping our drinks. Claudia looks elegant as usual. She truly is a striking woman. She's wearing a stunning green dress with gold braided straps that cross her collarbone, over her shoulder, down her bare back. Her makeup, blond-highlighted hair, and manicured nails are flawless. Her shiny green high-heeled shoes sparkle like emeralds. She is wearing a simple platinum necklace with a tasteful emerald pendent—probably a recent gift from Dad.

"You're quiet tonight," Owen says to me. "Is everything okay?"

"It will be," I tell him. I don't tell him what I spent all last night plotting. After months of feeling powerless, parts of me are beginning to feel stronger.

"Dennis," Claudia says, "I can't tell you what an honor it is that you could come to our house this evening." *Our* house.

"You've heard the joke," Dennis says. "An actor comes home to find his house burned down. The cops tell him, 'Your agent came here tonight and raped and murdered your wife and burned your house down.' The man says, 'My *agent* came to my *house*?'"

Everyone laughs, especially Claudia. "And Monica," she says, "I'm so pleased you could join him. Are you also in the industry? A film actress? TV?"

"I've done some stage plays, but so far not film or TV. Hopefully, Dennis will change that."

"She's genius. Pure genius," Dennis says.

That may be, but with her bulbous basketball breasts, I can't imagine what part she could land other than hooker, porn star, or The Other Woman.

"But of course, we're not here to talk about Monica," Dennis says.

"You're here to meet Gary Denner," Claudia says, and again everyone laughs.

"It's true that in this business, you can never have too many friends," Dennis says.

"Very true. Everyone, dinner is ready. Let's sit down, shall we?"

We move into the dining room and sit around the

huge oblong table. Owen sits to my left and a guy in his early thirties sits to my right. Dozens of candles in silver holders are spread out across the length of the table. The candlelight flickers sylph-like over the silver, china, and crystal.

The dinner, for the most part, is the usual awkward and overly formal ordeal. There is a moment, however, that almost puts me in a good mood.

It happens when Maria trips over Monica's chair, and the tray of gazpacho she was carrying goes flying.

It sprays several of the guests unfortunate enough to be sitting in close proximity to the detonation site, including Monica. The gazpacho drenches her hair and face and a large chunk of tomato gets wedged in between her steel-reinforced cleavage.

"Uh!" Monica splutters in shock and outrage.

Several guests go rushing to her aid, oblivious to the sheepish-looking Maria, who is tiptoeing backward out of the room, hoping to escape unnoticed. The guests are also oblivious to the quivering pools of gazpacho between them and the aghast Monica, so they go slipping around as if they were guest stars on an episode of *I Love Lucy*. One person's feet go flying out from underneath him, and he falls on his butt with a thunderous crash.

Within moments, a SWAT team of hired help swarms the affected area, brandishing bottles of Windex in one hand and cloths in the other.

While Monica is accompanied to the bathroom to clean up, the dining room is returned to its sparkling splendor in no time.

Owen and I keep giggling on and off for several minutes, but Dad does his best to quickly dampen any fun that's being had, and soon the dinner is back to being an endless, dreary affair, complete with relentless discussions about stock prices and the markets overseas and I don't even know what else as I quickly become comatose with boredom.

After dinner, Dad clinks his fork against his wine glass and stands.

"I brought you all together tonight because I have some very exciting news to share with you."

My heart pounds and I have trouble breathing as I realize this is it, this is my chance. I stand. Dad looks at me quizzically. "I have an announcement too. Dad, if it's okay, I'd like to share my news first." I plunge on so Dad doesn't have time to argue. "As many of you know, I'm a film major, and I have a very short home movie that I would like to share with you tonight. Maria?" Maria rolls in an entertainment stand with a large-screen television set and VCR. "In this world, reputation is everything. Gossip and innuendo can make or break you. Getting a job, getting ahead, it's all about who you know and who your references are. In a world where your reputation precedes you, gossip can be such cruel poison. I guess in some ways, I'm lucky to have been able to learn just how much damage a few lies or harsh words can cause. I know firsthand that when you try to speak out against the allegations leveled against you, people find your defensiveness further evidence of your guilt. People believe what they want to believe. In my house, for example, Claudia accused me of crashing my father's prized Mercedes into the garage."

"This is uncalled for," Dad says. "Helaina, sit down now."

"I'll get to my point, Dad. I'll just ask a few more minutes of your time, if you'd be so kind as to indulge a budding filmmaker's movie. As I was saying, perception is everything in this world. And in most cases, the word is far mightier than the sword. When Claudia accused me of crashing the car, Dad believed her without question. And why wouldn't he? I've been a depressed wreck since my mother's death nearly four months ago. It's easy to imagine that I would take my father's car, get wasted, and come back to bang it up a bit, maybe to vent some of my anger. However, as I told both Dad and Claudia, I was home last Friday night with five of my friends, and I never took the car out. What Dad and Claudia don't know, however, is that I had my video camera out at the very moment the car accident occurred." I hit play. "Dennis, I think you know that your client has a reputation for boozing it up and behaving badly, and I think you'll find this video particularly intriguing."

The tape begins playing at the point where I'm interviewing Hannah and we hear the crash. "Holy shit," I say, turning toward the garage. You can see the Mercedes backing up. "Jesus," Hannah's voice says behind me.

The camera stays focused on the garage and car; the picture is unsteady like footage on *Cops* as I race across the yard.

When I get closer, you can distinctly see Claudia in the driver's seat.

The real-time Claudia makes a noise that's something between a sigh and a scream. "That's a lie!" she says. But the tape keeps rolling . . .

"Follow me," my voice on the tape says in a whisper. On-screen what you see is grass, pairs of bare feet, then the door, then the granite kitchen floor. "Shhh!" You hear the slapping of bare feet against the tile and our murmurings as the six of us pile into the pantry. On-screen, you can see through the slats of the pantry door as Claudia staggers in. She drops the keys on the edge of the counter where they go bouncing to the floor. "Shit," Claudia slurs drunkenly. "She's tanked!" I whisper.

I turn the tape off.

"Why didn't you show me this before?" Dad asks. His voice is a tangled snarl of rage. His face is knotted in fury with furrowed eyebrows and twisted lips.

"Why didn't you believe your only child?"

I turn to the other guests.

"Well, thank you all for giving me your attention. I hope you enjoy the rest of your evening. Dennis, I wish you the best of luck with your new client."

My heart is pounding furiously, but I try to remain as composed as possible as I exit the dining room. As soon as the door closes behind me, I race across the living room floor, up the plush carpeted spiral staircase, down the hall to my bedroom. I slam the door and lock it behind me and struggle to catch my breath. I thought I would feel good after showing the video, I thought I would feel triumphant, but instead I feel childish. I feel terrible.

There's a knock at the door. "Who is it?"

"Me," Owen says. I unlock the door and let him in. "That was quite a stunt you pulled."

I shrug. "I didn't fix the brakes on her Lexus or frame her for a crime she didn't commit."

"So this is your revenge?"

"I was just showing the truth. Claudia was the one who lied, remember?"

Owen nods.

"What's going on down there?"

"Claudia stormed off and Dad apologized for the

disturbance and asked the guests to stay for brandy and cigars."

"You think I'm a terrible person, don't you?"

"No, I don't think I would have done it this way, but I understand your anger."

I start crying, and Owen takes me in his arms.

Chapter 18

Monday morning, I get an e-mail from Gilda with a message that says, "Let me know what you think." I click on the URL and am brought to the Web site of the paper that Gilda writes for.

The New York Citizen
THE HOLLYWOOD HEROINE AND THE TECHNOLOGY
  TYCOON
By Gilda Lee

Once upon a time, a long time ago, there was an actress who made a small splash in the movies. Her name was Claudia Merrill, and she made a few mediocre movies, one big hit, and then a series of box-office bombs. Hollywood can be very forgiving or very unforgiving depending how much money can be made, and with Claudia Merrill's losing streak, bad attitude, weight gain, and losing battle with alcoholism, directors decided not to give her the benefit of the doubt. She disappeared from Hollywood's radar overnight.

Also doing a disappearing act was her money, and soon after that, her briefly wedded husband.

Claudia spent the next few years racking up

credit card debt to get plastic surgery in an attempt to rekindle her career. With her enhanced bust and reduced waist, Claudia managed to catch the attention of Hayden Van Horn, heir of the Van Horn publishing dynasty. Van Horn was a poor little rich boy with money to burn. And he'd been burning it for years on B-movies filled with tits and ass and low-caliber wannabe actresses. Claudia was grateful to be able to join their ranks.

Claudia starred in his next three movies. Then Van Horn decided that he'd mastered the art of squandering millions of dollars on movies no one ever saw. He turned to venture capitalism when a smooth-talking entrepreneur talked him into funding a telecom company. For once, it appeared that Van Horn had done something right. In just a few years, Avec Communications became one of the overnight successes the Information Age produced in droves.

And where was Claudia during all of this? A few months before Able Technologies gobbled up Avec, the penniless and unemployed former actress showed up at her sister's door. Her sister just happened to be married to the CEO of Able Technologies. Several months after Claudia arrived, living off the generosity of her sister, Ellen, driving expensive cars, and wearing expensive clothes despite having no job and no discernable talent, Ellen conveniently (for Claudia anyway) died in a questionable car accident. Mere months after the funeral, rumors are that Claudia and Gary Denner are engaged. Whether or not nuptials are in the future, something is clearly rotten in the Denner household: Claudia has remained living with her brother-in-law four months after the death of her sister. Sources tell me that Gary and Claudia were sleeping together well before the untimely death of Ellen Merrill Denner. Was Claudia still in contact with her old buddy Hayden Van Horn? Was Claudia the one who encouraged her lover, Gary Denner, to spend 50 million dollars on a company whose stocks are now worth less than half that? Incidentally, Claudia just happened to own thousands of dollars of Avec stock at the time of the buy out. Tell me, how does an unemployed former actress acquire thousands of dollars of one of the hottest stocks around? Claudia Merrill has apparently found the equivalent of the alchemical recipe for gold—how to make money without having to work for it or risk a single cent.

The column would probably have been forgotten by the general public except for one thing: Able's quarterly earning reports were announced the next day.

Fortune
BUSINESS BRIEFS
By Judy Riley
July 1, 2006

As for Able's much-awaited earnings: Able announced that it will sell off its web hosting division to shrink its debt load. Equity investors seemed pleased—the stock gained 87 cents to $36.84— but Moody's notes that it has placed all of Able's long-term debt on review for a possible downgrade.

Chapter 19

Every day I read the online newspapers hoping for word on Able, and soon enough I get it.

Fortune
TELECOM INDUSTRY FEELS FULL IMPACT OF DOWNTURN
By Steve Tyson
July 15, 2006

. . . Denver-based Able Technologies' stock has faltered significantly in recent months.

The task of restoring Able's glory falls to chairman and CEO Gary Denner. It won't be easy. Able's "overall quality of earnings has deteriorated, its level of behind-the-scenes financial engineering has increased, and its overall standing with the Street has sunk," wrote UBS Warburg analyst Jim Schneider in a recent report. Despite Denner's insistence that all is well, investors are hesitant to bid the company back up. Able now trades at around $31, down some 40% from its 52-week high.

One reason Denner has his work cut out for him is because Able's financials are as clear as a concrete wall. While Wall Street was once willing

to take the company's word on financial performance, it no longer is. And because Able gives analysts so little to work with, building independent
models is next to impossible.

Then there is the apparent defection by Able's
top brass themselves. According to analyst Jeff
Atchley, insider selling has been brisk—and stock
prices have been falling. While Able execs still
hold major portions of stock, Denner himself has
sold $35 million worth of stock in the last year
alone, calling into question the possibility of criminal insider trading . . .

I read these pronouncements with a curious sense of
detachment. Since I never see my father, I have no idea
how he feels about any of this. Also, I don't know enough
about the business world to know if what's happening is
catastrophic or just business as usual. I seriously doubt I
had anything to do with this, but it makes me worry
about my father. I leave messages with his secretary and
on his personal cell phone number, but he doesn't return
my calls.

After work, Owen and I pick up some Chinese carry-
out on our way to his place. When we get there, we find
Polly looking better than she has since she got fired.

"You're looking good," I say.

She smiles. "I got a call out of the blue from a New
York publishing house. They want to give me a job! The
pay is a little more than I was making, but of course the
cost of living will increase, so I think everything will equal
out in the end. It sounds like a great position. Maybe I
won't have the kind of control I had at *Local Color*, but
you know, who really needs the stress? Anyway, isn't it
thrilling?"

"Polly, it is incredible," I say. "I am so happy for you. Really. You have no idea."

The night of the slam poetry festival, Owen and I head to the Mercury Café after work.

The Mercury Café has a restaurant and a bar and an upstairs with a stage for performances like the contest tonight.

Anyone can sign up, so Owen does. He fishes a number out of a hat and learns that he's number seven out of twelve. Each person gets two minutes to perform. There are three judges. One of them, a petite woman with short black hair and tiny glasses, explains the rules. "If you go over the time limit, you're disqualified. The poets who aren't disqualified will be judged on two things: the audience's reaction—enthusiasm, responsiveness, thunderous applause—and the judges' whims." The audience laughs. "Now let's get started with a poet from our very own Denver, Colorado . . . "

I like the first few poets more than I expected I would. A black guy performs this poem that's as lyrical as any traditional poem and has such a compelling beat the audience is practically forced to clap along to it. His poem is about how Hispanics are soon going to surpass blacks as the largest minority, but they haven't even had a TV show since *Chico and the Man*, when blacks practically have the entire UPN, which is of course hilarious, since it's not like that's such a great thing, it's not like the UPN is known for its wonderful, high-brow programming. The rest of the poem is about what Hispanics can learn from black people's mistakes, like how black activists kept switching from Negro to black to African-American back to black and even the "N" word. "Make up your mind/

what your gonna fight for/Save your rage/for a battle that means more," he finishes. "Good night and God bless, y'all." He waves and takes a bow.

Another poet is a woman whose poem is about a pregnancy scare, and how she's been taking the birth control pills every day for three years, but her period didn't come and her fate depended on whether a pink line formed on the pregnancy test stick. The poem actually manages to be pretty funny, though she's obviously angry about the extra burden women have to deal with. She says that as they waited for the results, her boyfriend said, "Someday we'll want the test to come out positive." She said, "What's this *we* shit? This is not about *we*, this is about *me*, my womb, blue pills, and pink lines."

Owen gets up next. His poem is about how his girl-friend was beaten up by a group of thugs, how sometimes she just retreats into herself, into the pain of the memory. He describes the scar from where one of the guys cut his initials into her thigh with a shard of broken glass from a bottle of Cutty Sark. The bulk of the poem is about how he feels so powerless to help her, to help the pain go away. I don't realize until he's up there that I was nervous. For him not to embarrass himself? Or for me, because I don't want to witness him make an ass of himself? But I feel relief, and, strangely, pride because he's good, really good. Not just as a poet but as an entertainer. He is artic-ulate; you can hear the pain in his voice, you can see the pain on his face and in his eyes. I don't know if it's the gut-wrenching imagery or his voice or his eyes, but I start crying. I try to wipe the tears away, but then he says another line and they come right back. I glance quickly across the room to seem if I'm the only freak crying—I've been crying like crazy since Mom died, so maybe it's just that I'll cry at any excuse—but it's not just me, at least a dozen members of the audience are crying, too.

He says it has been years since the assault, but she still wakes up screaming from nightmares. Sometimes she breaks down during sex or even while doing the dishes. He ends by saying that time doesn't heal all wounds, some wounds just keep festering, letting out a little more poison each time.

I'm in awe of the way Owen expresses his emotions. It occurs to me as he talks that he is the polar opposite of my father. Not only does Owen not give a rat's ass for money or power, he doesn't hide from his emotions; he revels in them. He studies them, dissects them, and then gets up on stage and shares them with anyone who will listen.

The applause is powerful. I join with everyone else, clapping so hard my palms sting.

As Owen gets off the stage, a judge pulls him aside and whispers in his ear. Owen comes back and sits down next to me.

"That was amazing," I say, wiping the tears away, "really amazing. You're going to win for sure. You got about a quarter of the audience crying."

"I got disqualified. I was almost two full minutes over."

"You're kidding."

"No, but it's no big deal. It wasn't important to win, it's just cool to have people hear what I have to say."

"Jesus, what a pisser." I look over at the next poet on-stage, then look at Owen again. "Have you at least sub-mitted the poem for publication in a journal?"

"No. I will though."

"When?"

"Tomorrow at work?"

I nod my approval.

The black guy wins and the pregnancy-scare chick comes in second. The prizes are free beers, two for the winner and one for the runner-up. Most of the poets and the audience stay to hang out after the show. We go downstairs to the now mostly empty restaurant and push several tables together. We talk about movies, books, politics, the best place to get a cup of coffee in Denver, things like that. Several people stop by to tell Owen what a talented poet he is. A few people encourage him to compete in the slam poetry festival in Taos later this year and remind him to be sure to time himself before he gets up on stage.

No one talks about their big expensive cars, no one talks about where they "winter" or "summer," as if these were verbs. No one talks about designer clothes or who their interior designer is, and I can't remember the last time I had so much fun.

It's two in the morning when we leave the café, and I suddenly realize that I'm exhausted. This stupid having-a-job thing is really messing with my social life. Having to wake up at seven in the morning is sadistic bullshit.

"I had so much fun tonight," I tell Owen.

"Good, I did too."

"I'm so glad I got to hear one of your poems. It was really amazing."

"It's the first time I've ever performed it. I haven't even workshopped it yet."

"By 'workshop' you mean send it through the firing line of your peers through the writer's workshop?"

He nods. "Students and teachers. Sometimes they can be brutal but I've learned a lot from their feedback."

"Was it true? The poem? Was it about your ex?"

He nods but doesn't say anything.

I want to know everything: how old she was when it

happened, where she was, if she called the police after-ward, and if it went to trial. Instead I say, "Couldn't she get plastic surgery for the initials?"

He closes his eyes for just a moment, smiles sadly. "When we were together, we didn't have a lot of money. One night, I was out with some friends, and she stayed home and got very wasted, and she cut out a chunk of her thigh where the initials were. So she still has a bad scar there, but I mean, it's not like if she gets rid of the scar she's not going to remember what happened. Maybe she'll get plastic surgery someday, I don't know. I think about it sometimes. I wonder what she says when she gets a new boyfriend and he asks how she got the scar. I'm pretty sure she makes up a story about how she was bitten by a shark or how she fell out of a boat when she was in a swamp in Australia and wrestled with an alligator or some-thing. You'd believe her too. She has a way with telling stories."

We go home and make slow, gentle love. Thoughts of his ex linger in my mind. How much anger she must have had.

What happened to my mother was a different kind of betrayal. Is it more or less painful when the betrayal comes from strangers or from people you know and care about?

It's too late for me to help my mother, but I vow to do something in her memory to show her that although my love was imperfect, it was deep and profound and very, very real.

Chapter 20

Denver Post
BUSINESS BRIEFS
July 20, 2006

On Thursday Able Technologies slashed its financial projections for this year and next, outlining a conservative approach that includes 7,000 lay-offs from a worldwide staff base of 50,000 and a scaled-back rollout of high-speed Internet service. Additionally, they will sell their web hosting division.

"How are you holding up?" Owen asks me from his seat across from me. I'm doing my new morning ritual of reading papers online.

"I'm not really sure. This is all really weird. I feel all these competing emotions. Like I'm still mad at my dad, but I'm also scared for him. At the same time, I think if he has been lying about all this stuff, he should get some kind of punishment. Do you think I'm awful?"

"No, but I also think that even though you're angry with your father, you still care about him very much."

Annoyingly, he's absolutely right.

That night, we order a pizza and eat it in his room, washing it down with a few beers.

After dinner we make love. Owen relishes every touch. I'm the impatient one. I don't want slow, tender caresses. I want to fuck, to get sweaty, bodies slamming, breath heaving. I want to forget about my mother and my life. I roll Owen on his back and lose my mind a little as I'm on top of him. I feel a powerful sensation welling up within me. It scares me and I slow down, but then I want the feeling back, so I start going faster again.

When I come I nearly scream. It feels like my body has exploded—or maybe imploded, I'm not sure which. I just know that my heart rate is skyrocketing and my breath is jagged and every part of me feels quivery.

Owen smiles. I roll over on my back, stunned, and pull Owen on top of me. He doesn't last long.

He snuggles beside me and looks at me with that same pleased smile.

"Don't look at me like that. It's embarrassing!"

"I'm sorry. You're a beautiful, sexy woman, and you look particularly beautiful and sexy after you've had an orgasm."

I hide my face in my hands. "Come on, this is embarrassing."

"It's not. It's wonderful."

I peek out from behind my hands. "You know what's weird? I could feel it happening and I got scared and slowed down. Isn't that stupid? Why would I feel scared?"

"Anything that's new is scary. You do realize that we can't rest on our laurels about what happened. We have to practice. We want to be sure this wasn't a one-time thing. Practice makes perfect."

I affect a thoughtful expression. "Well, I guess if we *have* to . . . " He tickles me. "Ack!" I laugh, trying to squirm away from his tickling fingers. "Stop it! Cut it out!"

"I love you." He kisses my lips, my neck, the curve of my right breast.

I smile at him. I realize what he's just said but decide to take it the way you'd say, "Boy, I really *love* potato chips."

"I'm thirsty," I say.

He gives me a half smile. We both know what has been said and we both know I'm ignoring it. "I'll get us some water."

"You're my hero."

Over the course of the next couple of weeks, Owen and I practice and practice and practice. Owen doesn't say the "L" word again, and I sure as hell don't bring it up.

There are times when I think that I'm getting on with my life. Other times out of nowhere grief threatens to overwhelm me. No matter how many people are in my life who I love and who I know love me, I get these feelings of being completely alone in the world. At moments like those in particular, I feel the need to reach out to my friends as if to confirm that they aren't figments of my imagination.

I try calling my father to let him know I'm worried and thinking about him, but he doesn't call me back. Then I think, *you know what, screw you. Rot in prison for all I care.*

Most of the time I don't have an orgasm. I think we both feel a little frustrated, but Owen seems to take it more personally than I do.

We lie in bed naked; Owen seems heartbreakingly disappointed. "Owen, don't worry about it, really. I just need to figure out my body. It's not your fault."

He sighs and embraces me. I feel hot and—not trapped

exactly, but confined. Closed in. "I know. I just want you to be happy."

"I know."

"Do you know why I want you to be happy?"

"Because you care about me."

"I more than care about you."

Again I say nothing.

"So what happens at the end of the summer?" he says.

"What do you mean?"

"I mean what's going to happen to us?"

"I don't know, what do you want to happen to us?"

"I'd like to stay together."

"You mean do the whole long-distance thing? Date exclusively?"

"It'll only be for nine months. I'll graduate in May, and I was planning to move out to New York anyway . . . "

"Like move in with me?"

"Maybe, but I mean, whatever, we can play it by ear."

"I don't know. I don't know if I can handle being in a relationship right now."

"What do you mean? How could it have escaped your notice that you're *in* a relationship right now? You've been staying at my house for more than a month. We spend every second together." His voice is infused with an anger I've never heard coming from him.

"We never said this was some committed thing . . . "

"Helaina, don't you love me? I love you."

"I don't know. I don't know how I feel about anything."

"How can you make love to someone you don't love?"

"Christ Owen, it's friction, it's fucking, don't take everything so fucking seriously."

"I can't believe I'm hearing this. Helaina, what about

those poems I wrote you? Didn't they mean anything to you?"

"They were beautiful. They were well written."

"'Well written,' Jesus, why don't you just leave your literary review before you go? It wasn't about the *writing*, it was from the heart. I really care about you."

"I didn't mean—"

"Helaina, I wasn't kidding. I'd like you to go."

"What do you mean?"

"I mean if you don't want this relationship to go anywhere, what's the point? How can I possibly look at you day in and day out knowing that you don't feel the same way about me that I feel about you?"

"Where am I supposed to go?"

"I don't know, home maybe. To one of your eight million friends. To a hotel. I don't care."

"I can't believe you're kicking me out."

"I need some time to think. I just can't see you right now."

Owen puts shorts on and walks out his bedroom door, leaving me alone. He can't be serious. Jesus, fifteen minutes ago we were screwing in a hot, sweaty, loud way that would steam up any movie screen and now we're breaking up? This is crazy!

It's not my fault my emotions are a convoluted wreck.

I get dressed, pack up my things, and drive to a hotel for the night. Owen will get over this. Everything will go back to normal in the morning.

Except the next morning, Owen is not at his desk, and just before noon, Jill comes to my desk and asks if I know what's going on, why Owen would quit so abruptly.

"I thought he was more responsible than that."

"Owen quit? You're kidding."

"Is he upset about Polly? I mean I guess I can understand that . . . "

"I don't know. Yeah, that's probably what it is." It
sounds much too lame to say we had a fight last night. It's
better if she thinks this is about Polly.

"You'd think if he was going to resign in protest he
would have done it right after she was let go."

"You'd think."

"Oh well, he only had a couple more weeks till he was
going to go back to school anyway. How's the story on
that old-time band coming?"

"Ah, good, I'll be done today. I'll bring you a draft by
early this afternoon."

"Great."

As soon as Jill leaves I pick up the phone to call him,
then I decide that maybe he needs some time to cool
down. Anyway, I have no idea what it is I want to say to
him.

Chapter 21

Denver Post
BUSINESS BRIEFS
August 3, 2006

After Able Technologies significantly reduced its financial projections and after one industry analyst told Fortune that Able's accounting practices could amount to little more than "smoke and mirrors," Able's stock plummeted to a low of $23.10 on Friday—Able traded in the $30s and $40s earlier this year.

Able Technologies has been a nightmare of rising debt and credit concerns since its acquisition of Avec Communications, angering investors and inciting bankruptcy fears among employees.

One of Able's primary concerns is its debt load, which has mushroomed 42 percent to $27 billion since the merger.

Much of this debt was raised to support initiatives that have yet to produce monetary returns. Combined with the ongoing cost of Able's fiber-optic communications network, the bill was massive.

Chapter 22

Owen doesn't call me that day or the next. I just go home to my hotel and think. I think about how much I miss his hugs and kisses and touch and his laugh. I miss talking to him and being with him. But what I keep asking myself is, "Is he a man I can't live without? Can I imagine my life without him?" If the answers were "Yes" and "No," respectively, then I'd know I loved him. The problem is, I'm not sure *what* my answers are.

But no matter how many times I go over it all, I feel no closer to understanding anything. Part of me almost feels relief that we've broken up. How could this have worked as a long-distance relationship?

And of course I think about Dad. That, too, is scary. No matter what, my father is my father. I had thought that if he suffered a financial loss, a hit to his image and prestige, somehow this might make him realize that what really matters in life are the people you love. If Dad is learning anything from all this, I bet it's about how to avoid getting caught using illegal accounting procedures. Still, there is a part of me that clings to the hope that at some point he'll realize what he's done to Mom is wrong and he'll come to me—the last vestige of her—and want to make amends.

Fortune
By Steve Tyson
August 14, 2006

Talk of insider trading and a possible criminal investigation by the FTC plunged Able's stock to a four-year low of $6.40, and there is talk of bankruptcy. Independent consultants from Erickson Consulting are currently tasked with reviewing Able's books. According to Erickson employee Laura Kirkland . . .

Laura Kirkland? As in the Laura Kirkland that is Owen's sister? She must have been called back from her consulting job in Europe.

I finish reading the article and the quote from Laura, but I don't get any more information. Laura's quote is far too evasive to shed any light.

According to Erickson employee Laura Kirkland, "We are investigating every angle and hope to have some answers before the end of the fiscal quarter."

I try calling Dad. Again. It has to be the twentieth or thirtieth time I've called him in the last few days.

I alternate between leaving messages with his assistant, his private cell phone number, and Maria. I mix up the order of which number I call next, like I'll somehow miraculously stumble on the secret combination that will let me figure out a way to be able to talk to my father.

I can't go home. I seriously worry that Claudia could go postal on me and attack me with a kitchen knife or one of those pearl-handled tiny guns made specifically to fit in a woman's handbag.

The office seems so quiet without Owen around. I can't concentrate on work so I pick up the phone and call Maria.

"Hey M., it's me again."

"I haven't seen your father to be able to give him your messages, I swear. Reporters have been swarming around the house for the last several days, so he's been staying at a hotel, and even I don't know where. It's all very hush-hush."

"How about Claudia, is she around?"

"I haven't seen her for the last few days. I don't know where she is."

"How are you doing?"

"The reporters are a drag. A few of them managed to get over the fence and they completely ruined the gardenia bed. They are trampling all over the lawn, they are a menace, but we'll get through this."

"I'm sorry, M., I'll talk to you later, okay? Hang in there."

I get off the phone and Goatee Guy comes up to me and says, "Heard about your dad. That's really heavy. Are things cool? He's not like, going to go to jail or anything, is he?"

"I try to stay out of my dad's business as much as possible. I don't really know anything about it." All of which, sad to say, is true.

I feel relieved when my phone rings. "I should take this," I tell him. He nods and walks away. "Hello?"

"May I speak with Helaina Denner?"

"This is she."

"My name is Lucy Randall. I'm with the *Denver Post*. I wanted to ask you a few questions about the situation your father . . . "

"How the hell did you get my number?" Did Maria or someone else from the household staff let her know? Of course, journalists in the area keep tabs on the goings-on of the wealthy elite. I'd been getting bylines in *Local Color* under my mother's maiden name. Everyone knows Gary has a daughter named Helaina. It's not like Helaina is a common name. Damn. "I don't have anything to say. Goodbye."

I slam down the phone, my heart racing. I let voice mail screen my calls for the rest of the day. Over the next several hours nearly every coworker stops by to see if I have any inside information. I wasn't going to quit working at the magazine until August 20, about two weeks before school starts, but I decide at last that I can't take this, and I go to Amanda and tell her that I'm sorry for the short notice, but with all that's happening, I just can't continue working here anymore.

"I'm sorry to leave you in a lurch. Maybe I could freelance? I don't want you to be stranded with both Owen and me leaving."

"It's okay. We've been interviewing new interns for the fall. Maybe one of them can start a little early. Frankly, with everything that's going on with your dad, it's probably for the best. I know you've been going through a lot lately. You need to take care of yourself. We'll be okay."

"Are you sure?"

She nods.

"It's been a great experience working here. I learned a lot. I liked working for you."

She smiles warmly. "You're a talented writer, Helaina. You're a bright kid. When you're a big movie director, you'll give me an exclusive interview, right?"

"Of course."

"Good luck to you."

"Thanks. For everything."

I pack up my few things and straighten up my desk. I say good-bye to Amanda and Jill, but otherwise decide to skip the good-byes and do my best to sneak out unnoticed. I think my coworkers will understand.

I return to my hotel room. I'm only there a few minutes when I start to feel restless. I try to work on my screenplay, but the truth is, I'm not sure what it's about or what should happen next. I try to imagine the movie in my mind. I can envision the characters but not what they should do or say or why anyone would want to watch the damn thing. I know that my first attempt at a screenplay isn't going to be easy or effortlessly brilliant, but somehow in my head I imagine it to be a work of genius. The reality is rather humbling, yet it does surprisingly little to stop the fantasy that every word of a screenplay I'm not actually working on is brilliance itself.

Maybe I just need to go out and see a good movie. Maybe that will inspire me. I call up Hannah.

"Oh my God, how are you?" she asks.

"I'm okay."

"Aren't you scared?"

"Scared?"

"About your dad. He could lose everything. What if he goes to jail and you . . . you don't think you'd need to get a job for real?"

"Hannah, my father sold thirty-five million dollar's worth of stock this year alone. I think we'll manage."

"I hope so."

"Listen, do you want to do something?"

"I'd love to, babe, but I have plans with Todd. We're going hiking."

"Hiking?"

"It's when you walk outside in a thing called *nature*."

"Ha ha. Dan used to drag me out hiking all the time. I just never thought you were much of the outdoorsy type."

"I never used to be, but lately I've found that exercise and being outside recharges me."

"Have you been overtaken by alien forces? Who is the person I'm speaking to?"

"People change."

"I guess. Have fun."

"I will."

I try Marni next. When she answers, it's obvious she's been crying. "Marni, what's wrong?"

"I had a fight with Jake."

"About what?"

"He wants to have four kids, but I only want two. I just think four pregnancies is a lot to ask. I'm going to be a doctor. I'm just worried that I won't have time to be a good mother to four kids. Honestly, I'm not sure I can be a good enough mother to two."

This is what they are fighting about? Unbelievable. "I'm sure you guys will figure it out. Your parents did a pretty good job with you."

"But they only had one of me, don't you see?"

"Do you want to go out with me, get your mind off things?"

"Yes."

"What are you in the mood for?"

"Let's go to Brendan's and listen to some blues."

"Sounds good. I'll pick you up in an hour."

I pick her up and we drive down to the bar. It's early, but already the place is filled with smoke. At least we're able to get a table close to the stage. We'll have the perfect seats when the music starts. We order a pitcher of beer and two glasses of water. I want to pace myself and not get drunk.

"Okay, tell me everything," I say. I watch Marni down half her beer in a single sip. That's not her typical MO.

She shrugs. "I don't know. We were talking about our future. We've always talked about the kids we'll have one day. We've talked about how I'll wait until I've been practicing medicine for two years, but until today, we never talked about how many kids we'll want to have. I always assumed two. Two is the perfect number. But then he said he wants four. Four. We've never fought like we did today."

"Sweetie, it's going to be okay. You've got a while to figure this out."

"But what if he doesn't want to marry me? What will I do?"

"Let's not get crazy. You both need a few days to calm down. Maybe you could compromise and have three kids."

Marni pours herself another beer. "No. We both agree that odd numbers are no good."

"Sometimes you can't control these things, you know."

"I can't think about this right now. How are things with you and Owen?"

"Not good." I tell her what happened.

"You don't love him?"

"Honestly, I really care about him. I miss him a lot. But love? I'm just not sure."

"You always were emotionally constipated."

"What's that supposed to mean?"

"I mean you're guarded. I think you are afraid of really letting go and getting close to someone. I think you're afraid to really let yourself *feel* your emotions."

"All I have these days are emotions."

"But are you really dealing with them? Or are you trying to avoid what you're feeling?"

I have the urge to dump the rest of the pitcher of beer over her head. What the hell does she want from me? I'm doing the best I can.

The band gets up on stage, relieving me from the need to answer her. The singer is a broad-shouldered black man with a thick face and a bald, shiny head. The bar is dimly lit, but what lights it does have reflect in bright circles on his glossy forehead. His voice is deep and soothing and husky. I lose myself gratefully in the music.

Marni orders another pitcher of beer when I'm only on my second glass. I give her a concerned glance, but she ignores me.

The bar grows more and more packed until every table and chair is claimed and the dance floor is alive with bodies swaying to the music.

I'm feeling lightly, pleasantly buzzed when the band takes a break. I look over at Marni and realize she's trashed. I can't believe she could get so upset over how many children she may or may not have several years from now. I think she's so damn lucky to have such a clear idea of how her future is going to go. But I feel like a shitty friend that I obviously wasn't able to do a better job cheering her up. "Are you okay?" I ask.

"I have to go to the bathroom."

"Do you want me to come with?"

She glares at me. "I'll be fine."

"Okay, sorry."

Marni stumbles to the bathroom.

She's only been gone a minute when I hear a voice say, "Can I buy you a drink?"

I look up and see a handsome man with dark curly hair. He looks Italian. He's wearing a cream-colored shirt that has a stain on it and well-worn jeans. "Thanks, I'm okay."

"The music is great, isn't it?"

I nod. "You have the tiniest bit of an accent. Where are you from?"

"Rome."

"You're just visiting?"

"I'm a travel writer."

"Really? What a cool job. Who do you write for?"

"Have you ever heard of *Lonely Planet* guides?"

"Of course. You write for them? Wow. How long are you in Denver for?"

"Just till next week. I've been here all summer. I can't wait to get out of here."

I laugh. "Denver is no Rome, that's for sure. Where are you headed next?"

"I do a couple weeks in British Columbia, then I'm off to Thailand and Indonesia."

"That's great."

I look over at the bathroom door. There is no sign of Marni. It's too early to go searching for her, but it's been long enough to make me start worrying about whether she's okay.

"I've never been to those places," I say. "I've been to Europe though." After the words come out, I realize how very unimpressive this little tidbit of information is going to be to a European, especially a European who makes his living by traveling.

"How long were you there for?"

"A summer. Well, about two months."

"You need two months just to explore Rome."

"I'm sure you're right. I didn't have two months for Rome, unfortunately. I had about three days. I liked it though. Look," I say, looking at the bathroom again, "I'd like to talk to you more, but I'm a little worried about my friend. She's been in the bathroom for a long time. I want to check on her. Do you want to have a seat?"

He nods. "I'm Matteo." He extends his hand and I shake it.

"It's nice to meet you. I'm Helaina. I'll be right back."

I go to the bathroom and peer under the stall doors for Marni's size six feet. "Marni, are you okay in there? Marni? Can you open the door?"

The door swings open and I see Marni slumped against the side of the stall door, her shorts around her ankles.

"Are you okay?"

"I'm just resting."

"Come on. Let's get up."

I help her stand. She fumbles for her shorts. "Can you help me?"

Um, no, put your own damn clothes back on. "Lean on me. I won't let you fall."

With a great deal of effort and fumbling she manages to successfully get dressed. I help her wash her hands, and then I try to help her back out to the table. I'll just say goodbye to Matteo, and then I'll take Marni home.

"I can walk by myself!" she insists once we exit the bathroom.

"Are you sure?"

"Yesss!"

"All right." I let go of her and she sways a little. As I walk, I notice I have toilet paper stuck to the bottom of my shoe. I'm trying to covertly get it off when Marni tackles me so hard the both of us almost go tumbling down as she screams, "You have toilet paper on your shoe!"

Thanks. Very subtle. I smile at Matteo, who is grinning at our folly. "Matteo, it was really nice talking to you, but I need to take my friend home."

"Of course. It was nice meeting you."

I walk Marni out to the car. The second we get in she falls asleep, her head propped up against the passenger door, snoring loudly. I pull the seatbelt across her, click it closed, and drive her home.

After I drop Marni off, helping her get inside to her bedroom, I return to my hotel room feeling more sad than when I left to go out and have "fun."

I strip out of my clothes and wash my face and brush my teeth, then I climb under the covers with a heavy heart.

I need to get out of this funk. I need to be able to think clearly about Owen and my mother and my father and my life. To feel happy again, I just need to focus on the things that are good in my life: I'm in good health. I'm young. I have good friends. I have a nice, warm bed. It feels so good to nestle up in the fresh, clean sheets. Although I do miss my own feather comforter at home that is so soft it's like being wrapped in a cumulous cloud . . .

Oh drat, I'm already focusing on what I don't have. I have to focus on the positive.

Oh screw it. Being happy takes too much work. It's easier just to be sad. I don't have to do anything to feel sad. It just comes naturally.

In the morning, I try to work on my screenplay but don't get anywhere. My concentration is shot. Thoughts of Owen keep interrupting. I miss him. I really miss him. That's a good sign, isn't it? It means that I'm not an emotional black hole like my father.

The truth is, I'm pissed at Owen. He's acting so immature. Why isn't he calling me?

I think I love him. But I'm so confused. About everything. Is love supposed to be so hard, or is it just when love comes on top of a traumatic event it makes it more difficult than it's really supposed to be?

I bring my laptop to a café. It's a locally owned place filled with students and writers. It's the kind of place that encourages people to hang out. Unlike chain coffee shops that want you in and out as fast as possible, this café has a bookshelf filled with books to read and chess sets and board games for people to play. There are outlet strips all over the place for people to plug their laptops in and work for hours.

I get myself a large mocha with whipped cream. I'm still having trouble keeping down solid food, and while I admit that whipped cream and chocolate-flavored caffeine isn't the healthiest way to get calories, at least it will help keep me from disappearing completely. I try to really taste the chocolate and the sweetness of the whipped cream, but it's like my taste buds have been boarded up and shut down for the summer. Nothing really tastes like anything.

I sit down, open up my Final Draft software, and stare at the infuriating cursor blinking tauntingly back at me.

I'm strategizing my plot (i.e., staring off into space) when a man in his late forties stops in front of my table.

"What are you working on?" he asks.

"Hmm? Oh, I'm trying to write a screenplay."

"A writer! How wonderful." He nods at me. I smile. "War is a terrible thing, isn't it?"

I eye him, confused. Was that a logical transition in our conversation? "Um, yes."

"I have an article about the importance of peace in my car. I'll go get it."

Did I ask him to? It's like he thought we were having a conversation that we were not, in fact, having. He doesn't look crazy. He looks like Woody Allen—a thin, neurotic-looking man with glasses and thinning hair.

I return my attention to my computer, trying very hard to concentrate as if that will deter the strange man who has, for whatever reason, set his sights on me.

It doesn't work. He returns with a photocopy of an article from what I imagine must be some magazine. I glance at the single sheet of paper quickly. The title of the piece is "The Peace Tree" and the article is by a man with an East Indian name that I don't recognize.

"I'll write down my name and number," the strange man says. He takes the sheet of paper and writes his name and number at the bottom. "Call me sometime. Maybe we can go to a movie."

Is he asking me out on a date? Doesn't he realize that he's at least twenty years older than I am and not remotely attractive? How could this have eluded his notice? Men are such fascinating creatures.

"Um, thanks," I say, because I don't know what else to say. "I should get back to work."

"Sure, sure." He stands but doesn't make a move to leave. He just looks at me. "What's your name?"

"Helaina."

"What a beautiful name. How unusual."

I shrug.

"Call me," he says again.

I smile without conviction and he leaves. I turn my attention once again to my manuscript, but I can't lose myself in a made-up story because I have no idea what story it is I want to tell. Everyone around me seems so industrious and deep in thought. I kill as much time as I can pretending to be busy.

"Hey! Helaina!"

"Oh my God! Matteo! How are you? Have a seat." I gesture to the empty chair across from me.

"Thank you." He pulls the chair out and sits down. "How's your friend?"

"I'm pretty sure she'll live."

"What are you working on?"

"I want to write a screenplay. In my mind it's very moving and funny and beautifully written. Unfortunately, in real life I've only written about twenty pages and they are the worst twenty pages in screenplay history."

"What's it about?"

"Well, that's actually my problem. I don't have a clue."

He laughs. "That'll slow you down."

"Actually, I'm very glad I bumped into you. You're a wonderful distraction. Tell me all about Rome."

We talk about Italy and America and the differences between our cultures for maybe half an hour. Then he says, "Do you think you'll go to Italy again?"

"Oh sure."

"If you'd like to hear all my suggestions for the best places to go, I'd be happy to tell you over dinner."

Matteo is hot as hell. I know he's leaving for British Columbia any second now, but even a chaste dinner seems like cheating on Owen. But I don't even know what's going on with Owen.

"Is something wrong?" Matteo asks with a sexy, flirty smile.

I realize that regardless of what's going on with Owen and me, I can't go out with anyone else until I figure it out. "Oh . . . um, I'm actually sort of seeing someone."

"I understand. I'll let you get back to work. Good luck with your screenplay, my *bella* Helaina."

"Thanks. Have fun on your trip."

"Always. What's the point otherwise?"

After Matteo leaves, I wonder why I turned him down. He's gorgeous and it would have been fascinating to spend the night talking about the world with a guy who has seen a good portion of it firsthand. My turning him down means I really care about Owen. Right?

Why are my feelings such a mystery to me? I wish they made a user's manual for the human heart. I could really use some guidance.

Chapter 23

I wake up at seven the next morning. I try valiantly to fall back asleep, not because I'm tired—I'm not, I went to bed at ten last night—but because I don't know what to do with all the hours in the day. There are too many of them. I don't know how to fill them.

Suddenly, without work and without Owen, with just these long, long days in which I have nothing to do but think, my depression deepens. It swallows me. I've been in a dark fugue state since Mom died, but right now, in this hotel room, it swells up with a new intensity. What can you do when your mind betrays you so much that you want to defy all laws of survival and kill yourself? It's insanity.

Isn't time supposed to make things better? But I'm only feeling worse.

I look around my room—the creamy walls, burgundy carpeting, comfortable chairs in burgundy with ivory flowers. I have the thick curtains open to let in the sunlight, in hopes that the light will brighten my mood. Here in my room, I can pretend like the outside world doesn't exist. I don't care if my father's business is crumbling. I don't care what's going on in the world.

I decide that I need to get out or I'll go insane, so I go

to the amusement park thinking that I could use some amusement. Then I realize amusement parks are actually rather sad places when you're by yourself. There is no one to talk to as you wait in line to go on the rides and almost all the rides are set up to seat two people. It is fun to people watch, though—the teenage boys gripped in a fever of testosterone; the skinny teenage girls in braces and too-short shorts, their accessories a riot of pink and glitter, setting the women's movement back thirty years or so; the adorable little white girls with short, prickly ponytails sticking straight out of their heads like straw on a scarecrow; the adorable little black girls with their hair full of round plastic balls and plastic barrettes shaped like ducks or butterflies, making them look like little Christmas trees.

I wait in line for a roller coaster and I see a couple up ahead of me who are all over each other. They kiss and have their arms linked around each other's backs and they are pressed up close together. Every now and then they turn and hug and kiss deeply, passionately, their pelvises smashed up against each other. They are young—about my age. I wonder if this is their first love. She has an impressive mane of shocking red hair. He looks a little like Owen, and it twists my heart up to watch him with another woman, even though I know it's not Owen.

I wonder what he is doing. I wonder if he's okay.

Do I love him? I know I miss him. I think about him constantly. If I were going to fall in love with someone, Owen would certainly make sense. He's kind and smart and sexy . . .

"Oof!" It happens in a flash. At first all I know is that a body rams into me with painful force, sending me sprawling to the ground where I catch myself with my hand.

The skin on the palm of my right hand ignites with red-hot pain as it's shaved across the pebbly asphalt.

"Are you okay?" someone asks.

I sit on my butt and turn to inspect my hand, which is covered in blood. Bits of my shredded skin curl up like ribbons. I look up to see a group of abashed-looking teenage boys, and then I understand what happened. One of them pushed another one right into me, but I was the one who took the dive.

Why did I leave my stinking hotel room?

"I'm really sorry," one of the boys says.

"It was his fault," another says.

"Are you all right?" the voice asks again. It's a girl who is maybe my age or a little older. She has a young child with her.

"Um, I'm sure I'll be okay. I just need to get cleaned up."

"Here, I've got a travel thing of rubbing alcohol in my purse. Give me your hand."

"You carry rubbing alcohol with you? Are you a boy scout in training?"

"No, I'm a mother. But we follow the same motto about always being prepared."

I stand up and extend my hand. She pours the alcohol over it, which sends fiery sparks of agony through my arm. Fortunately the worst of the pain ebbs quickly.

"I think you're going to be okay. It doesn't look like the cuts go very deep. I'm Abby, by the way."

"I'm Helaina."

Abby takes three normal-sized Band-Aids from her purse and puts them on to cover the worst of the cuts on my hand.

"I had a girlfriend who was drinking and she tripped on some railroad tracks and cut her hand," Abby says.

"Apparently on railroad tracks there are all these chemicals and some of the chemicals got into her bloodstream. She got blood poisoning and was out of work for six weeks."

"You're kidding."

She shook her head. "About a year ago, I fell from a stool that was just six inches high but I landed on my hand just so and broke my wrist. I had to have surgery. I was out of work for six months. They had to shave the bone in my wrist."

"Oh! Ouch!"

"So my point is, I think you're lucky. You'll be okay."

"I hope so." Although now I'm wondering if maybe there are some chemicals that I can't see that are slowly creeping through my veins and by this time tomorrow I'll be on my deathbed, thrashing around in a fevered sweat as my organs shut down one by one. Were her little anecdotes supposed to cheer me up? Because if so, it didn't work.

"Well thanks for the on-the-spot Florence Nightingale treatment. Can I buy you and your daughter some I-C-E C-R-E-A-M or something?"

Abby's daughter begins jumping up and down, clapping her hands. "Ice cream, ice cream, ice cream!"

"Oh, gosh, sorry, I didn't think kids that small could spell. Are you raising some kind of prodigy?" I say.

"Children learn how to spell key phrases young. It's like how a dog can only understand words like 'walk' and 'food' and 'treat.'" She laughs. "Anyway, thanks for the offer. That's nice of you, but you don't have to. Really, it was no trouble."

"Ice cream!" the little girl cries.

"I'm really sorry," I say again.

"It's no problem. We can get ice cream."

"Yeah!"

We get out of line for the roller coaster and head for the nearest ice cream stand.

"What's your little one's name?"

"I'm not little!" the girl declares in a fever pitch of indignation.

Abby laughed. "This is Morgan, my little angel. Are you a student?"

"I study film at NYU. Are you?"

Abby nodded. "I'm going to college part time. It's not easy with Morgan and a full-time job, but I'll be done with school next year and it will all have been worth it."

"Can I ask you how old you are?"

"Twenty-three."

"How old is Morgan?"

"She's four."

I order three DoveBars and struggle to get some cash out of my wallet using only one hand.

"Can you help me?" I ask. Abby helps me put my change back in my wallet, my wallet back in my purse, and my purse back on my shoulder.

"I see a table. Mommy, I see a table!"

"Okay, why don't you run and save it for us and we'll be right there."

When Abby was my age three years ago, she was caring for a one-year-old infant. It's amazing to me. In a world where you can trip and get blood poisoning that keeps you in bed for six weeks or you fall and need surgery to have your wrist bone shaved, the task of keeping such a tiny human alive and healthy seems nearly insurmountable.

Abby and I sit at the table with Morgan, whose face and shirt become almost instantly covered in ice cream. As I watch Abby wipe off Morgan's face with a tiny square of a napkin, I remember my own mother doing the same thing to me. The memory is so sharp and acute it feels like a punch to the stomach. Grief suddenly threatens to overwhelm me.

"Well, thanks for helping me out with my hand," I say. "I should really get going." I clear my throat in an attempt to keep from crying.

"Are you sure you're okay? You didn't finish your ice cream."

"Yeah, you know, I'm actually not that hungry. Thanks. Thanks again. Morgan, it was nice meeting you."

"Thank you for the ice cream. Morgan, what do you say?"

"Sank you."

"No problem. You guys have fun, okay?"

Even though I've only been at the park for an hour and haven't gone on a single ride, I go back to the hotel.

I lie in the bed and the pain rips through me. I feel like my skin has been flayed off and every nerve ending is so hypersensitive that even the cool breeze of the air conditioner is excruciating. I feel like those characters on the *X-Files* when they were poisoned by the alien creatures and their eyes and bodies filled with that black oily substance. I feel like this dark poison is overtaking every cell in my body.

I start to cry and in moments the crying explodes into racking sobs. I cry and cry, and I'm not even totally sure what it is I'm crying about.

I think of Mom when I was little and I think of the parties, weddings, and other events that will happen without her. I think of my dad and the way he ignored my movie and the way he didn't even listen to my side of the story about the car but just threatened to ship me off to rehab. I think of Owen, of his poems, of the way he looks when he's sleeping, of his grin. I can't lose him. I can't.

I look at my mother's journal and flip through the pages. Her final thoughts, trapped on paper, because she didn't have the courage or the strength to say them out loud.

All these thoughts. They won't stop tormenting me. They flash through my mind, and as soon as I push one away, another takes its place.

I wish I had been a better daughter. I wish I could say that I was a whiz on the piano. A child math prodigy. A contender for the Olympic Gold in gymnastics.

I suffered through countless hours of piano lessons and ballet classes, but I never showed the least bit of promise. Mom did her best to make me well rounded and despite having every advantage I'd turned out to be hopelessly average.

I don't know how long it is that I'm crying, but when I finally stop, I'm utterly exhausted. I fall asleep with damp eyes, tears caught in my eyelashes.

I dream that Owen and I are in New Zealand, in its plush green forests alight with brilliantly colored exotic flowers and birds. Both of our families are there. Mom and Dad are there. Owen's father and mother are there. (I've never met his parents, obviously, and I don't see them in the dream, I simply know they are there.) I have no idea why both our families are there, some of whom have traveled all the way from the dead to go across the globe to New Zealand. All of us are in a Jeep, driving around, seeing the beauty of the country. Then we return to the hotel. Owen and I go to our room, close the door, and by some unsaid mutual agreement, go straight to the bed and make love. I'm not a sex-dream person usually. I think I've had maybe two somewhat sexy dreams before, but in them, I never did anything more than kiss some guy—at least I don't remember anything more. But in this dream, the sex is explicit—slow, sensual, wonderful.

When I wake up, I feel this wonderful sense of calm, something I haven't felt in months.

I lie in bed in that groggy daze before awakening and replay the dream in my mind. I wonder what it means. Hannah would know. I sit up and grab my cell phone.

"Hello?" she says.

"Hey babe, it's me."

"What's up?"

"I had a dream."

"Uh-huh. Give me details."

I sit back down on the bed, settling in to get comfortable. "I dreamed Owen and my family all went to New Zealand. Both Mom and Dad were there, and both of Owen's parents were there even though they are dead. We all drove around together, looking at the beautiful country, then we came back to the hotel. Owen and I went back to our hotel room and made love, and it was awesome. I never have sex dreams, and this one was really detailed and drawn out. Isn't that weird? That both our families take us halfway around the world, just so Owen and I can get some? That our parents would return from the dead so we could do it? So what does it mean?"

"Is something wrong between you and Owen?"

"How did you know that? I'm actually staying at a hotel."

"You're kidding. What happened?"

"Owen was talking about commitment, about how he'd like to do the long-distance thing until he moved to New York after graduation, which he was planning to do anyway. I said I wasn't ready to commit, and he sort of wigged and kicked me out, telling me he needed space to think."

"Why aren't you ready to commit? I've never seen you as into a guy as you are with Owen. He's cute, he's nice, what gives?"

"Han, my mom just died, I can't think straight, I can't plan on what I'm going to have for lunch today, let alone how I'm going to feel ten months from now when he graduates."

"I don't buy it."

"What do you mean you don't buy it?" I say, filled with a sudden flash of anger that I have to defend myself.

"I think you're scared. You've never felt this way about a guy and you're freaking out. It's the whole male-commitment thing, except, you know, you're a girl."

"That's a load of shit. What about Dan?"

"You didn't love Dan. You certainly never looked at Dan the way you look at Owen. What I think is that your dream is about your parents trying to tell you that you are putting up all these barriers to your happiness. Beauty and happiness are all around you. Your parents want you to see the world, they want you to love and be loved, they want you to stop feeling sad all the time."

I think her reading of the dream is pretty far-fetched, but I like the idea that my mother can still visit me, even if it's in my dreams, and give me advice, show me the way.

I don't say anything for several seconds. "You really think so? Maybe you should consult one of your books."

"Babe, your dream was not as weird as you think. It's pretty common. Travel is an obvious metaphor for free-dom and change, not just change in your surroundings but in your attitude. And sex is obviously a sign of love and wanting to be close to someone. And as for your mom coming back? You miss her. You want her back. It's not a big mystery."

"Maybe," I say, the idea growing on me. "Thanks, Han."

"You know I'm always here."

She was right. I did know she was always there for me.

"Let's get together soon," she says. "This disappearing act of yours is getting old."

"Sure. Later."

I hang up the phone and lie down again. I look at my mother's journal.

Just now, I wish my mother had been buried after all so I had some physical place where I could visit her grave. I really need to talk to her.

Wait. There *is* a place I can talk to her.

I slip on some clothes and bring my mother's journal with me. I go to the parking garage and get the Viper and drive the hour and a half to Rocky Mountain National Park. On the drive, I feel this sense of urgency and purpose, though I have no idea what it is I want to say to my mother or what I will accomplish by going to the mountains where her ashes were released.

The road gets progressively windier as I get close to the mountains, and I have to slow down to 30 miles per hour, which seems so slow it's like I'm not even moving at all.

At last I get to the edge of the park. My ex, Dan, was a big hiker, and he knew all the trails here that weren't on the maps. Even though I'm not much of a hiker, I remember that this path was particularly beautiful.

The first part of the trail is easy and I start jogging, listening to the leaves crackle beneath my feet. I go faster and faster until I'm in a full-blown sprint. Out of nowhere,

I start crying. The tears blur my vision and I can't see the trees or the view of the mountains.

I run faster, as if I can somehow run away from all this pain and sorrow, from all my mistakes and disappointments, from this all-encompassing grief.

The trail gets progressively steeper and my lungs ache, so I slow down to a fast hike, battling to catch my breath. My palms are so sweaty I almost drop Mom's journal.

It takes about an hour to get to the waterfall, but even though my lungs hurt and my leg muscles burn with exhaustion, I welcome feeling physically drained. I've been mentally drained for so long, this feels strangely good.

The waterfall pours into a small, emerald green lake, and I sit on a boulder and listen to the cadence of the falling water. Mom would have loved this. She would have loved to paint this. The lush green trees reflecting in the lake; leaves floating delicately on its surface.

The tears start again, flooding out of me like the waterfall. I try to speak, my voice husky from tears and fatigue. "Mom. This. Hurts." I take the back of my hand and try to brush away the veil of snot and tears. "But you know, Mom, I can't do what you did. I can't stop living and stop feeling. There's this guy, Mom. You'd like him. He's really great, but, but I . . . I've been scared to love him." I let out a choked laugh. I laugh because it's so damn obvious. It's. So. Damn. Obvious. "It's scary, loving, because the people we love can up and die on us without warning.

"I wish I could go back. I wish I could spend more time with you. I miss you so much. So much." My voice cracks with the intensity of my pain; I miss my mother and I want her back. I feel the weight of so many mistakes, so many opportunities thrown away. It's so unfair—it's so unfair that she was taken from me when she was so young. When I am so young and still need so much mothering, so much guidance, so much love.

"The thing is, Mom, I will never forget you, but I need . . . I need to let you go." I clamp my hand over my mouth reflexively when I let out a strangled sob, then I sniffle back the tears and throw the journal into the lake. I watch the water ripple where it landed, sinking deep into the water's depths, taking Mom's final pains and mangled dreams away.

I finally gain control of my voice. "I will never forget you, Mom. But I need to let you go."

Chapter 24

"Hello?" Owen answers.

"Hey stranger."

He doesn't say anything for a moment, but he doesn't hang up either. "What is it?" he says at last.

"I've been thinking." I chew on my lower lip for a moment, trying to think of the right words to say what I want to say. "For the last several days I've been hiding out in this hotel room. I'm hiding, just like Dad has spent his whole life hiding in his work and Mom hid by playing a charade of living the perfect life. But nobody was fooled. What did staying in a sham marriage get her? It got her miserable, that's what. Here's the thing. I don't know much about love. No, that's not exactly true. I know I love my mom and Hannah and Marni and Kendra and Lynne." I pause, trying to drum up courage that doesn't come. I force myself to stumble on anyway. "I know I love you," I say quietly. I realize I'm holding my breath, like I'm expecting the ground to swallow me up for saying these words. I exhale and the words come pouring out of me in one long breath, "I'm pretty sure I'm going to mess up this relationship somehow, but I mean, if you're willing, I'd like to try. It seems silly not to try."

"Yes, it does," he says simply, calmly.

"Yes it does what? Seem silly not to try?"

"It's downright ridiculous."

"Yeah?"

"I've really missed you. I've been waiting for you to come to your senses. The way I feel about you—that doesn't happen every day."

"There's one small problem."

"What?"

"If I date a guy who is the polar opposite of my father, how am I going to work out all my father–daughter issues? I'm supposed to find a guy like my father and try to change him and of course you can't change someone so I'll always be disappointed and spend my life trying. So what am I gonna do?"

"I guess you'll just have to have a healthy, fulfilling relationship."

"Call the press! Headline news!" I smile.

"I love you, Helaina."

"I love you, too. I want to see you. Can I take you out to dinner tonight?"

"There's nothing I'd like more in the world."

When I see Owen, a light, airy feeling fills me. I feel happier than I have in months. He looks so good. His eyes, his smile—he's gorgeous. I hug him and he hugs me tightly, for a long time, crushing his strong body into mine. It feels so good, I can't help but smile. It feels so good to smile.

I take Owen to one of my favorite restaurants.

"Ever been here before?" I ask him as the waiter hands us our menus.

Owen shakes his head.

"You're in for a treat."

"It looks good."

"Do you want to split the goat cheese salad?"

"Sure."

The waiter puts down a basket of bread and an olive spread, and I take a roll and begin devouring it. It doesn't stick in my throat. I realize that I'm ravenous.

I eat one roll after another, and when our salad comes, Owen has to fight for his share. It's all I can do not to just shovel it in.

"Hungry?" Owen asks, smiling.

"Famished."

"Good. You need to put some weight on."

I nod, swallowing a big bite of salad. "I know."

"How have you been?"

I take a moment between bites. "Well, the last couple of weeks really sucked. But I think I'm better now."

"Good."

"What about you?"

"The last couple of weeks pretty much sucked," he agrees. "But I'm better now."

"Is your sister back in town?"

He nods. "She's part of the consulting firm that's supposed to figure out whether Able cooked the books. I've barely seen her. She's working around the clock."

"Did she enjoy her time in Europe?"

"It sounds to me like she just worked while she was there. She loves her work. I kind of get the idea she's getting a charge out of working on Able. It's such a big news story."

"Mmmm," I agree.

My meal comes. Grilled vegetables with a cheese sauce, polenta, and rice. I eat every last bite of it and wash it down with two glasses of wine. I'm stuffed. Painfully so. But it feels good to be able to eat again, to be able to taste again.

I reach across the table and take Owen's hand. We look into each other's eyes and smile.

Chapter 25

After dinner, Owen and I go back to his place. "I forgot to tell you," he says as he unlocks the door. "Polly sold the house. She's closing on the place a few days before I leave for school. I'm going to drive with her in a U-Haul to New York."

"Yeesh, that'll be a long drive."

"I bought a bunch of books on tape to entertain us. We'll manage. You're welcome to join us."

"I'd rather stick a fork in my eye, but thanks. You're a good stepson, Owen."

Boxes are everywhere. The paintings and photos have all been taken down.

Owen and I make slow love. I don't have an orgasm. I don't really understand the capricious whims of orgasms just yet, but with practice I imagine I'll understand more, and I'm all for practicing as much as necessary.

I feel so damn happy and at peace lying here in Owen's arms. I feel blessed.

The ring of my cell phone wakes me up the next morning. I answer it quickly. Owen shifts in his sleep but doesn't wake up.

"Hello?" I say quietly as I scurry out to the hallway to avoid waking Owen.

"Hey, how are you?" Marni says.

"Good. I'm at Owen's."

"That's great. So everything is good between you two?"

"Everything is great."

"Come out shopping with me and Hannah today."

"I don't know . . . "

"Come on. You need to buy clothes for school. We'll just go shopping for clothes and shoes and handbags and makeup and stuff. Just the essentials. Anyway, it's going to be months before the three of us can hang out again."

"Yeah, okay, you're right."

A few hours later, Hannah, Marni, and I go to Park Meadows Mall. People shouldn't recognize me—my picture has hardly been in the papers at all—but I still feel like people are staring at me and saying things behind my back. I know I'm just being paranoid, but I can't help myself.

We're there about an hour, and Hannah has already spent $2,000 on a handful of items, which is pretty impressive considering none of the clothes or shoes she buys covers more than a few inches of skin. That much money would keep both Kendra and Lynne with food, entertainment, and a roof over their heads for an entire month, and Hannah has shelled it out in a single hour.

Marni has spent about $800 on more sensible items.

I haven't been able to buy myself anything yet, and it's driving Hannah nuts. I eye this one black shirt, and Hannah encourages me to buy it.

"But I already have like twenty black shirts," I say.

"But you don't own this one."

"I guess I'm not really in the shopping mood."

"Why don't you try getting that shirt in another color? You wear too much damn black."

"I don't know."

"Red would look good on you."

"Maybe, but I'm just too skinny right now. I'll buy more clothes when I've put some weight back on."

"You promise?"

"I promise."

"Speaking of putting on weight, can we stop and get something to eat? I'm famished," Marni says.

We go to the food court and get sandwiches and chips from a deli.

"So Hannah, are you and Todd going to keep seeing each other?" I ask.

"No. The truth is, I was getting pretty bored with him. I'm glad he's going back to Chicago and I'm going back to school. This way we can leave on good terms instead of having to do that awful breaking-up thing."

"Well, I guess it's good that there won't be any tears."

As we talk, we glance around and people watch. A mall brings together such an intriguing mix of people, and the three of us eat our lunch and watch the moms with their kids and the boyfriends and the girlfriends as if we're watching the monkey exhibit at the zoo.

"My God. There has never been a better example of why dentists are important," Hannah says, tilting her head to her right. We look in the direction she's "pointing" and there, sure enough, is a woman with a severe underbite and the most crooked teeth I've ever seen.

I'm about to say something bitchy when I catch myself and remember *this is not the kind of person I want to be. This is not the way I want to lead my life.*

"I'm leaving for school on Thursday," I say instead.

Hanna nods. "I leave Saturday."

"I take off next Tuesday."

"I'm going to miss you guys."

"I'm going to miss you, too," Marni says.

"Come on, let's not get all mushy," Hannah says, then, rolling her eyes, adds, "I'll miss you, too."

Owen and I spend every free moment of our last few days together. I leave the morning before Owen and Polly are going to drive to New York. His plans are to drive her across the country and move her in, and then fly to Chicago where a friend will pick him up and drive him the four hours to Iowa City. Owen drives me to the airport. He takes me to the passenger drop-off area, opens the trunk, and gets my suitcase out for me. Then we stand there, me studying the ground, unsure what it is exactly that I want to say.

"I can fly you out to New York any weekend you can get away," I say. "I need to put my inheritance to good use. Anyway, you should get to know New York before you decide for sure to live there."

"If you're there, I'm sure I'll love it."

"I'll miss you desperately."

"I'll e-mail you all the time and call you whenever I can."

"Oh! That reminds me." I take my backpack off my shoulder and open it up, pulling out a small box that I'd wrapped in shiny red paper and a red ribbon.

"I feel terrible," Owen says, cringing. "I didn't get you anything."

"This gift is really more for me than it is for you."

He gives me a curious look and unwraps the gift. "A cell phone?"

"You have like a zillion anytime minutes and free calls after seven and on weekends."

"I can't accept this."

"Owen, it just makes sense. This way we can call each other all the time and it will hardly cost a thing. Again: inheritance. Don't worry about it."

"Thank you, Helaina."

"I love you, Owen."

"I love you."

We hug, tightly. I can feel the tears welling up in me so I break away and clear my throat. "Have a good trip to New York. Call me as soon as you get there."

"I will. Have a safe flight."

I look at him one last time, and then I turn and go.

Chapter 26

It feels good to be back in New York and to see Kendra and Lynne again, but from the moment I get there I walk around with a constant ache in my heart. It sounds cliché but that's how it feels—a physical manifestation for how much I miss Owen.

Even though Owen and I e-mail constantly and call each other every other day, it's just not the same thing as being able to see him.

I start working on my movie script again. It's going in a direction I hadn't expected. Instead of "Clare" and "Gaven" being these evil monsters, the movie is about "Elaine." In the beginning of the film, she's depressed. She's trapped in an unhappy marriage and an unhappy life. She begins painting as a way to fill the many long hours of her day. One painting is of a woman dancing at *Carnaval* in Rio, smiling broadly; another is of a woman hiking in the mountains; another is of a woman drinking a cappuccino at an outdoor café in France as she paints. When Elaine finishes the last one, she finally sees that all three women in her paintings are her. It gives her the strength she needs to leave her husband and become the women she paints.

Every morning I start my day by reading the business

section of the newspaper. It's funny, I spent my whole life turning my nose up at business, thinking that the corporate world is something a person would find herself in only if she couldn't do something worthwhile, like be an actress or a writer or a photographer or an artist. But I don't know, this stuff is better than soap operas. All these underhanded goings-on and nefarious double dealings, I'm kind of getting into it.

Denver Post
MELTDOWN FOR ABLE TECHNOLOGIES
By Alison Peterson
October 1, 2006

Able Technologies, once held up to MBA students as the quintessential model of how to build a successful company, now may make the textbooks again—this time as a cautionary tale.

In the last five years, Able has spent $15 billion to build a worldwide network of high-speed Internet and telephone lines and has yet to find enough customers to make the network profitable.

To cover up their losses, it now appears that Able used creative accounting techniques. According to Senator Tina Simon, D-Vermont, "Able's books have been so cooked they are little more than grime and ash."

The New York Times
October 18, 2006

Able technologies filed for Chapter 11 bankruptcy yesterday, in what may be the biggest collapse in the history of corporate America.

Thousands of employees lost their jobs, their savings, and much of their retirement accounts. Able, like many businesses, had a stock-matching program for its 401k program. Employees would have, say, $50 a month deducted from their paycheck every month to buy Able stock, and Able would match it with another $50. Because all the money went to Able stock instead of diversifying the fund, all that money is gone.

Some employees are making light of the fall of the telecom giant, selling t-shirts that say "Able— Isn't" and mocking Able's "See where you can go" tagline with one of their own, "See yourself go to the unemployment line."

Other employees are having a tough time seeing the humor in the situation.

"I feel betrayed," said Sheila Wheeler, a programmer from Aurora, Colorado. "I worked 50- to 60-hour weeks for ten years for them, and now I have no job, no health insurance, and no retirement savings. I've got two kids to feed. I don't know what I'm going to do."

Fortune
THE FALL OF A COMMUNICATIONS GIANT
By Steve Tyson
October 18, 2006

When I began working on the story that would ultimately call into question Able's valuation, I interviewed CEO Gary Denner over the phone, asking what I thought were standard questions. I simply wanted to understand the company's complex

earnings statement, yet Denner told me I was being belligerent and argumentative and hung up
on me.

In the wake of Able's stunning collapse, it appears I wasn't distrustful enough. None of us was.
No one was calling into question the financial
sleight of hand that left shareholders with worthless stock and employees without savings, jobs,
or pensions.

Senator Tina Simon, D-Vermont, isn't going to
accept Able executives' version of the story. In
her eyes, the time for trust is over. She's calling for
a congressional investigation. "Able didn't have
to lie outright, they just obfuscated the truth with
extremely complex financial reports. But they probably lied, too. That's what we're going to find out."

BusinessWeek
October 18, 2006

Able's bankruptcy may have wiped out most of
the retirement savings of most of its workers. But
one thing it didn't take away were the pensions of
its most senior executives. Financial filings disclose
that CEO Gary Denner used a private partnership
to protect millions of dollars' worth of executive
pension benefits . . .

The New York Citizen
THE PLOT THICKENS
By Gilda Lee

With reports that Able Technologies is taking a
beating, thanks in part because of its acquisition

last year of the debt-ridden Avec Communications, speculation is rising about the role Claudia Merrill may have played in persuading her sister's husband, her alleged lover, CEO Gary Denner, to purchase the company from one of Claudia's old Hollywood chums, Hayden Van Horn.

Claudia's gifts for persuasion are many. Despite having no journalistic background or writing experience to speak of, Claudia managed to swing a gig as a columnist in the upscale Colorado publication *Local Color*. Said one editor who worked with her, "She's essentially illiterate. Every month she'd call in with a few haphazard ideas stolen directly from the pages of *Vogue* or *Mademoiselle* and it would be up to us staff writers to construct a cogent column. Yet it was her pretty face on the page with her byline and her bio pimping for her alleged company. I can't say I'm sorry that the truth about Claudia Merrill has finally come to light."

Claudia had considerable stock in Avec Communications, which, for a time, would have made her very comfortable indeed. Now, those stocks are worthless.

People
FOX CANCELS *STAYING POWER* IN WAKE OF ABLE COLLAPSE

In light of the Able Technologies debacle, Fox Studios has decided not to pilot *Staying Power*, the sitcom starring former blockbuster movie star Claudia Merrill. The show was about an over-the-hill actress struggling to remain vital in an industry that has little room for actresses over the age of thirty.

Fox spokeswoman Karen Regan said, "The fall-out of Able Technologies has meant financial ruin for thousands of Able Technologies employees. It's wiped out their retirement savings, it's left them unemployed and struggling. Evidence seems to suggest that Claudia Merrill was in some way tied to the deception that helped corporate executives and board members like her profit at the expense of the working man."

Newsweek
A CULTURE OF GREED
October 22, 2006

Until recently, it went without saying that wealthy men in power had a tendency toward dalliances with young secretaries and eager blond interns. A frustration for executives' wives, no doubt, but hardly a national concern. But when executives' decisions rob shareholders and leave thousands of employees without pensions or savings, maybe the time to scrutinize the personal lives of corporate executives like billionaire Gary Denner has come.

A few months ago, it appeared that Denner had it all. One of the world's wealthiest people, CEO of a Fortune 100 company, Denner was the kind of person we hold up as an icon, someone we aspire for our children to become, someone we wish we ourselves could be.

When we heard rumors of his wife's unusual

(suspicious? Silkwoodesque?) death, we shook our heads and said, "What a shame." When we heard about his sister-in-law, a former actress named Claudia Merrill, known for her partying lifestyle, living with him after his wife's death, we thought, "Boys will be boys" and "High-powered executives can have whatever they want—isn't that why we want to be them?" But maybe now we should be examining whether this culture of greed that celebrates having whatever we want whenever we want it and tosses aside ethics and family values is really something worth emulating.

Denner's alleged dalliance with Merrill might have been worth nothing more than fodder for the gossip mill if it weren't for one thing: Merrill's appointment to Able's board of directors last summer shortly after Able acquired Avec Communications. Merrill had close ties with Hayden Van Horn, Avec's primary stockholder and chairman of the board. The acquisition paid off well for all three. Denner, Merrill, and Van Horn all sold significant portions of their stock holdings in the months prior to Able's collapse, leading to questions of possible criminal wrongdoing.

Criminal or not, the culture of greed that led to ever-rising profits has fallen under scrutiny.

Greed was evident, even in the early days. "More than anything else, they talked about how much money we would make," says someone who worked for Denner. Compensation plans often seemed oriented toward enriching executives rather than generating profits for shareholders. Executives were compensated based on a market valuation formula that relied on internal estimates. As a result, says one former executive, there was pressure to inflate the value of the contracts—even though it had no impact on the actual cash that was generated . . .

I suppose that my identity as Helaina Denner has probably been shattered right along with my father's. I feel fortunate that I had adopted the identity of Helaina Merrill when I came to school. Around my liberal artsy friends, my father and Able Technologies may as well be in cahoots with the devil.

I'm sitting at the kitchen table in my robe, sipping my coffee and reading the business section of the newspaper when Kendra comes out of her bedroom wearing boxer shorts and a tiny heather-gray t-shirt that shows off her flat, perfect tummy. Even though her blond hair is all mussed, she looks gorgeous as always.

"Is there any coffee left?" she asks.

"Yep."

She pours herself a cup and joins me at the table. I set the business section down—I always go straight to that section these days—and reach for the front page.

"Those executives better damn well spend some time in jail," Kendra says, glancing at the section I just set down. "They stole people's life savings. Hundreds, no, *thousands* of people will have to put off retirement. If those execs get off . . . uh! It makes me so mad just thinking about it. They'll lock up some black kid who stole somebody's wallet that had a hundred bucks in it, but they never punish the white-collar criminals who steal thousands of dollars and people's futures."

I don't want my father to go to jail, but at the same

time I agree with her and tell her so. When I unfold the front section, I immediately zero in on a photograph of my father. My jaw drops as I read the headline.

"What? What is it?" Kendra asks.

I can't believe I have to *read*—I didn't get a phone call from Maria or Claudia or one of Dad's assistants—that Rick Harwell has shot my father. I have to read in the paper that my father is in the hospital, paralyzed, and will likely never walk again.

The New York Times
ANGER OVER LOSS OF JOB TURNS VIOLENT
By Kevin Keller

Cofounder and CEO of Denver-based Able Technologies was shot yesterday morning by an unemployed computer programmer.

Witnesses report that 24-year-old Rick Harwell shot Gary Denner as Denner was walking from his car to Able Technologies headquarters.

Police caught Harwell within minutes of the shooting. Police report that Harwell was walking leisurely away from the crime scene, shouting epithets and threats, apparently at Gary Denner in particular and corporate America in general.

Denner is out of the ICU, but doctors fear that he has been paralyzed from the waist down and will never walk again.

Harwell told police that he has hated Denner since Able laid off Harwell's father, James P. Harwell, as part of a company-wide downsizing ten years ago. James Harwell killed himself ten months after being laid off. He had not been able to secure another job.

Harwell's girlfriend, Marie Munoz, was among the thousands of Able employees who lost their jobs—as well as millions of dollars in stocks and retirement plans—in the wake of Able's bankruptcy. During the last few weeks scandal has rocked Able . . .

"Helaina, what's wrong?" Kendra asks again.

Mutely, I hand over the paper and point to the article. "Gary Denner is my father."

"Gary Denner of Able Technologies?" She glances at the article. "Holy shit. Helaina, I'm so sorry."

I suppose I should feel grateful that she doesn't ask me why I kept my father a secret for so long. Someday I will explain everything, but now, with wobbly legs, I stand up and get my cell phone. I call Owen first and tell him what's happened and that I'm going to catch the next flight out. Then I call Maria.

"I can't believe no one called to tell me what happened!" I shout as soon as she picks up the phone.

"I'm so sorry, I couldn't find your mother's address book. I called information, but there was no Helaina Denner listed. I couldn't remember your friends' last names."

It hadn't occurred to me that our phone number is under Kendra's name. Anyway, everyone else out here knows me as Helaina Merrill. And of course Dad wouldn't have my number. He's never called.

"I'm sorry, Maria. It was just such a shock . . . How is he?"

She pauses. "I don't know."

"I'm flying out there on the next flight. I'll go directly to the hospital. What hospital is he at?" If the article had mentioned it, I've forgotten already.

I write down the information, thank her, and click my

phone off. I throw a few clothes in a bag. I'm packed and in a taxi racing to the airport in record time.

I'm on standby for four hours, but it feels like years.

I spend another four hours on the plane. I have far too much time to think about Dad. I wonder—and as soon as it pops into my head I'm mad at myself for possibly jinxing it—I wonder if maybe he will change as a result of this. That's how it would happen in the movies. He'd be so grateful to see me; he'd realize that family and friends were more important than any amount of money.

I keep picturing our reunion. He'll be sleepy, his eyes opening and shutting, as if groggily trying to decide whether he wants to sleep or wake. The sound of beeping machines will surround us. He will open his eyes and see me, and his eyes will light up. He will smile and outstretch his arms. He will apologize for everything and ask my forgiveness, and I will give it to him.

When my plane lands, it's nearly five o'clock. I sprint across the airport, cell phone in hand, calling Maria.

"What time do visiting hours end?" Seven, she tells me. "What room is he in?" Room 317. "Thanks." I click my phone shut, throw it in my purse, and race to a taxi.

We get to the hospital an hour later. I overpay the cab driver ridiculously and race inside, nearly careening into an old man in a wheelchair.

"Sorry, sorry," I tell the man and the stern-faced nurse behind him. I reduce my pace to a race walk and hit the elevator button five times, like that'll make the door open any faster.

As soon as the elevator door opens, I run down the hallway, my purse banging against my side, my suitcase rolling behind me. I'm actually smiling. I'm in a great mood, as if the reunion scenario I'd imagined has actually already happened.

"Dad!" I say, bursting into his room.

He's flat on his back, attached to several beeping machines and torture-chamber-device-looking contraptions, talking on his cell phone. He looks at me only long enough to give me a stern glare for interrupting him and gives me the "one minute" sign with his index finger raised. At once, my good mood vanishes and I feel like a meddlesome nine-year-old again, being scolded for trying to get some attention from her daddy.

I stand next to my suitcase, shifting from one foot to the other, looking around the room. He has a private room, and I'm sure it's much nicer than most hospital rooms, but it still seems austere. Far too stark and plain for my father.

Five minutes pass, and I hear my father say, "Bob, hang on, I've got to take this, it's Byron."

I listen to his frantic conversation, but I can't understand what they are talking about. I've been sitting all day, but already my feet are sore. There is a chair against the wall. I consider sitting in it, but I don't want Dad to forget I'm here. I decide to move the chair closer to him.

The chair makes a horrible metallic screech against the floor as I move it. Again, Dad glares at me like I'm a pesky child.

Ten minutes pass, twenty. I consult my watch every two minutes. Visiting hours will be up in half an hour. Couldn't he finish his conversations then? I know his company is in serious turmoil. Hell, his life is in serious turmoil, considering that he may be brought to court on charges of knowingly approving falsified documents. Still, I dropped everything and flew here to be with him.

Couldn't he acknowledge me with something friendlier than an angry glare? He was shot yesterday. He could have died. But nothing's changed. He hasn't reevaluated his priorities one iota.

I stand up, point to my watch, and mouth, "Visiting hours are almost over." I mouth it again, but he isn't looking at me, just yelling into the phone and giving me that "I'll be with you in a minute" finger.

I sit down again. Maybe the battery on his cell phone will die and he'll be forced to talk to me.

That's when the tears come. Tears of embarrassment and sadness. I blink them away, but my eyes fill up again right away.

I'm such an idiot for thinking Dad would change. I look at my watch. Fifteen minutes.

Ten minutes. I can't do this to myself anymore. I can't keep hoping, keep coming home eager for the slightest shred of attention or affection. I have to accept that my father just isn't capable of love. It's not me. It's not my fault.

A nurse comes by and says there are only ten minutes left of visiting hours. I wait for a reaction from Dad, but he keeps talking on the phone, as if he hadn't noticed her.

6:59.

7:00.

7:01.

7:02. The nurse opens the door and says visiting hours are over. I stand and look at my father. He doesn't meet my gaze. I roll my suitcase out the door, down the hall. I take the elevator downstairs, walk through the automatic doors, and hail a taxi. I ask the cab driver to take me to a hotel near the airport.

It seems to take a million years to check into the Hilton. It's all I can do to hold in the tears long enough to get to my room.

The elevator goes slowly up to my floor.

Finally, finally, I get to my room, collapse on the bed, and cry. When I finally get a hold of myself, I call Owen.

"How is he?"

"I don't know. He talked on the phone the entire time I was there, and then visiting hours were over and I had to leave. I mean he's attached to a bunch of scary-looking machinery, but I figure if he can talk business, he can't be that bad."

"He was talking about the business? Didn't the accident just happen yesterday?"

"Yeah, and I guess he was out of commission for a few hours so he had to make up for lost time. He didn't even give me two minutes of his time, Owen."

"I'm sorry, hon. I'll fly out tomorrow. I've already booked . . . "

"Don't bother. I'm going back to New York first thing in the morning. I'll reimburse you for the ticket."

"What do you mean? Why are you going home already?"

"Because I'm sick of standing on my head and doing cartwheels to get my dad to notice me. I sat there for the longest hour of my entire life, just waiting for him to give me a smile, and all he did was glare at me for daring to interrupt him when he was working. I've got to stop doing this to myself. I just . . . I think I should just forget Gary Denner is my father. Don't you think that would be the healthiest thing, to stop setting myself up for this constant disappointment?"

"Helaina . . . you don't have to decide this right now. No matter how much it hurts, family is family. You may feel differently in a few months."

"We can't choose our family. I got lucky with Mom; I can't have everything. It's like, just because we're born somewhere, it doesn't mean we belong there. When we grow up, we can find the city where we really feel at home. We make our friends; they become our family. Just because I have Dad's genes doesn't mean he's my family.

I fly home early the next morning. The plane shudders as we land. The mechanical whine of the wings repositioning themselves fills my ears. As we taxi along the runway, I think of Owen's poem:

You know you're going the wrong way
Living life half-awake
Hand hovering over the break
Considering, seeking courage

Slow down, slow down
Turnaround
There is still time
To go the other way

I think I've turned my life around in the last several tumultuous months. I've stopped drinking, started eating and sleeping, met a guy worth loving.

I still mourn, but I'm better.

Somehow I don't feel victorious about Claudia and Dad's careers crumbling. Revenge is really such a silly urge. You think it'll make up for your pain, but it's just something to distract you from the hurt for a while. Nothing can make up for Mom's death.

I walk through the airport, listening to the hum and buzz of the throng of people. Outside I'm greeted by the sound of horns honking, sirens blaring, and people shouting. I smile.

I'm home.